Depraved

THE DEVIL'S SYNDICATE
BOOK FIVE

SARAH BAILEY

Please note the spelling throughout is British English.

Cover Art by Sarah Bailey

Published by Twisted Tree Publications
www.twistedtreepublications.com
info@twistedtreepublications.com

Paperback ISBN: 978-1-913217-15-0

To my dark and depraved Quintet
Your story has given me life, love and laughter
I'm so glad you've finally found your way
home to each other

CHAPTER ONE

Quinn

The video Geoff had sent me shook me to my core. Except I wasn't the one who was the worst off here. That was Ash. She fumed in her seat and the declaration she would be the one who slit Russo's throat was a little chilling, to say the least. But, honestly, I couldn't blame her. Not after seeing that shit. Not after Russo had taken Isabella and slapped her around. And not after he'd said all those things about Ash. Calling her a whore and a slut. She was neither of those things.

Reaching out, I cupped her face and turned it to me. Her blue eyes were wild and the rage in them almost made me flinch.

"Little girl…"

"I hate him."

"I know."

"We need to get her away from him."

I stroked her cheek. Whilst I wanted to get angry, she needed me to remain calm and we needed to get both her and

Rory to Viktor. They were injured and as much as Ash might want to go rushing off after Isabella, she couldn't.

"You're going to let me, E and Xav handle this."

"But Quinn—"

"No buts. You were just in a car accident and need to be looked over by a doctor, as does Rory. So you and he are sitting this out, do you understand?"

She looked mutinous. My girl might be strong, but if she thought for a second I'd allow her to further injure herself, she had another thing coming. She needed rest and recuperation.

"Ash, do you understand?"

"Yes."

"Good girl."

Her eyes flashed momentarily with pleasure at my praise. Ash might not like it, but she had to deal with it.

"E, how much longer until we're at Viktor's?" I asked, turning to him and dropping my hand from Ash's cheek.

"We're just hitting the outskirts now, should be like maybe twenty minutes."

"Okay, good."

I had a few choice words for her father who was meant to be keeping Isabella safe for Ash. Fiddling with my phone, I forwarded him the video Geoff sent me along with a message.

QUINN: You were meant to keep her safe.

I didn't care if it antagonised him. The responsibility lay with him. He assured Ash he'd make sure nothing happened to her mother. His personal feelings about Isabella and what she'd done didn't matter. Only Ash's happiness did, and that meant keeping the people she loved and cared for safe.

I felt like shit she even thought for one second we weren't in this with her for good. That she wasn't enough for me and the boys. Didn't she realise she completed us? Didn't she know we'd all fucking well die for her if it came to it? Fuck marriage and all the other bullshit. All we needed was her and that was fucking that.

I could see Xav and Rory looking at Ash with sympathy, as if they understood how much this pained her. As if our girl hadn't suffered enough today. Now she had this bullshit on top of it. I didn't care how but I would fix this for her. I'd make sure I got Isabella away from Frank. It might take some fucking time, but I'd do it. And then we'd destroy Frank for good. If she wanted to be the one who ended him then who was I to stop her doing it? Of course, I still worried since this was my girl and I didn't want shit on her conscience she couldn't handle. We'd have to see if Ash really wanted to go through with it when the time came.

"I don't want her to die," she whispered.

"She won't. He's not going to kill her."

It's what he'd said, but who knew when it came to Frank fucking Russo. The man was psychotic and a cold-blooded killer. Couldn't trust him as far as I could throw him.

"I'm in so much pain. I didn't want to say anything, but my chest is so sore."

"Little girl…"

"I couldn't think about me, not when Ror needed my help."

I tugged her against me upon seeing the tears welling in her eyes. Rory met my eyes over her head. The abject misery in them made me aware he hated he'd had no other choice but to rely on her. I didn't blame him for what happened. None of us could know her cousin would follow them. But it did go to show I was right about her not being safe in the outside world. It didn't make me feel remotely vindicated knowing both Rory and Ash had got hurt though.

"It's okay, sweetheart, when we get to Viktor's the doctor will be there and I'm sure he'll get you some painkillers."

I stroked her hair, not wanting to aggravate her injuries any further.

"I love you, Quinn," she sobbed, her tears soaking through my shirt.

I rested my cheek against her head.

"Shh, I know."

Xav and Eric would have to help me sort out this mess once we got to Viktor's, but I could afford to give Ash the comfort she needed right now. And there was no fucking way I would let her drown.

Eric and Xav spoke in low murmurs the rest of the journey, but the three of us in the back were quiet. Ash had stopped crying, but I kept holding her, reassuring her without words she had me to rely on. I'd never let her go.

Eric got out first and went up to knock on the front door whilst Xav helped Rory out of the car and I took care of Ash. She winced as we went up the steps, the movement aggravating her chest. I thought about carrying her, but Ash might not agree to me doing so. The door was already open and I led her right through into Viktor's living room with Rory and Xav behind me. Eric was there with grim-faced Viktor and Doctor Alekhin. He immediately came over to check on Ash but she waved him off, telling him Rory was more important.

"Your father wishes I examine you first," he protested.

"Little girl, let him do his job," I told her.

She scowled but allowed him to lead her over towards the sofa. Xav took Rory over with him. Viktor intercepted Ash and Alekhin, wrapping a hand around the back of her head and looking her over himself.

"*Kotik*," he murmured.

"Rory should be checked first, Dad," she whispered.

He shook his head and I think she got the message. Her health was paramount to him. I watched her let Alekhin examine her, insisting he needed her to remove her top to which had Ash scowling. Viktor turned away, giving them some privacy. Considering the rest of us were intimately involved with her, we didn't matter so much.

I stepped up to where Eric was standing next to Viktor. His eyes fell on me and I could see the concern in his features.

"Before you ask, yes, I am aware of how Isabella was taken. My men were subdued and will be thoroughly reprimanded for losing her. I apologise for this. She was under my protection and I failed her and Ash."

The fact I didn't even have to say anything went to show what kind of man Viktor was. Willing to admit his mistakes without a second thought. Then again, we were his daughter's partners and I think the apology was more for Ash's sake than ours.

"That said, retrieving her from Frank will be… difficult."

"We're aware," I replied. "We have to do it though, for Ash."

He gave me a sharp nod, then he glanced over at Xav and Rory.

"What happened?"

"She didn't explain?"

"A little. Do not worry, my men are on their way to deal with the vehicle as we speak. It is the least I can do under the circumstances."

I rubbed the back of my neck, glancing at Alekhin and Ash. He was busy looking her over to make sure she didn't have any external injuries.

"Our plans are going to have to change in light of all of this."

He nodded, his face growing solemn.

"My only concern right now is my daughter."

To be honest, it was mine too. I had concerns about Rory too. He was looking paler by the moment and it worried me. Alekhin finished up with Ash, giving her some painkillers to take and helping her back into her t-shirt. Then he turned to where Xav sat with Rory.

"You're going to have to be careful with him," Xav said. "He doesn't like being touched."

"It's okay," Rory mumbled. "I'll deal."

"You sure, man?"

"If my fucking wrist is broken I'd rather know, okay?"

Alekhin approached him carefully and asked Xav to untie the makeshift sling Ash had created for him. Viktor went over to Ash and sat in the armchair next to her. They spoke in low tones, but right now I was more interested in making sure my best friend was okay.

"Ow, Jesus, fuck," Rory growled as Alekhin looked his wrist over.

"I was going to ask if it hurt when I moved it like this, but I can see it is an issue. You need an x-ray."

"You're not taking him to a hospital," I ground out. "We can't explain his injuries."

Alekhin looked up at me.

"If I take him to a private one, they will not ask questions." He glanced at Viktor. "We have taken men here before."

Viktor stared at Rory for a long moment as if contemplating whether or not to allow this before giving a nod and turning back to Ash. Alekhin proceeded to check Rory over for other injuries, including his head wound.

"Have you had any dizziness, headaches, blurred vision, vomiting?"

"Headache and a little dizziness. My vision was a little blurred right after the accident. Also having trouble staying awake. You'd have to ask Ash how long I was out for."

Alekhin looked over at her.

"Um at least twenty minutes at a guess," Ash said with trepidation.

"You may have a concussion," he said, turning back to Rory. "We must get this x-rayed in the meantime."

"He's not going without me."

We all looked at Ash, whose eyes were fixed on Rory. I knew that look. She wasn't going to back down from this.

"They can't go alone," I said directly to Viktor.

"André will take them and bring them back once the x-ray is done. It is safer for them to remain here with me."

"What? We're not staying here," Ash protested immediately. "Not without Xav, Eric and Quinn."

Viktor raised his eyebrows and my chest filled with pride. Ash refused to be without us.

"You want me to put you all up?"

"No, I want to go home, but if you're going to make me stay here, then I won't do it without them. Regardless, I have to be where Ror is so I can take care of him."

Alekhin stood up and put his hands in his pockets.

"You need to rest, Ash, so someone else will have to see to him, I'm afraid."

"I'll make sure Rory has what he needs, little girl."

Ash's eyes fell on me and the appreciation in them warmed my heart.

"Okay, fine, but we're going home after we've been to the hospital."

She looked at Viktor as if daring him to say otherwise, and he wisely kept his mouth shut.

"E and I can look after Ash then," Xav said with a smirk.

"She doesn't need two of you to do it," Rory muttered.

"Whatever, she's going to be treated like a queen whilst she recovers and you just have to suck it up."

I swear Rory might have attacked Xav if he wasn't in pain and injured judging by his scowl.

"Instead of bickering like children, we should get going," I said, not wanting this to escalate when tensions were already high.

Viktor got up and went out into the hallway, presumably to speak to André. He was back shortly with the man himself and we all made a move. Viktor pulled me aside before I could get out of the door with Xav and Eric.

"We still need to discuss what will happen next."

"I know. I'll bring her over tomorrow if she's feeling up to it or you could come to us."

"She needs her rest."

"Then come to dinner and we'll talk then."

Why I'd just invited Ash's damn father to dinner again was a mystery to me, but at the end of the day, Viktor was in our lives.

"Yes, that would be best."

I nodded and he let me go. Ash was standing outside a car when I made it out of the door. She looked up at me with sad eyes so I went to her, stroking her cheek.

"Take care of him for me, little girl."

"Ror?"

I nodded.

"I will."

I leant down and kissed her softly, which I think reassured her. Then I helped her into the car and watched it pull away before getting into the Range Rover with Eric and Xav.

"Do you think they'll be okay?" Xav asked when we pulled away.

"They have to be."

"Should one of us have gone with them?"

"No, I need you two so we can start making a fucking plan to get Isabella back."

"Do we really have to?"

I looked back at Xav, who was scowling.

"Yes. Do you want to explain to our girlfriend why we allowed her mother to remain with Russo?"

He looked away and shook his head.

"I didn't think so." It was time we got home and sorted out this mess. "And don't think I've forgotten about Julian. That's a whole other fucked up mess we're going to have to fix."

"It's not my fault he escaped."

"I didn't say that."

Xav met my eyes again.

"I'm going to put him back in prison where he belongs, Quinn. Mark my fucking words."

And I believed him.

We had to get a handle on this shitshow and fast before everything fell apart around us. I wasn't going to let Russo have the upper hand any longer. The man was going down and his whole family with him.

CHAPTER TWO

Ash

I sat in the private room with André waiting for Rory to come back from getting an x-ray. Alekhin had spoken to the private hospital we were at on the way here, so we had no issues when we arrived. I was seriously worried about what would happen next when it came to Frank and my mother but focusing on Rory helped keep me grounded. I didn't care what the others and the doctor had said. Rory's care would be my responsibility. My boyfriend needed me.

"Are you tired?" André asked me.

"A little."

In all honesty, exhaustion plagued me. The painkillers Alekhin gave me were strong and the ordeal I'd gone through had drained me. Running on empty was never a good idea.

"Hungry?"

I nodded. Rory and I hadn't eaten since breakfast. Who knew how long ago that was. André got up and went outside into the hallway. I rested my head back against the wall and closed my eyes. My chest still ached intolerably, but the drugs had helped some. Tomorrow I would feel it worse. Way worse. So even as I hated it, I couldn't begrudge Quinn for insisting I sit out any attempts at rescuing my mother. My body was in no fit state to do a single thing, let alone go after Frank fucking Russo.

Voices made me open my eyes. Alekhin, Rory and André walked into the room. Rory was made to sit up in the bed whilst André brought me a pack of crisps, a Cadbury's caramel bar and a cup of tea.

"Thank you."

He nodded and sat back next to me.

"I've looked over the x-rays and you have a hairline fracture in your both your radius and ulna. You're lucky the breaks are not more severe. You'll have to wear a splint for at least four weeks whilst they heal. I do not think you'll need a cast, but once the swelling goes down, we will reassess."

Four weeks. It seemed like a lifetime, but at least Rory wasn't worse off. What if he'd had a severe break and had to have surgery? I don't think I could've handled it. Not after everything else. Having more shit news today would destroy me completely.

"I also ran tests with you whilst we were waiting for the x-rays and I do believe you have a mild concussion. I shall go over what you need to do but of course, I will come to see you and examine you again in a couple of days."

Alekhin proceeded to run over everything we needed to know, like making sure Rory limited his activities for at least two days and having someone with him to check on him. I listened intently so I could relay the information to Quinn when we got back. But if he thought I wouldn't be staying with Rory whilst he recovered, Quinn had another thing coming.

André made sure I ate and had my tea, then Alekhin prescribed both of us pain meds and we got them from the pharmacy before we went home. I made sure to pick up Rory a snack for the car and had to help him eat it on the way home since he was too tired to do anything himself. My heart was in pieces seeing him like this but remaining strong for him was all I could do.

André helped Rory up to the house whilst I unlocked the front door. I didn't know where the others were, but figured they were busy since they didn't come to meet us. André assisted me in getting Rory upstairs and onto the bed. Quinn appeared in the doorway. A good thing since I couldn't help Rory into a change of clothes in my own injured state.

"I shall let Viktor know you're both okay," André said to me before he departed.

Quinn approached us cautiously.

"Can you help him get into something more comfortable?" I asked as I gathered up pillows and stacked them to elevate his wrist. "He needs to sleep."

"What's the prognosis, little girl?"

"Hairline fractures in both wrist bones and a mild concussion. Alekhin left strict instructions about his care." He'd written them down for me, so I dug them out of my purse and handed them to Quinn. "He needs monitoring."

Rory had been especially quiet whilst all of this had been going on. I could see the exhaustion plaguing his features.

"You can read it later, we need to settle him first."

Wordlessly, Quinn popped the pages down on the bed before unstrapping the sling from Rory and helping him out of his t-shirt, jeans and shoes. He then tugged a clean t-shirt over Rory's head and we got him on the bed under the covers with his arm propped up. Before Quinn could object, I stripped down to my knickers, grabbed another one of Rory's clean t-shirts and climbed in next to him, resting my hand on his free arm. Rory gave me a half-smile before closing his eyes.

"You can't stay here with him."

I glared at Quinn.

"Yes, I can. He needs me. And I'm exhausted. Let us sleep, please."

I could see Quinn wanted to object, but he shook his head and picked up the pages as he sat on the edge of the bed. Rory's breathing turned steady and even, so I knew he'd drifted off. Quinn ran a hand through his hair, looking distinctly harassed.

"When I heard you couldn't wake him up, I thought I'd lost him," he said, his voice quiet and gruff.

"Quinn…"

"Rory means everything to me, little girl. He's a brother to me. One I've taken care of our whole lives. A part of me would die if he did."

I desperately wanted to reach out to him. His shoulders shook, but his back was to me so I couldn't see his expression.

"I did it… you know… everyone who hurt him when he was a kid, I made sure Rory had his revenge against them. I made sure the four of us ended them for good."

My voice got stuck in my throat. His foster parents… but no, Quinn meant everyone. That meant the kid who'd scarred Rory's abdomen too and whoever else had been involved.

"They all begged for their lives at the end of it. Begged us not to. Said they were sorry." He laughed, but it was hollow. "They weren't sorry for burning him with an iron. They weren't fucking sorry for beating him so badly, he couldn't get out of bed for two days. They didn't care how they scarred him physically, psychologically and emotionally. But I did. I cared so damn much. I saved him. I got him help from a psychologist. I made sure he didn't implode. He didn't deserve any of it. None. He did nothing but have the misfortune of his parents dying when he was too young to understand anything."

Tears leaked out of my eyes, dripping down onto the pillow where I'd laid my head next to Rory. Next to the broken, damaged man I loved with my whole heart and soul.

"What did you do to them?" I whispered.

Quinn didn't turn around. He placed the pages on the bed and dropped his head into his hands.

"What didn't we do?"

I shivered.

"It was bloody and gruesome… depraved."

"Quinn…"

"You don't want the details, little girl. Trust me. Xav and E were sick when we were done. It reminded Xav of the aftermath of Julian's crimes. Except none of us felt sorry for them. Not when we knew how they'd caused irrecoverable damage to Rory. And it gave him a sense of closure, you know. Rory, whilst still burdened with his memories, didn't seem so… lost any longer. He had a reason to go on since we'd eradicated them from the world."

I stroked Rory's arm, staring at his peaceful face as he slept.

"I don't know how I feel about that."

"What? Knowing we're all killers? That we're capable of butchering people like Frank? It was a one time deal, Ash. One night where we didn't hold back and then we got rid of the evidence. That part was worse than what we did to them. They're unsolved missing person cases. No one knows they're dead but us and now… you."

It's not like I'd tell anyone. Hell, I already was an accessory to murder because of Frank. Not like I wanted anyone asking questions of what I'd done in my life.

"I don't care that you've killed. Do you think it'd make me love you all any less?"

"I don't know. It's why none of us wanted to tell you."

"Then why tell me now?"

Maybe I was fucked up in the head. I guess my upbringing made it hard for me to judge them for it. Especially in light of what I knew about what Rory's foster parents had done to him. And I wanted to murder the man who raised me before he could do the same to me. So who the hell was I to talk?

"Secrets have a way of coming out whether or not we want them to. Honesty is what you've always asked of us. Maybe I'm done hiding behind the shit I've done in life. Maybe almost losing you and Rory has made me realise just how fleeting everything is."

He raised his head and turned it towards me, eyes dark and expression hollow.

"So you have to believe me when I tell you I won't let this shit go on any longer. I want a normal life or as fucking normal as it can be with whatever we are. I want out of the criminal underworld. So two things need to happen. One, we get your mother away from Frank and two, Frank dies. That's it. When it's done, I'm fucking out. *Il Diavolo* retires and we go on with our lives away from all that bullshit. You, me, Xav, E and Rory. Together."

I reached out my hand to him since I was too exhausted to move any longer. Quinn got up and came around the other side of the bed, sitting next to me and brushing my hair back from my face. He wiped away the tears under my eyes.

"I'll give you anything you desire, little girl, just promise you'll let me take care of the both of you."

"I promise, Quinn… I love you."

He looked exhausted himself and I didn't want him to leave, but there wasn't room in Rory's bed for the three of us with the pillows propping up his arm. Leaning down, he kissed my forehead and tucked me up further under the covers.

"Sleep, I'll be right here when you wake."

So I closed my eyes, turning back to Rory and letting myself drift away on a sea of pain meds, knowing Quinn would watch over us. Whatever they'd done in the past didn't matter to me. Our future was the thing we had to secure. Our future together as a quintet. The four of them and I were in this together until the end.

CHAPTER THREE

RORY

I awoke to my shoulder being shaken. Blinking, I found Quinn leaning over me with concern on his face. Why was he waking me up? Didn't he know the pain stopped when I was out? Why was it so bright in this room?

"What do you want?" I grumbled.

"Just checking to see if you're still alive."

"Do I look dead to you?"

"All right, grumpy, chill out."

He straightened and grinned.

"Where's Ash?"

He pointed to the form next to me, which I hadn't noticed. Ash's blonde hair poked out from under the covers. I might feel groggy and out of it, but having her there soothed me.

"How long have we been asleep?"

"Few hours… She needs waking up too as Eric's made dinner."

I looked at her again. My little star curled up against my side with her hand resting over my chest. How I hadn't noticed her there before was beyond me, but then again, the doctor said I had a concussion.

"It's too bright in here."

"Sorry, hold on…"

Quinn turned on the bedside lamps before turning out the main light. After a few minutes, I didn't feel so dazed. I shifted, pain shooting up my arm as I did so. The movement caused the girl next to me to rouse. She opened her eyes and rubbed my chest.

"Ror," she breathed.

I attempted to smile, but my head was still fuzzy.

"Little girl, you need to help me sit him up as E's bringing dinner up for you."

She shifted and yawned before sitting up. Then the two of them helped me up with Ash fluffing the pillows behind me.

"How are you feeling?" she asked, rubbing my shoulder.

"Fucked."

A smile played across her lips and I realised what she was thinking.

Dirty girl.

"Not like that."

"I know." She turned to Quinn. "Are we going to have to help him eat?"

"Depends on what E's made."

Being right-handed meant this would be a little intolerable. I'd let Ash feed me in the car earlier as her expression brokered no objections. Besides, I'd been exhausted. I didn't want to be babied, but we'd been told I had to be monitored to make sure my symptoms didn't worsen or for changes in my behaviour.

"Knock, knock." Eric came in with a tray in his hands with two plates and two glasses of water. "Dinner for my invalids."

"I'm not a fucking invalid," I all but growled.

"Well, someone woke up on the wrong side of bed."

I almost retorted but kept my mouth shut since he popped the tray down on my lap and it was mac and cheese. Something I could eat with one hand.

"Thank you."

Eric smiled and turned to Quinn.

"You'll have to go get your own, Xav's watching TV so you can eat with him and I'll sit with these two, yeah?"

Quinn looked like he was about to dispute Eric's suggestion, but then he realised there was no point so he ambled out of the room. Eric sat down next to me, shifting the pillows where my arm was resting.

"Careful," I muttered, even though he hadn't disturbed my wrist.

"You going to be a baby and throw your food everywhere if I'm not?"

"Ha-fucking-ha."

"At least you've not lost your sense of humour, eh?"

Ash shook her head and gathered up her bowl and started digging in. I picked up the spoon Eric had thoughtfully provided me with my left hand and scooped up a helping for myself, shoving it in my mouth before half of it fell off.

"Oh good, I don't have to play the aeroplane game with you," Eric said with a grin.

I scowled. Why these idiots were trying to wind me up when I was already feeling irritable was beyond me.

"Do you really have to be here when I have Ash?"

"She needs keeping an eye on too, in case you'd forgotten our girlfriend was in the same crash as you."

I hadn't. Turning to her, I found Ash giving me a soft smile.

"I'm okay, I promise. A little stiff, but Alekhin said it would be much worse for me tomorrow." She glanced at Eric. "I hope Quinn won't force me into my own room. I don't want to leave Ror… unless he wants that."

They both looked at me expectantly.

"Huh? No, she can stay… you can stay, little star… I want you here. Even if Quinn gets pissy."

Ash's grin made my heart thump, but I turned back to my meal since I was ravenous.

"I'm surprised Xav isn't up here cracking jokes," Ash said with a shake of her head.

"Trust me, I had a hard time making him go watch TV instead of us all piling in here for dinner. Didn't think our Rory here would have appreciated it," Eric replied.

I most definitely wouldn't have. It was enough having two people in here at the same time. I couldn't complain too much since I knew it was for my own good and for Ash's. As much as I'd like to kick Eric out, her well-being was paramount to me. I couldn't take care of her in my unsteady state.

"Xav actually listened to you? That's a surprise."

"He does on occasion… especially when bribed with sex."

Ash snorted and almost spat her mouthful out. She swallowed hard and laughed, rubbing her chest.

"Oh god, don't make me laugh… it hurts. Xav can't ever resist the promise of sex."

"The things I do for you."

He waggled his eyebrows. It just set her off even more.

"Must be such a hardship to have sex with your boyfriend who you've been in love with our whole lives," I muttered.

That made it worse for Ash. She clutched her chest and waved us both off.

"Stop, stop. I can't take it… god, please, it hurts so much."

"Should I get your pain pills?" Eric asked.

She gave a nod, all the while still trying to stifle her giggles. He got up and gathered the two bags we'd brought from the pharmacy off my bedside table, going through each one to familiarise himself with what we needed. Then he popped off two pills for Ash, handing them to her now she'd settled down.

"It is a hardship, you know. Xav is greedy as fuck," he said as he sat back down.

"It's true, he's always in the mood and if he's not, then you know something's wrong with him," Ash added.

"Spare me the sob story," I said with an eye roll.

The two of them shared a glance. I wasn't really surprised about Xav considering how he'd brag about his sexcapades to me, Eric and Quinn all the time. I swear between him and Quinn it was like a fucking competition as to who could get laid the most. And they had shared the same woman in the past, but never at the same time, as they had with Ash. She was different. We loved her. She was our fucking queen.

I continued eating as silence descended on us, albeit slowly as it was hard to fucking well eat with one hand. Eric ended up holding the bowl for me and I almost asked him to feed me, but I didn't want to look or feel weak even if I felt it. Why I was worried about saving face in front of him and Ash was a mystery to me. It still felt wrong to ask other people for help, even if I needed it.

By the time I was finished, Quinn and Xav came upstairs and crowded into my room, leaving me feeling a little overwhelmed.

"How are my invalids feeling?" Xav asked as he stroked Eric's hair mindlessly.

"Careful, Rory might bite your head off for calling him that," Eric said, leaning into Xav's touch.

"He's grumpy and I'm okay," Ash said, sorting out the empty plates onto the tray and helping me drink my water.

"Question… how long until both of you can get down and dirty again?" Xav asked with a wink.

"Fuck off," I grumbled.

I didn't want to be reminded of the fact I wasn't allowed to do any strenuous activity. Having Ash in my bed and not being able to touch her? Yeah, that was going to be fucking painful.

"Is that really all you care about?" Ash said with a frown. "Your girlfriend is in pain and you turn it to sex?"

Xav's face fell.

"Angel…"

"No, don't you 'angel' me right now."

He came around to her side of the bed and sat down, taking her face in his hands.

"I'm sorry, I don't like seeing you in pain so I'm deflecting… I know."

Ash let him kiss her before he leant his forehead against hers.

"I love you," he whispered. "I just want you better."

She nodded, stroking his cheek. I looked between Eric and Quinn, who was sitting on the end of my bed now.

"Can I ask if there's a reason why you're all crowding my bed at the same time?"

"I wanted to see Ash and this one is in mother hen mode," Xav said, pointing at Quinn.

I almost sighed.

"Fuck off," Quinn grumbled, scowling at him.

"Okay, all of you can shoo out of here now, Ror needs his rest," Ash said, giving them all a look which told them no would not be the right answer.

Xav got up, ruffling her hair before saluting me. Then he grabbed Eric on the way out. The two of them were looking at each other like they were about to race to one of their bedrooms.

Yeah, definitely not a fucking hardship.

That left me, Quinn and Ash. And I wasn't about to throw him out since I knew he wouldn't listen.

"I'll take this downstairs then I'll be back," Quinn said as he picked up the tray and left.

"Thank fuck for that," I muttered.

Ash rubbed my arm and leant her head on my shoulder.

"Aww, Ror, they're worried about us."

"They can be worried somewhere else."

She stroked my face but didn't say anything. I was trying not to be irritable. Didn't help my head was fuzzy and all I wanted to do was sleep.

"Sorry, little star… I'm not feeling myself."

"I know, it's okay. Do you want to sleep again?"

I nodded so she helped me out of sitting position, getting the covers settled over me. Leaning down, she kissed my cheek and stroked my hair back.

"You're going to be okay. I'm right here watching over you. I love you, Ror."

"Love you too."

I closed my eyes and let my exhaustion take me under again. Maybe tomorrow I wouldn't feel so groggy and annoyed. I could fucking hope, couldn't I?

CHAPTER FOUR

Xavier

The past couple of days in our household had been particularly quiet. Nothing we'd planned to get done actually happened. I suppose when you've got two car crash victims to look after, the rest of the shit goes out the window. We hadn't dealt with the Isabella or Julian situation yet as we'd been taking care of Rory and Ash.

The day after the crash, Eric and I had found the other three fast asleep in Rory's bed. Quinn was squashed up against Ash's back with barely any room. How he was remotely comfortable was a question to me. When we woke them up, Ash had been stiff and sore, complaining about how much her chest hurt. Rory was quiet and moody. And Quinn had been up half the night keeping an eye on them. Eric and I went to scrounge up breakfast. When Quinn came down, he asked for a vat of coffee to keep him awake and said he'd cancel dinner with Viktor. Instead, it'd been rearranged for today so we could discuss Julian.

Fucking Julian. As if I wanted to deal with him being on the run. The manhunt for him had intensified. We'd had the police over yesterday asking questions about whether I'd seen or heard from him. Fucking lucky I hadn't, so could easily give them the truth. The last time I'd been in the same room as Julian was the day he'd been admitted to hospital and he'd fucked us over royally. All I wanted was for him to be back in prison where he belonged so he couldn't hurt anyone else. I doubted he'd actually try to attack anyone like he had done Mum and Katie, but you never knew with him. He had been an enforcer for Russo.

Ash had helped Rory have a shower earlier since he couldn't do it by himself. He was on the sofa downstairs now as he was feeling a little better after being in bed for two days doing very little. Eric was making dinner and keeping an eye on Rory in the process whilst Quinn was in his office.

Ash and I were in Eric's bathroom. She was nestled in the bath and I had my sleeves rolled up as I washed her hair. As she was still in a lot of pain, I offered to help her. For once, I was not perving over my girlfriend since she'd told me off about it.

"Did anyone ever tell you, you're good with your hands?" she asked as I massaged shampoo into her scalp.

"Only all the time."

"I should have known that would be your answer."

"You know only you and E have access to these fingers these days."

I waggled them in front of her face only to have her bat them away.

"Better be the case or I'll be hunting these men and women down and putting them in a headlock for daring to go near you."

I snorted and shook my head as I got a jug to rinse her hair out. Inside, I fell a thrill of delight she'd go to all that trouble if someone attempted to steal me away. She had nothing to worry about there. I loved this girl to death.

"Possessive much?"

"You're mine."

"You're beginning to sound like Quinn."

Ash bit her lip and looked up at me as I poured water over her head, careful not to get it in her eyes.

"I would only sound like Quinn if I threatened to kill them."

"That's not what you were doing?"

She shrugged and didn't say another word whilst I finished rising out her hair. Then I applied the conditioner. She moaned whilst I massaged it into her hair.

"Damn, angel, quit making sex noises or you're going to get my dick hard."

"Can't help you with that, you know."

I grumbled but continued to massage her hair. Ash needed to get better. That was far more important than fucking.

"Besides, E said he'd been keeping you occupied."

Admittedly he and I spent every night we weren't with Ash together, but it didn't mean we fucked all the time. They might accuse me of being sex-mad, but more often than not I just wanted to cuddle and fall asleep. Being with Eric was comforting in a lot of ways. He kept me grounded and sane, especially whilst I worried about Ash, Rory and the fucking Julian situation.

"We were talking about how we'd like it if you slept in between us last night."

Ash had been with Rory since they'd got home from the hospital.

"Just sleeping?"

"Yes, just sleeping. You know, E likes being the big spoon."

She grinned as I began to rinse the conditioner from her hair.

"Oh, I know. I wake up with him draped over me, hands all possessive and shit."

"Snap."

You'd think it'd be me who was all over him like that considering how I liked to top. The number of times I'd woken up on my side with him curled around my back, hand wrapped around my abs like they might disappear any second didn't bear thinking about. The man got possessive as fuck at night.

"You're all different. You like to have my face and tits pressed up against your chest. Quinn likes to sleep on his back with me half across his chest. Ror… well, he's the clingiest of all."

"No shit, our Rory?"

"Oh yes, it's like these tits are mine, this pussy is mine, this arse is mine. Doesn't matter how we fall asleep, he's always grabbing hold of something as if I might bolt any second."

I could see it. He'd never slept next to a girl before. Probably his subconscious telling him to keep Ash by his side.

I wouldn't rib him about it though. Rory was sensitive as fuck when it came to Ash and him. He'd never been in love before, the poor sod. Then again, neither had I until Ash and Eric, but at least I knew how to be with another person. Now I had two. As much as it'd fucked me up for a while with jealousy and insecurity, I was over it. Ash and Eric had their own relationship with each other, but it didn't mean they loved me any less. Didn't mean they compared what they had to what we had.

"That's cute. Our baby Rory has grown a pair finally."

"Don't say that to him, he might bite your head off."

"Oh Jesus, don't remind me. Old grumpy balls has put a damper on my libido."

"I didn't think *anything* could achieve that."

"You try getting it up when getting a death glare from him for so much as looking at you."

I'd finished rinsing her hair. Ash laid her head back against the lip of the bath and looked at me with understanding in her blue eyes.

"He's been worrying about my recovery when he should be worried about his own."

"Yeah well, he's suffered worse, angel. He's got a thick skin when it comes to physical pain."

She flinched. I knew Rory had told her some of what happened to him and Quinn fessing up to the night where we'd done unspeakable things to everyone who'd abused Rory. It felt easier now Ash wasn't ignorant of the truth. Like one of the worst nights of our lives wasn't a sordid secret any longer. For a long time, it worried me I'd turned into Julian, but Eric reassured me that could never be the case. Julian was psychotic whereas I had still maintained my morals despite what we'd done.

All I could say now was never a-fucking-gain.

"I wish he didn't."

"Me too."

If we could've spared Rory all that pain, we would've done it in a heartbeat. Being kids made it impossible. At least we'd given him a sense of closure.

"Right, time to get out since Daddy V will be here soon."

"Oh god, don't call him that!"

"Why not? He is your Daddy."

She splashed me, which had me laughing.

"Stop it. That's just wrong. He's Dad not… I can't even say it. And don't you dare say it to his face. Ever."

I put my hands up in defeat.

"I promise. Though I do wonder if Isabella ever called him Daddy."

I jumped up and got out of the way before Ash full-on attacked me.

"Xavier!"

"Ooh, am I in trouble, my queen? Should I bow down and grovel at your feet for making you think such disturbing thoughts about your parents?"

"Fuck off."

I grinned and winked.

"You sure? Don't you need my help getting out the bath and dried off?"

She gave me daggers.

"You are fucking lucky I love you so much."

"Oh, I know. I'm one incredibly lucky fucker."

"And don't you forget it, *tesoro*."

There was no way in hell I ever could. When I looked into those beautiful baby blue eyes of hers, I saw my future mapped out. Me, Ash and the boys… and perhaps a few little ones running around after us too. Now all I had to do was make sure that picture-perfect snapshot became a reality for us.

CHAPTER FIVE

Ash

The minute my dad walked in with the doctor and André, my face grew hot remembering what Xav said to me earlier in the bath. I could murder him for it and the disturbing images of Viktor and Isabella flashing through my head. Sometimes, just sometimes, Xav took his jokes way too far.

As if Quinn noticed my discomfort, he leant over to me, "What's wrong?"

"Nothing," I muttered.

"You seem hesitant to say hello."

"So would you if you'd been subjected to Xav and his jokes earlier."

I plastered on a smile when my dad approached and embraced me. His hug was very gentle, as if he was scared of hurting me further.

"How are you feeling, *kotik*?"

"Sore, but okay."

The muscles in my chest had loosened up a little, but I still felt like I'd been run over or something. Alekhin had said something about the seatbelt having likely given me internal bruising.

"I'm glad to hear it." Viktor turned to Quinn. "Good evening."

Quinn nodded but was still eying me with a raised eyebrow. He wasn't about to let what I'd said go.

Great. Just fucking great.

Viktor moved on to say hello to the others whilst Alekhin had made a beeline straight for Rory to check him over and André stood off to the side.

"Little girl…"

"No. Just no."

"Tell me what he said."

I shook my head, zipping my lips with my fingers. Quinn decided that wasn't acceptable as his hand, which had been on my waist, fell to my arse and he gave me a warning pat.

"None of that," I hissed. "Not until I'm better."

His eyes darkened and I knew I was pissing him off.

"Do I need to remind you, secrets aren't allowed?"

I scowled and almost turned away.

"Xav suggested my mother had a daddy dynamic with Viktor," I whispered, wishing the ground would swallow me whole. "He called him Daddy V and, quite frankly, I'd rather die than hear that come out of anyone's mouth ever again."

Quinn let out a snort and covered it up with a cough. I noticed Xav grinning at me and indicating Viktor with his head. I almost stuck my middle finger up at him. The little shit was determined to ruin my evening with this crap.

"I swear that man will be the death of me."

"Xav? I've thought that on many occasions myself," Quinn mused with a stupid smile on his face. He clearly found this situation far more amusing than I did.

"Can we get this evening over with before everyone ruins my dad for me?"

Quinn raised his hand from my behind and cupped my head, pressing a kiss to my temple.

"Of course, little girl."

Eric had slipped out to go get a drink for Viktor and Alekhin was still looking Rory over. I wanted to go to him, but we'd know soon enough whether he felt Rory needed a cast. He'd been feeling a lot better today with his concussion. Hadn't been so irritable and was able to come downstairs after I'd helped him shower. He'd been adamant none of the boys were going to do it. I think it had more to do with him not wanting to be vulnerable around them even though they were his family.

"Do you think he's going to be okay?"

"Considering what he went through as a kid, I think so."

I shuddered. The reminder of Rory's childhood and what Quinn had told me leaving a sour taste in my mouth. I didn't care about what they'd done to Rory's foster family, but the thought of how much pain and suffering my man had gone through made me sick. No one should go through that, least of all a defenceless child.

"You've changed your tune, what happened to 'I might lose him'?"

I looked up at Quinn in time to see his brows drop and his face turn grim.

"He's going to be fine," he replied through gritted teeth.

I leant closer to him, wrapping my arm around his waist and pressing my face into his side.

"He's got us, we won't let him be anything but fine."

Quinn met my eyes. His were dark with frustration.

"If your father wasn't here, I'd kiss you for that."

I bit my lip. Viktor had seen how much they all cared about me, so I didn't think it would be a big deal if Quinn kissed me.

"What's he going to say? Get your hands off my daughter?"

"You know very well the way I want to kiss you is far from innocent, little girl."

I ran my free hand up his chest.

"Yes, sir. I do."

A low growl sounded in the back of his throat. Next thing I knew, my feet were dragging along behind me as Quinn hustled me out of the room and almost pinned me to the wall of the dining room. His touch was gentle so as not to hurt me, but his mouth crashed against mine and I lost all sense of pain. Everything morphed into pleasure. Pleasure I hadn't felt in days. I gripped his shirt, tugging him closer. His body caged me in. He dominated my mouth, making my toes curl and my skin tingle all over.

"Quinn," I moaned breathlessly as he kissed down my jaw and the column of my throat.

"You're such a bad girl," he muttered. "The things you do to me."

There was a cough from behind us. Quinn pulled back slightly but kept me against the wall with his body as he turned his head. Eric was standing a few feet away from us with a raised eyebrow and a drink in his hand.

"Are you two quite done? Dinner's ready."

I snuck out from under Quinn's arm and sauntered over to Eric, which only made his eyebrow raise higher. Raising on my tiptoes, I kissed his cheek before hovering over his mouth with mine.

"Did you want one too?"

"What?" he breathed.

"A kiss."

The flush across his face spread from his cheeks down his neck and if I looked, I was in no doubt the tips of his ears would be red too. So I took the drink out of his hand and carefully placed it on the dining table next to us. Then my hands were in his hair, dragging him closer as our lips met in a clash of urgency. He fisted my t-shirt in his hands at my waist, holding me still as he deepened the kiss. I felt an extra set of hands curling around my hips and a mouth planted against my neck, teasing and sucking at my skin.

Oh. Holy. Fuck.

Sandwiched between Quinn and Eric was somewhere I could stay forever. The soreness of my chest didn't matter when I had their hands and mouths on me. I turned my head as Eric kissed down my jaw and Quinn was there, kissing my lips and making me feel like I really was their queen.

"You have to stop," I all but moaned when both of them ground against me. "We have guests."

"We'll continue this later," Quinn said although he didn't pull away.

"What, the three of us?" Eric questioned as he nuzzled my neck.

"Yes."

"But I'm still not better," I interjected.

Quinn chuckled.

"Don't worry, little girl, there are many ways we can pleasure you that don't involve fucking the two of us at the same time."

I wriggled my way out from between them and scowled.

"No. Bad boys… And I suggest you sort yourselves out unless you want my dad to know what we were doing in there."

I pointedly looked at the distinct bulges in both their crotches. Quinn looked nonplussed whilst Eric shuffled away from him, his face still very much on fire.

"You can't talk, little girl. Perhaps try checking yourself in the mirror."

My scowl deepened and I flew over to the mirror above one of the cabinets, realising he was right. My pupils were dilated, my face flushed and I had that glow about me.

"For fuck's sake," I muttered before storming away into the living room. I didn't have time to hide it.

Of course, the moment I walked in, Xav winked at me and gave me a thumbs up, which only prompted me to give him the middle finger in return. I tried to compose myself when Alekhin stood up and levelled his gaze on me.

"What's the prognosis?" I asked with a shaky voice.

"The swelling is going down but I don't think he needs a cast. He needs further rest and to stick to light activity. It is still early days, but I think your friend will make a full recovery."

I was about to retort he wasn't just my friend but kept my mouth shut. Instead, I went straight to Rory and checked him over myself, running my hand across his cheek. His hazel eyes had been dull since the crash but a spark of life was there as I touched him which flooded me with relief.

"I'll be going then, enjoy the rest of your evening," Alekhin said.

I sort of waved at him as I stared into Rory's eyes.

"Little star…"

"Shh, let me be happy you're going to be okay, Ror."

Leaning forward, I pressed a kiss to his cheek which made him sigh quietly.

"I've been so fucking worried," I whispered. "Seeing you hurt ripped my heart out of my chest."

"Little star, please."

It was probably making him uncomfortable having me all over him when my dad was here. I kissed his cheek again before pulling away.

"I love you."

Then I got up and turned to Xav and Viktor, who were both watching us. Xav with a smirk and Viktor with understanding.

"Dinner's ready, should we go through?"

CHAPTER SIX

Eric

"You owe me," Xav hissed at me right after we sat down.

I glanced at him with a frown.

"Why?"

He rolled his eyes and served himself roast potatoes. I'd made sure to make extra since I knew they were the boys' favourites.

"Who do you think kept Daddy V's attention away from you and Quinn mauling his daughter?"

I almost choked.

"What did you just call him?"

"Viktor."

I scowled as he grinned. I didn't care he'd had to keep Viktor's attention away from us. Hell, that kiss had been hot. But Xav calling the man who was essentially our father-in-law a stupid name which was bound to piss off Ash? Yeah, I had a problem with it.

"Have you said that to Ash?"

He shrugged as he continued to serve himself after Quinn passed him carrots. I'd gone all out and made a roast dinner for this evening with both beef and chicken.

"Yes, and I swear she would've beaten me up if she wasn't hurting."

I eyed Ash who was making sure to serve Rory. It wouldn't surprise me if she cut up his food for him. Something I knew Rory wouldn't exactly be happy about but would allow. Ash could be a little scary when she went off on one.

"It's a bit creepy… even for you."

"What do you mean? I'm not creepy."

"Creepy, pervy, same thing."

He pointed his fork at me.

"It is not."

"Would you two stop bickering?" Quinn interjected.

Xav turned to him with a grin and I knew there'd be trouble ahead regardless of the fact we were entertaining Ash's dad tonight.

"Sorry, *Dad*, the missus and I will try to keep it down."

"Excuse me? Why am I the wife in this situation?" I asked, midway between serving myself some parsnips.

Xav patted my arm as Quinn glared at him.

"We both know why that is, dear."

"Jesus Christ," Quinn muttered.

Just because I bottomed didn't make me his fucking wife. I poked Xav in the ribs as a warning. If he didn't cut it out, then I'd use his ticklishness against him. I spared a glance at Viktor, who looked outright amused by what was happening at the table. This was nothing compared to what it could be like with Xav, his incessant jokes and relentless teasing.

Viktor leant over towards Ash, "Are they always like this?"

"This is them on their best behaviour," she replied, rolling her eyes.

"I would like to see them at their worst."

Ash hid a smile behind her fork.

"I'm sure you'd be scandalised."

Viktor's grin got wider.

"I assure you, I have seen a lot of very scandalous things in my time."

Ash flushed and looked down at her plate.

"Husband and wife isn't far off what Xav and E are," she all but whispered.

Since Xav was too busy stuffing his face and Quinn was scowling into his plate, I doubted they heard her. Rory was busy trying to eat with one hand until Ash noticed and practically ripped his cutlery out of his hand so she could cut his meat up for him. He looked like he was going to protest, then he saw her face. He sat back and let her get on with it, making me grin.

You really do love that girl, Rory. More than you'll ever let on.

Quinn looked up and raised an eyebrow at Rory, who scowled. Then Quinn grinned and shook his head. Our quiet boy didn't like being forced to have Ash babysit him like this. Then again, if it had been one of us, he'd have outright refused.

Viktor sat back and eyed me and Xav for a moment before comprehension crossed his features. I couldn't say our situation was the norm or that many people would approve of it. I mean for starters, the four of us shared a girlfriend and then there was Xav and me to contend with on top of it.

Complicated didn't even begin to cut it. But we were it for each other. The five of us. Four friends forged in the fucking pits of hell and one girl who'd been broken until we fitted her pieces back together again.

"Okay since all you are being quiet as shit about this, I guess I'll start," Xav said, waving his fork around. "We need to do something about Julian and fast because I for one don't want him fucking well out on the streets any longer."

I winced. We'd been avoiding talking about him whilst Ash and Rory recovered over the past couple of days, but it was the reason Viktor was even here other than to see his daughter.

"Julian would be your father," Viktor said.

"Yes, a father who should be in prison… not to mention he has cancer and is meant to have treatment for it. And who knows if he's still on his medication for his lung clot. We need to find him. Julian might be a psycho, but I don't want him dead."

I rubbed Xav's arm, realising perhaps this whole situation bothered him more than he'd been willing to let on. His conflict surrounding Julian was no secret to me, but with everything going on, he'd not said anything about how he felt regarding this situation.

"Do you have an idea of where he'd have gone?"

Xav looked down at his plate.

"I'm sure you know he used to be an enforcer for Russo. I imagine he's with his old associates, but I have no clue where they'd be. We didn't think to keep tabs on them after Julian got sent down."

"Then that's what we do first," Quinn said. "Look for them and work out if they're still loyal to Russo, then we lean on them. I can pull in favours from a few people to help us track him down."

It seemed like the only plan of action we had regarding Julian. The police were hunting for him, but if Russo's men had helped him escape, they knew very well how to evade the police. Julian wasn't stupid. He knew he needed to keep a low profile until he was ready to strike. Whatever plans he had couldn't be good. Our focus should be on keeping Ash inside and away from everyone else until further notice.

"Okay, I can get started on that."

"Have you thought further about Isabella?" Viktor asked.

Quinn's mouth settled into a thin line.

"We don't know where Russo is holding her," I said, saving Quinn from answering. "And our contact within his organisation has gone dark. The only other intel we've managed to acquire is from Fabio, but even he has no clue what's going on."

Viktor rubbed his chin.

"Yes, he told me as much. It seems Russo isn't taking chances."

"Are you saying you can't get a hold of Nate?" Ash asked, looking up from where she was helping Rory eat.

"No, not for lack of trying," Quinn replied.

Ash's face fell a little and her brow furrowed.

"That's not good. Do you think Frank knows he's your mole?"

Quinn's expression turned grim.

"Could well be. I think we have to assume the worst and turn to other avenues to find out what's happening in Russo's inner circle."

Ash's face paled a little and she turned back to Rory. His eyes were intent on her as she resumed helping him with his food. I could only imagine what was running through her mind right then. She might be ours now and angry at Nate, but I don't think she wanted him to die at Russo's hands. We'd have to wait and see what happened next as much as it pained me. We'd had so many plans ruined recently. Everything was up in the air and who the fuck knew how things would go from here on out.

"You can't put Fabi in any further danger," Ash said quietly, her eyes on Rory rather than the rest of us.

"We might not have a choice."

"There's always a choice. He has a family. If there's anyone I care about who is a part of this world outside of this room, it's him. So please… for me."

"*Kotik*, we need him," Viktor said.

I watched her hand tremble as she curled it into a fist on the table.

"Mandy and Ricardo need him more."

"He knows what he's signed up for."

The fork she was holding clattered on the plate. She pushed her chair back and stood up abruptly.

"Excuse me."

I saw the pain in her blue eyes before she walked out of the room. Before anyone else could do a thing, I rose to my feet and followed her. Ash was in the kitchen, pacing and running her hands through her hair as I closed the door behind us.

"They can't," she said, not stopping to look at me. "It's not fair."

I approached her slowly, not wanting her to get spooked and lash out at me considering I understood her predicament.

"How can they act like Fabi is collateral in this?"

I stopped her pacing and tugged her against my chest, running my hand down her back. She didn't exactly melt into my embrace, but she didn't try to escape either.

"He was my only friend growing up, E, my only friend. The only person who gave a shit about me."

I had a feeling there was more to it than that, so I said nothing.

"I can't let him die. He's done so much for me. So fucking much. God. This sucks. Fuck. I hate this situation. I hate everything about it. I fucking hate stupid fucking Frank and his bullshit."

Her hands buried themselves in my jumper, fisting the fabric at my waist.

"What happened between you and Fabio?"

She let out a shuddering breath before the tension left her body and she buried her face in my chest.

"He was my first," she whispered. "It was my first act of defiance against my father… I wanted to decide who it was. He meant the world to me, you know. Not romantically, but as a friend. When he met Mandy, he couldn't be around me as much, but I never forgot what he did for me. How much he cared. How gentle he'd been with me. He did that for me so isn't it only fair I do this for him?"

I held her tighter, understanding what drove her. Why she didn't want her friend hurt in this war, but war had a way of hurting everyone involved. And there would be collateral damage no matter what.

"Sometimes we have to make very tough choices in life. He knows what he signed up for, Ash. He chose to work with Viktor as well as Russo. We can't protect everyone we love."

I didn't want to say those things to her, but they were true.

"I know. I hate it, but I know."

She pulled back and stared up at me. The tension and anxiety flittering across her features made me want to take her away from all of this so she wouldn't have to suffer any longer.

"We're going to get through this, aren't we? None of us will be safe until we destroy Frank. I want him gone, but I'm still terrified he'll hurt everyone I love in the process. He's not a man people mess with for good reason."

Reaching up, I cupped her cheek and stroked her face with my thumb.

"I think we have to hope for the best but prepare for the worst. We've made so many plans and all of them have failed to take him down. What we do next will ultimately decide our fates in this war. And make no mistake, Ash, this is a war and one we have to win no matter the cost."

"What if the cost is one of us?"

I almost shuddered thinking about it. We could not afford for that to happen. The cost would be too high. Far too fucking high. So even as I'd said, no matter the cost, I didn't mean us. We had to find a way to survive. We needed each other.

"How about we don't think about it unless we have to cross that bridge? We already have enough to worry about without the possibility of one of us not making it through this."

She leant into my hand, her eyes darkening.

"You're right. There's already enough on the line."

"You ready to go back in?"

Ash took the opportunity to raise up on her tiptoes and reach for me. I leant down willingly, letting her brush her lips over my jaw.

"I am… Thank you… you always know how to calm me down."

I turned my face into her mouth and kissed her, cupping the back of her head gently. My beautiful girl sometimes needed a minute to gather her thoughts.

"I love you," she murmured against my lips.

My heart thundered whenever she said it. I'd never get over hearing those words coming from her.

"I love you too."

I pulled away and she dropped back down to her feet.

"Guess I should tell them I understand why Fabi has to put himself in danger."

Taking her hand, I pulled her back towards the dining room.

"It's going to be okay, Ash. You'll see."

I wish I could see it too. My words felt hollow and empty. Who knew whether or not things would be okay. Who knew if any of us would come out of this unscathed. Only time would tell. And time was not on our side at all.

CHAPTER SEVEN

Xavier

I glanced at the clock, realising it was almost dinner time. Having spent most of the day researching Julian's old contacts and doing website maintenance, I was starving. I stood up and stretched before ambling downstairs into the kitchen. It was deserted, making me frown. Eric was normally cooking dinner at this time.

I walked into the living room, finding Ash and Rory on the sofa. She seemed to be reading to him but stopped mid-sentence when I arrived. Considering Rory was still under strict orders to keep his activity to a minimum, to see Ash looking after him and him letting her was sweet.

"Hey lovebirds, you seen E?"

"He went to the casino a few hours ago," Ash replied.

"He should've been back by now though," Rory added.

I slumped down next to Ash and stroked her shoulder.

"Did Quinn go with him?"

"No, he's in his office… I think he's in a mood which is why we're hiding in here."

I grinned as she leant into me.

"What's Mr Uptight's problem this time?"

"Something about Mac McCarthy."

"Fucking Irish gangsters."

Ash shrugged and popped her Kindle down in her lap. I glanced at it, seeing the paragraph she was on.

'His fingers wrapped around my neck, squeezing until I could hardly breathe. My heart pounded violently in my ears as my body trembled with need. The wicked look in his eyes set fire to my veins. There was no doubt in my mind, this man would devour me whole with his cock and his tongue.'

"Are you reading porn to Rory?"

Ash fumbled with the off button, clearing the text off the screen as her face flushed.

"No! It's a romance book."

"That's what's in romance books? Jesus, I need to get me some of that."

She rolled her eyes and shoved me.

"Not all of them…"

I glanced at Rory over the top of her head.

"This is the shit you're into? Man, I wish I'd known this earlier."

"Fuck off," he muttered.

"Hey, I'm not judging. Hell, angel, you can read this shit to me any day."

"I'd rather not. You'd complain about it the whole time except for the sexy parts and then you'd get distracted and want to get in my knickers."

She hit the nail on the head right there. Just the thought of hearing dirty shit from that pretty mouth of hers had my cock stirring. None of us had been able to touch Ash intimately since the car crash. I couldn't exactly complain, but fuck did I miss her lithe body wrapped around mine.

"Mmm, did the doctor say when you can resume normal activities again?" I asked, leaning towards her and nuzzling my nose against her neck.

"Xav…"

"I can't deny I'd use any excuse to get you naked and hearing you read dirty sex out loud would definitely constitute as an excuse."

She squirmed as I kissed her neck. I took her hand and pressed it against me, not caring at all Rory was right there.

"I'm surprised Rory here isn't getting all hot and bothered by it."

"He's not allowed to do any strenuous activity," Ash panted out as her fingers wrapped around my cock.

"I'm relatively sure if you did all the work, it wouldn't be an issue."

"Would you leave her alone?" Rory interjected. "She's still in pain."

I pulled away and gave him a sly smile.

"She's not complaining."

He glanced down at where Ash's hand was in my lap and rolled his eyes.

My phone buzzed. I fished it out of my pocket whilst Ash pulled her hand away, shifting closer to Rory with a very red face. She gave him an apologetic look.

I frowned as I noticed it was a picture message from Eric. Opening it, I felt an icy chill run down my spine. Sitting in a chair was Eric, his head bowed against his chest and blood trickling down his forehead. It looked as though his hands were secured behind the back of the chair, which is what was still holding him up.

ERIC: Your boyfriend and I are going to get further acquainted today. As if we're not already. Lots of love, Dad x

"Xav? Are you okay?" Ash asked.

I didn't even know what the fuck to say, so I gave her the phone. Julian had taken Eric. My worst fear confirmed. Here we were worrying about Ash and I should've fucking well been worrying about the rest of us. All of us should've been on fucking high alert.

"Wait… Julian has E?"

Rory peered over Ash's shoulder, staring down at the message and picture.

Why the fuck was I sitting here like a lemon? I needed to do something. I needed to save him. Like right now.

I jumped up, ready to spring into action until I remembered I didn't have a fucking clue where Eric was.

"We need to get Quinn," Rory said, his expression turning grim.

"I'll go," Ash said, getting up and handing Rory my phone.

She was out of the room before I could say a word. Rory looked up at me. I didn't know what to do or say. If I thought too hard about how much danger Eric was in, I might break the fuck down. All I knew was I had to get to him.

"Where do you think this is?" He pointed at the photo as he held up the phone to me. "Because that picture in the background looks familiar."

I took it from him and stared at it, zooming in as I realised he was right. Then my hand trembled. The realisation hit me like a ton of bricks. When Julian went to prison, he still owned the house I grew up in. The house where he murdered Mum and Katie. It'd remained empty for twelve years as I refused to step foot in it after Julian had transferred the deed into my name. I didn't want to sell it because the thought of anyone living in that house after what Julian had done in it made me ill.

"Fuck. Fuck, it's… FUCK!"

Quinn and Ash appeared in the doorway.

"Show me," he demanded, coming over to the sofa.

I handed him the phone.

"He's taken him to the house…"

Quinn looked over the photo and the message. His expression hardened and his fist clenched at his side.

"Don't reply to him. He doesn't know we know where he is or maybe he knew we'd recognise it. Fuck. Okay, first, we need weapons, then we'll go after him."

"What?" Ash said, her eyes widening.

"You and Rory are staying here whilst we deal with this."

"You and Xav can't go after Julian by yourselves!"

Quinn turned to Ash, his eyes dark.

"What else do you expect us to do? We're not leaving E with Julian. Rory and you can't help us, you're both injured."

Ash looked as incensed as I felt. Julian taking Eric made my blood boil. Hatred laced my veins as well as fear. Fear for my best friend and soulmate.

"I'm calling my dad."

"What? No, do not call Viktor."

"For fuck's sake, Quinn. You're not going to call the police to deal with it, are you? So I'm not letting you go running off and being all heroic without backup, you hear me?"

I didn't have time for their argument. I stomped out of the room and went into Quinn's office. Opening one cupboard, I pulled out two guns, a baseball bat, rope and two sets of handcuffs, stuffing them into a bag. We needed to subdue Julian before he hurt any of us. I didn't want to kill my father. He needed to go back to prison. But if the worst happened, then I would fucking kill the man before he could kill us.

I walked out into the hallway, finding Quinn grabbing the car keys off the side table. Now the Audi was done for, we only had two cars. I knew Eric would've taken the BMW so we'd be in the Range Rover.

"Is she going to call Viktor?"

"Yes… I can't fucking stop her, but at least she's not demanding she comes with. I realise she's upset about it being E, but we can't afford to get emotional over this."

Quinn was right which is why I kept a lid on mine. I channelled my fear into anger.

Ash came rushing out of the living room and wrapped her arms around me.

"Bring him home, please," she whispered. "And tell him I love him."

"I promise I'll bring him back, angel, if it's the last fucking thing I do."

"Don't get yourself killed, okay? Please, both of you stay safe."

I leant down and kissed her, sealing my promise I'd bring Eric back home to her. Ash went to Quinn and hugged him too. He stroked her hair and then we were walking out of the house.

It was fucking time we dealt with my piece of shit father for good. That man was not going to get away with this shit. Not on my fucking watch.

CHAPTER EIGHT

Eric

The pounding in my head was like a fucking base drum. What the hell happened? The last thing I remember was opening the backdoor to the casino to jump in the car and drive home. After that? A complete blank.

I cracked my eyes open finding a man standing with his back to me a few feet away. My head snapped back and I tried to move. Looking down, I realised it would be impossible. My arms were tied behind my back and my legs to the chair legs. As I moved my wrists, it felt like cable ties digging into my skin.

I looked around the room next and recognition filled me instantly. How could it not? I'd grown up in and out of this fucking house.

"I see you're awake," came the voice of the man who'd terrorised my best friend's entire childhood.

Julian turned and stared at me with unnerving intensity. The manic look in his eyes had me swallowing hard. I'd seen that look a hundred times and it didn't signal good things. It gave me the distinct impression he'd taken me for the purpose of getting back at Xav as opposed to doing it for Russo.

"I thought we could all have a little reunion. Just like the old days, hey? You boys always used to cause such trouble when you were kids. Xavier was always coming home with letters from the headteacher regarding his behaviour. Some might say… like father, like son."

Xav was nothing like Julian. He wasn't psychotic. If anything, Xav had more compassion and understanding in his little finger than Julian possessed in his entire body. He might like to joke a lot, but humour was his defence mechanism. He didn't like to take life too seriously except when it was needed. Like when shit was life or death. Like right now.

Do they know Julian took me?

"If you think Xav is anything like you, you're fucking delusional."

Julian threw back his head and laughed. It was maniacal. A chill ran down my spine. Being tied up with a psychotic killer didn't sit well with me. Who knew what Julian would do. The man was fucking unhinged. I didn't think prison had softened him. He could hide his darker urges behind a façade if he wanted to. That was part of his charm. Except I knew better.

"Oh, Eric, you've changed. What happened to the shy timid boy who liked to follow my son around like a puppy dog?"

He grew up and learnt how to stand up for himself.

I clenched my jaw shut. Talking to Julian wouldn't get me anywhere. What did he have planned? A reunion? Too bad he wouldn't get that. If Julian had contacted Xav, then it'd be him and Quinn who came after me. Rory still had his concussion to contend with. And Quinn wouldn't let Ash out of the house.

"No wonder Xavier sat up and took notice. Can't say I'm surprised the four of you stayed together. Not as if anyone else gave a shit about you, especially not your parents."

I flinched. Julian had known them. And even though I hated it, he took me in since he didn't have an issue with my sexuality nor Xav's. I wouldn't ever be grateful to the man in front of me. Not when he beat his own children and wife before murdering them. Not a day went by I wasn't thankful Xav had been out with us that night. If he hadn't, who knows if he would still be with us today.

"What do you want?" I ground out.

He waved his hands around.

"So many things."

"Care to narrow it down a little?"

His sly smile chilled me to my very core.

"I want my son to pay for putting me behind bars."

"So what? You want him dead?"

Julian shook his head and paced away.

"Oh no, no, no, no, no, Eric. I don't want to *kill* Xavier. I want him to suffer. And how can I do that, you ask? Oh well… many, many ways." He turned back to me, the wild look in his eyes returning. "Starting with you, of course… Now, I wanted to take Ashleigh, but she never leaves your house. You're all so busy trying to protect that girl, you forgot to protect yourselves."

It's not as if we didn't view Julian as a threat. We'd been actively trying to track him down, but it didn't mean we could neglect our businesses. The only reason I'd gone to the casino alone was to meet with Geoff regarding an urgent financial matter. There'd been a need to pull out of one of our investments before it went south.

"Congratulating yourself on taking me unawares, are you?"

I shouldn't be baiting him, but, quite frankly, I'd had enough of being treated like I couldn't handle myself. I'd known Julian most of my life. Whilst he scared me on some level, I also knew he'd want Xav here to witness my suffering. He wasn't going to do anything too drastic just yet.

I hoped.

"Perhaps."

"What's the hold up then, Julian? Afraid to hurt me?"

He advanced on me and grabbed me by the face, staring down at me with no small amount of hatred in his eyes.

"You think you're so fucking smart, do you?"

He let go of my face and backhanded me, causing my head to snap back. It hurt, but not to the point where I thought it might bruise. It was clear he didn't like me smiling at him when I looked at his face as he stalked away, clenching his fists.

"Calm down," he muttered to himself. "Not yet… not yet."

"Have you even told him where we are?"

Were they coming for me? No doubt Quinn and Xav wouldn't hesitate if they knew where Julian had taken me. Not that Xav ever wanted to set foot in this house again. Hell, we were in the room where Julian had taken Erin and Katie's lives. Of course, the blood no longer remained, but the atmosphere in here suffocated me. Ominous.

How is he going to cope with being here again?

"No, and I'm not going to. He needs to learn a little lesson in humility."

I almost scoffed. Xav could never be called humble. He had an ego the size of England and wasn't shy about it. Probably why he and Quinn were always at odds. Their clashing egos had always been a problem in our household. Which was why it'd come as a surprise the two of them had buried the hatchet when it came to Ash. Though now I knew. Ash had that way about her. She kept the peace as much as I did, if not more now we were all together.

My heart sank. I missed the fuck out of her. Last night after Viktor had left, she'd put Rory to bed and crawled into her own, quickly followed by me and Quinn. Whilst we hadn't gone any further than just kissing and touching, we'd all fallen asleep together like it was the new normal. It seemed the closer we got, the less the four of us cared about sharing beds. Ash had been nestled between us this morning, her blonde hair a mess over the pillows and her face at peace. She'd looked so damn beautiful. At this rate, we were going to need bigger beds to accommodate our new sleeping arrangements. That's if I even got out of this fucking situation I was in with Julian.

"Does he know you have me?"

"Of course, I sent him proof so he knows I'm not fucking around."

I had to hope Xav wasn't losing his shit right now. All of them probably were. My heart ached at the very thought of it.

"And what are your plans now?"

Julian glared at me.

"As if I'm going to tell you that."

I smiled, which I don't think made him any happier. Julian was far too easy to rile up. I had to be careful not to push him too hard. Didn't want him to snap and hurt me worse than he already planned to.

"How long was I out for?"

He glanced down at the phone in his hand, which was mine. The fucking bastard had taken it. Probably how he got in contact with Xav.

"An hour or so, perhaps. Took time to bring you here."

"Oh yeah? How d'you manage it?"

Julian looked like he was preening himself as he grinned.

"Oh well, I took your car, after all, the keys were on you. You're not so heavy I couldn't stuff you in the back."

Julian was built like Xav even though his son was far bigger in terms of muscle mass.

"And how did you even escape the hospital?"

He grinned wider as he paced away, putting his hands out.

"Easy, one of those stupid guards didn't notice when a nurse smuggled me a phone. Got in contact with Russo, told him everything he needed to know to guarantee my escape and here we are. Pretty simple to wind people around your finger when you've got as much charm as I do."

I stifled my amusement. He was so fucking full of himself. Even though I hated comparing Xav to Julian, you could see how much they were alike. Xav wasn't psychotic and whilst he might act like he was the dog's bollocks, he was still endearing, kind and understanding. Julian didn't have a good fucking bone in his body.

"I'm sure."

Keeping him talking about himself was probably the best way I was going to buy myself some time. And I needed all the time I could get if Quinn and Xav were ever going to find me.

"Just because I've been in prison for twelve years, don't mean I haven't seen a woman. The female officers find me endearing. Some of them can't believe I could kill so brutally, but I suppose they don't know me quite like you do."

Too fucking right.

"If you want me to congratulate you on fooling half the fucking world, then you're barking up the wrong tree."

As he turned, I could see the gleam in his eyes.

"They'll realise just how much of a bastard I am when they find you… They think I have the capacity to change. Fools." He scoffed. "This place has seen so much blood… and I wonder how much more it'll see before I'm done. I love the smell of it, watching it seep into every nook and cranny. It's so beautiful. Crimson red… but you know what's more beautiful?"

I didn't move, feeling more than a little ill as he approached me.

"It's the look in a person's eyes when they realised they're going to die."

I swallowed hard. If Xav and Quinn didn't find me soon… I was pretty sure they'd be left with pieces of me rather than a whole alive version judging by Julian's expression.

I had to fucking hope and pray they'd get here before that happened.

Or I'd be utterly fucked.

CHAPTER NINE

Xavier

My leg bounced as I scanned the houses whilst Quinn drove. He kept glancing at me as if he was worried I might trash the car in a rage or something. Hell, I wanted to but right now, I had to focus on us getting to Eric in time. The only person who deserved my ire right now was Julian.

"Can't you drive fucking faster?"

"And what, Xav? Earn us a fucking car chase from the police? I don't think so. We need to stay fucking calm."

"How the fuck do you expect me to be calm when E is in danger a-fucking-gain?"

After the incident with fucking Gregor Bykov, I'd sworn to myself I'd never let Eric get caught out like that. He shouldn't have gone to the fucking casino alone. We lived in dangerous times and none of us were safe. We needed to stick together. And once I got him back, I wouldn't bloody well let him go out alone until this shit with Russo was over.

You sound like Quinn.

Who gave a shit? Eric was everything to me. I couldn't allow anything to happen to him. My fucking soulmate was in trouble and it killed me.

Quinn's phone started ringing and he tossed it to me. It'd been going off for the past five minutes, but he'd been ignoring it up until then. It seemed he'd finally got fed up with it.

"Answer it."

I fumbled with it for a moment before putting it to my ear.

"Hello?"

"Xav… where's Quinn?"

"He's driving, angel."

Should've known it would be Ash calling. She hadn't wanted us going after Eric alone.

"Are you there yet?"

"No, we're about five minutes away."

I wished we were fucking there so I could damn well make sure Eric wasn't in danger any longer. My heart felt tight and my hand shook in my lap.

Focus. Don't fucking let yourself get emotional. Don't do it.

"Tell him we have a problem."

"What? What's happened?"

"You know how he was complaining about Mac McCarthy earlier? Well, Geoff called Rory when he couldn't get hold of Quinn. Mac is at the Syndicate demanding an audience."

"For fuck's sake! We can't go. We have to get to E."

"What's wrong?" Quinn asked, glancing at me again.

I put my hand over the speaker.

"According to Ash, McCarthy is at the casino demanding we see him."

Quinn slammed a hand down on the steering wheel.

"Jesus fucking Christ. I do not need this shit."

"What do we do?"

"He can fucking well wait. I am not leaving E with your psychopathic father under any circumstances."

It's what I'd hoped Quinn would say. We couldn't leave Eric with Julian any longer than we had to. No telling what he'd do. My question was why the fuck was McCarthy getting on our case? The man was a fucking fool.

"Did you hear that, angel?"

"I did… Xav… he's not just demanding an audience…"

I felt my stomach drop. We didn't need any further shitty news today, but apparently, the world was having a laugh at our expense.

"What exactly is he doing?"

"He's holding up the place… at gunpoint."

I took a breath.

"Are you serious?"

"Yes, Geoff is there. He's locked himself in the main office and is monitoring the situation. Rory is still talking to him."

I turned to Quinn, who looked thunderous. He would blow his fucking top off when he learnt of this development. And I didn't want to be the bearer of such news, but fuck it. We now had two fucked up situations to deal with.

"What does that Irish cunt actually want?"

"He's been asking me for a meeting ever since he found out who I was," Quinn gritted out. "Says I owe him for all the trouble we've caused his fucking operations. Wouldn't have fucked with him if he wasn't one of Russo's main suppliers of drugs and weapons."

"Wait, what? You never fucking told me that."

"There was no need."

I clenched my jaw shut. Quinn always kept important shit to himself.

"Well, if you had told me, then I could've fucking well kept tabs on him and his gang, right? Because now he's holding up our fucking business at gunpoint."

"What? What the fuck?"

"Yeah, Geoff is hauled up in the fucking office watching, that's why he's been calling."

Quinn pulled up outside the house I grew up in. I stared at the building, feeling sick to my stomach.

"Fuck. Fucking fuck… fuck, we do not need this shit." He ran a hand through his hair. "That's it. We're going in, we're getting E, then we're going after the Irish cunt. If he thinks for a second he's not going down, he's a fucking idiot."

Before I had a chance to say anything, he opened the car door and jumped out, slamming it behind him. Quinn was raging and I honestly couldn't blame him. We had enough on our plate without this shit to contend with.

"Angel, we need to get E then I'll call you, okay? Did you get a hold of Viktor?"

"Not yet, but I'll call him now. Is Quinn okay?"

"No, but I imagine he might take his anger out on Julian. Not sure I care any longer. Just tell Geoff we'll be there as soon as we can, but don't mention the E shit, okay?"

"Okay, *tesoro*, please don't let Quinn do anything stupid."

It was liable to be me who did something reckless at this point but I decided not to point that out as I said goodbye to her and hopped out the car myself. Quinn had already pulled out a gun and the baseball bat, which he was tapping against his leg as he waited for me.

"Let's go."

"Wait, we can't go in without a plan," I said as he started towards the house after handing me the bag.

"We can because no doubt your psycho father will hurt E and that's not fucking happening, got it?"

I pulled out the second gun and slung the bag over my shoulder. Quinn kicked the front door in with little care as the wood splintered under the impact. He wasn't fucking around.

"Julian, where the fuck are you?" he shouted as he stepped through the destroyed wood into the hallway.

I swallowed hard and stepped in after him. There came a muffled sound from the living room and I wanted to die. That was where Julian had killed my mum and Katie. I tried to block out the images of blood, but they were there, haunting me. As if I couldn't hate my father any more right now.

The moment we walked into the living room, my heart fucking dropped. Eric was tied up with his face bruised as if Julian had been beating on him. I almost saw fucking red. Julian was standing by the dining table, twirling a knife.

"So you worked it out, did you?" he said quietly as he stepped up to Eric and put the knife to his neck. "I should've known."

"Get the fuck away from him," I ground out as I raised my gun.

"Now, now, Xavier, where's the fun in that?" He stared at the gun. "You wouldn't shoot your own father."

"He might not, but I fucking will," Quinn said, aiming his gun at Julian's head.

"Ah, Quinn… and here I thought you were the one who thinks before he acts." Julian looked behind us. "What? No Rory?"

"He's with Ash," I said. "You think we'd leave her completely defenceless?"

I didn't want to tell Julian, Rory was injured and that's why he'd stayed at home.

"I suppose not. You are rather protective of your little woman. Surprises me really, considering she's the daughter of your sworn enemy."

Quinn practically growled and my eyes fixed firmly on Julian. I could feel Eric's eyes on me but right now, my focus was on making sure Julian didn't hurt him further. I needed my man to come out of this alive and fucking well.

"Didn't you get the fucking memo, psycho? Russo is a dead man walking. And so are you at this rate. Let him go."

Julian grinned and winked at Quinn.

"Don't shoot him," I hissed.

Might seem ridiculous, but a dead Julian wasn't what I wanted at all. Why the hell did I feel so conflicted after all this time? The man was fucking evil. Quinn shot me a dark look but gave a subtle nod. We couldn't take the chance anyway. Not when Julian had a knife to Eric's neck.

My eyes finally fell on him and my heart fucking died on the spot. My beautiful man looked as if he'd been through the wars. His chestnut hair was plastered to his forehead, sweat beading across it. A trail of blood dripped down the side of his face from his hairline and his eye was rapidly swelling.

I clenched my jaw shut. There was a certain steely determination in his eyes, as if telling me it'd be okay. How the fuck could he know that? He had a knife to his throat and my cunt of a father had beaten him.

Then he mouthed the words which almost destroyed me.

"I love you, Xavi."

Nothing could prepare me for the pain in my chest. Eric was the world to me. If I lost him, I wouldn't cope. I needed the five of us together. He was an integral piece of our relationship.

"Isn't this lovely? Here we all are again. My son is too scared to end me, aren't you, Xavier? Doesn't the guilt eat you up inside? You had your chance when you found me. I would've let you. Then it would've been you who'd be behind bars rather than me." He pointed his free hand at me. "You stole the last twelve years from me."

His words tore into me. I hated they were true. Except the thought of killing my own father still didn't sit well with me. Hell, I knew Ash wanted to murder the man who raised her, but Russo wasn't actually her father. But Julian? Julian would always be my flesh and blood.

"You belong behind bars."

Julian's eyes flicked to Quinn and noted the baseball bat in his hand, which he tapped against his leg with irritation.

"Ironic, is it not? Bringing that with you. Do you remember it, Xavier? Remember how her blood stained the wood. You'll never feel the satisfying crunch as the bat connects with the skull again and again until there's nothing but brains and blood left. She was my final masterpiece."

I swallowed back bile. How he could even talk so candidly about murdering my mother, his wife, disgusted me.

"And in court when they held it up as evidence. Oh, the jury was horrified because no matter what they did, the blood still remained."

"Stop it. Just stop it."

Julian's grin was pure evil.

"Why? Does it still haunt you? Does it eat you up inside? All that blood."

"Shut up."

I could see Eric's eyes telling me to calm down, but I couldn't. The images assaulted me. Tearing me apart from the inside out. I could almost see Katie on the sofa and Mum on the floor. Dead. Gone.

"They screamed and begged me not to do it. Begged, Xavier."

That was fucking it. I couldn't take this any longer. His words were like knives across my skin. Tearing it from my flesh. I wanted him gone. Gone for fucking good.

Before I had a chance to move, Quinn stepped closer to me and gave me a warning stare.

"Don't," he hissed. "Just don't, Xav. He's taunting you… Do you trust me?"

I nodded. Quinn would do anything for me, just as I would for him. Despite me constantly giving him shit, he was one of my best friends and the person I'd go to hell and back for.

"Then let me handle this."

I clenched my fist around the gun pointed at my father's chest. Quinn would get us out of this. He deserved my trust and dedication. Always.

"He can't be taking his medication for his lung clot, which means he's weakened," I whispered. "I can see it in his eyes…

if we can get him away from E, then we can tie him up and leave him for the police."

Quinn's expression turned grim, but he understood what I was saying. Our only hope was to overpower my father and keep him from slitting my soulmate's throat.

"Conspiring, are you?" Julian said, the corners of his mouth turning up.

Quinn lowered his gun and slid it into the waistband of his trousers. Then he chucked the baseball bat from hand to hand, watching Julian with no small amount of hatred in his eyes.

"What do you want from us?"

"What do I want? Ha, now you ask… I want Xavier to suffer."

Quinn gripped the bat in his right hand and put his left one out.

"Do you not think being here isn't torture enough? Seeing the love of his life tied up with a knife to his throat?" He took a step forward. "Being in the place where his family died a painful, agonising death. How much more suffering do you think he needs to go through?"

Julian's eyes narrowed.

"It's not enough. It'll never be enough."

Quinn's lip curled up in a sneer as he pointed the bat at Julian.

"All you've ever wanted in life is to cause suffering and pain. I can see it in your fucking eyes… Well, guess what… I'm going to make you suffer more than you've ever known. Do you think you're the only one who's maimed and tortured whilst your victim slowly deteriorates? Whilst the blood drains from their body and they're in so much pain, they beg to die."

Julian stared at Quinn with confusion as he took another step forward.

My stomach turned. He was talking about the night with Rory's foster family. And I couldn't say I wanted the reminder but Quinn was doing all he could to protect Eric from Julian. So I just had to suck it up.

"I have, Julian… in fact, we all have. We were better at covering it up. Xav might not hurt you, but I will. I will destroy you for everything you've done."

Quinn's expression remained hard, but I knew he was as worried as me about Eric's safety. He had to remain calm and stay the course. We weren't going to hurt Julian, but he didn't know that.

"I'm going to enjoy watching the life drain from your eyes."

Julian's eyebrows shot up and that's when Quinn struck. The bat went flying and smacked Julian in the shoulder, catching him off guard. Then Quinn launched himself towards Eric and Julian. The chair went toppling backwards as Quinn ripped Julian's hand away from Eric's neck. The three of them were in a pile on the floor within seconds. I leap into action, charging towards them as Quinn grappled with Julian who was pinned underneath Eric and the chair.

I slammed down on the floor next to them, putting the gun down before diving into the bag and pulling out the handcuffs.

"Get his hands above his head."

Quinn struggled with the attempt, but then I was there, holding one of Julian's hands down on the floor. After a minute's struggle between the three of us, we managed to get them cuffed.

"You fucking bastard!" Julian roared, struggling and trying to hit us both in the face with his cuffed hands.

Quinn and I got Eric and the chair dragged off Julian. He bucked and scrambled on the floor before I got the rope from the bag and tied his legs together at his ankles. He shouted all sorts at me until I stuffed a rag in his mouth. Didn't need to listen to his shit any longer. All he spewed was venom anyway.

Whilst I dealt with Julian, Quinn got the chair upright and hacked into the cable ties holding Eric to it until he got them free. I was there the next moment, pulling him up and holding him to me. I couldn't deal with the emotions rushing through my veins. They overwhelmed me. Especially the sense of relief. My man was okay. He was okay. We'd got him. We'd fucking saved him.

"Eric," I choked out.

He wrapped his arms around me, burying his face in my shoulder. He had to be in pain, but he clung to me without saying a word.

"I've got you," I whispered. "I'm right here. I love you. I love you so much."

"I hate to break up this little party, but we need to get to the casino," Quinn said after a moment.

I looked at him over Eric's head.

"We need to phone the police and get them to pick up this fucking piece of shit first."

"Fine, I'll call them. You have two minutes, then we're going, right?"

I nodded, holding Eric tighter. He needed me. I could hear the muffled sounds of Julian, but I ignored them. He'd be back behind bars in no time at all.

"You came," Eric whispered.

"Did you think I wouldn't?"

"He said he hadn't told you where we were."

"The idiot sent a photo of you and Rory recognised the room in the background."

Eric pulled away. He had one bruised eye, a cut on his forehead, but otherwise, he was mostly uninjured. I reached up and stroked his face gently.

"Are you okay?"

He nodded slowly, leaning into my touch.

"I don't care what Quinn says, we're taking you back home before we go to the fucking casino."

"What's going on?"

"I'll tell you in the car," I replied as Quinn approached us.

"They're on their way. Let's make sure he can't go anywhere and then we're out of this fucking place."

The three of us turned and stared down at Julian who, for the first time in his life, had fear in his eyes. The fucker was going back to prison where he belonged. He should be scared. He was never coming out again. And I was done. Officially done. He could burn in fucking hell before I gave him anything else. The fucker was going to rot until the day he died.

I simply smiled down at him.

Goodbye Julian. Goodbye forever.

CHAPTER TEN

Quinn

We didn't have time to stick around and wait for the police. I'd refused to tell them who I was, merely dropping an anonymous tip about where Julian was. We'd made sure to tie him to the chair and secure the gag properly. Just as we pulled away from the house in the Range Rover, I could see blue lights at the end of the street. At least they'd been quick about it. No doubt Julian would be back in prison where he belonged soon enough.

Xav was in the back with Eric, who didn't look too worse for wear, but he was very quiet. Almost as quiet as Rory.

"Take us home first," Xav said as I turned out of the road.

"What? We can't leave fucking McCarthy holding up our fucking casino any longer."

"We have to leave E with Ash and Rory."

I gripped the steering wheel harder. As much as I wanted Eric to be looked after, I had no choice but to go straight to the Syndicate. We needed to deal with this situation quickly before it got out of hand. We'd already taken enough time rescuing Eric from Julian's clutches.

"No. E will be fine whilst we deal with this shit, Xav. Do you want to put our fucking employees in further danger? And what about our members?"

"I'm fine, Xavi," Eric said. "The casino comes first."

I glanced in the rearview mirror, finding Eric rubbing Xav's shoulder and giving him a sad smile. I'd connected my phone to the Bluetooth this time before we left, so I decided it would be better to find out what the fuck was going on now. Hitting dial on Ash's number first as I wanted to let her know about Eric, I waited.

"Quinn! Are you okay? Is E okay? What's happening?" her voice filled the car a moment later.

"We're fine, little girl. The police are picking Julian up and we're on the way to the casino."

"Is he there? Let me talk to him."

Eric leant forward.

"I'm here… I'm okay, hellcat."

"Oh my god! I've been so worried. Are you sure? Did he hurt you?"

Eric flinched and I glanced back at Xav, whose expression darkened. Our poor girl was fretting.

"I'm fine, Ash."

"You're not fucking fine," Xav ground out. "Don't lie to her."

It would be worse if we did. Ash hated it when we lied to her.

"Julian gave him a black eye and he has a gash on his head which I'm going to assume is from Julian knocking him out, but otherwise he's just shaken up," I said, not caring to prolong this conversation longer than I had to. "Now, little girl, is Geoff okay? And have you spoken to Viktor?"

"Geoff is fine and yes, my dad is sending André and some of his men to the Syndicate to back you up against Mac."

It was unexpected, but not unwelcome. Taking on McCarthy and his men alone wouldn't be a good idea. We had security at the Syndicate, but if they were being held up at gunpoint, they wouldn't be much help.

"They'll likely be there before you… and Dad sends his regards."

"I'll have to thank him later."

Ash didn't respond for a beat and it occurred to me she couldn't be too happy with Eric trying to hide the truth of his injuries from her. She'd see soon enough when we got home, so there was no point denying he'd got hurt.

"I don't ask for too many things from the four of you but I wish you wouldn't lie to me. Haven't I shown you I can handle it? I'm a big girl. I knew the moment he took you it'd be inevitable he'd hurt you. So please, don't sugar-coat shit for me. I deserve to know what's happening to the loves of my life, okay?"

My heart lurched. All the times I'd tried to keep things from her, she'd got them out of me anyway. Now I knew better. And I fucking hoped the rest of them learnt that lesson too.

"I love you, beautiful… when we get back, I'll prove to you how much," Eric said, his voice a little choked up.

"I love you too and I don't need you to prove anything to me. I just need honesty."

"I'm okay, I promise. Our idiot is looking after me."

Xav glared whilst the tinkle of Ash's giggles filled the car. The sound relaxed my tense muscles somewhat. She just did something to me. Brightened every moment with her youthful soul.

"Is that what you two call me behind my back?" Xav ground out.

"No, we say it to your face too."

I swear if Eric wasn't injured, Xav would've slapped him around the back of his head for that comment.

"Okay, enough jokes, we need to go, little girl. You and Rory stay safe, you hear me?"

"Yes, sir. Ror is fine. He's got me watching the casino monitors remotely. We have eyes on the situation, okay? Mac is getting impatient, but I know you'll be there soon."

Damn right we would. There was no fucking way I'd let him give me shit when I got there either. My employees were not pawns for him to play with. If he wanted a conversation, he'd have to lower his fucking weapons and be reasonable.

"We will. See you when it's over."

I hung up. Somehow knowing she had her eyes on the situation made me feel more at ease. Not that Ash could do anything from our house, but she and Rory could be there in fucking spirit. It kept me going. I would do anything to protect our future together. And it happened to include keeping our casino intact.

"A word of advice, next time, just be straight up with her. She isn't fragile. She can handle knowing one of us is hurt, okay? Look at what happened with Rory," I said to the two fools in the back when Eric settled himself against the seat again.

"She dotes on the poor fucker," Xav replied. "I swear if one of us tried to coddle him, he'd kill us."

"He loves her."

"And? Rory loves us but we don't get special treatment."

I glanced back at them, finding Eric grinning.

"We don't have magic pussies, Xavi."

Xav's eyes widened.

"What the fuck is that supposed to mean?"

"I think it's quite obvious."

I rolled my eyes, knowing exactly what Eric was getting at.

"He means our girlfriend has the pussy to end all pussies and therefore Rory is enamoured with her because of that."

Xav scoffed.

"Well, her pussy is pretty fucking special."

"Can't deny that," I grinned.

"Me either," Eric put in.

Not sure Ash would appreciate us talking about her pussy like that, but hell, it was the fucking truth.

"Anyway, my point is, when we get this one home, Ash will be all over him, making sure he's tucked up in bed and shit just like she does with Rory."

"Huh, you're right. You're in for a treat, E, I caught Ash reading Rory smut earlier. Maybe she'll give you a rendition too."

I snorted.

"Are you serious?"

"Yup, I think they both share a love of dirty books."

It hardly surprised me. Ash and Rory did like to read together a lot. It was their thing. It was only a matter of time before he told her about his secret love of romance novels.

"I'd rather she curled up next to me," Eric muttered. "Don't need to be read to."

Xav nudged Eric.

"You just want her to straddle you and do all the work."

"What? No! She's still recovering."

"I'm sure Ash would be very obliging if you told her it'd help you get better."

I bit my lip. Ash would tell them to shut up and stop being idiots if one of them suggested such a thing. She didn't take shit off us, especially not Xav, but he deserved to be taken down a peg or two.

"Jesus, Xavi, do you ever think about anything other than sex?"

"Of course, I fucking do."

"Could've fooled me. Have I not given you enough whilst Ash has been unable to?"

I stifled my amusement at the two of them having a spat. They did this a lot. Ash usually broke it up, but she wasn't here.

"You're more than enough for me, E."

"Yeah, whatever. You're just desperate to get between our girlfriend's legs again."

Glancing in the rearview mirror, I caught Xav shrugging and raising his eyebrow.

"You going to tell me you don't miss it too?"

"That's not the point!"

Xav rubbed Eric's shoulder.

"Are you getting jealous? Did the knock to the head scramble your brain suddenly?"

"No. I'm not fucking jealous. For fuck's sake, just shut up."

"You know I'd rather not have to hear your marital spat right now," I put in, waving my hand at them.

"Fuck off, Quinn," Xav ground out. "E, I'm sorry. I love you and you know very well I love our sex life."

Eric didn't respond. Instead, he looked out the window.

"Eric, please don't do this with me right now. I just got you back from Julian."

"I just want to go home," Eric mumbled.

"I know. We will… right after we deal with the Irish cunt."

I felt shit for having to bring him with, but it couldn't be helped. We had to sort this fucker out once and for all. It crossed my mind we might be walking into a fucking ambush by Russo, but considering Geoff had eyes on the situation as did Ash and Rory, I highly doubted he was there. Wouldn't put it past him though. The man was nothing if not resourceful. Perhaps he'd put McCarthy up to it. Or perhaps the fucker decided he'd had enough of my interference in his business.

When I glanced at the boys again, Xav was hugging Eric and the two of them had their heads bowed together. *Thank fuck for that.* I was beginning to think I might have to call Ash up again to sort them out. Then I'd have had to tell her what they were fighting over and that would never have ended well.

The rest of the journey to the casino was relatively silent, all of us contemplating what we might deal with when we got there. Another car was parked around the back and I recognised André leaning against it with a couple of other burly men.

The three of us got out. André's eyes fell on Eric first and he frowned. We had to get him cleaned up in the office where he'd be safe with Geoff.

"What's the latest?" I asked walking towards the backdoor and punching in the code.

"According to your man, they've taken all your members hostage and are demanding an audience with you. They won't leave until you come down," André replied following on my heels.

The rest of the men including Xav and Eric walked into the casino behind me. We couldn't all fit in the lift, so I took Xav, Eric and André with me to the top floor. I unlocked the office door when we got upstairs and found Geoff staring up at the screens. He immediately looked relieved when he spied me. He said nothing as I walked over to his side and studied the monitors.

"He's not fucking around then."

"No, he's really not," Geoff agreed.

I sighed. There were men everywhere and our members did not look happy. I was going to have to compensate them for their trouble, which was fine, we could afford it. Still didn't sit well with me. Our casino was meant to be neutral ground where this kind of shit didn't happen.

"We need to get McCarthy in the VIP area so I can talk to him." I turned to André. "If this goes south, I'm going to need your men."

He gave me a sharp nod.

"Can you bandage up E for me?" I said, turning to Geoff again.

He eyed Eric.

"Yes… do I even want to know what happened?"

"No, probably not."

Xav took Eric over to the desk and got him sat down, rubbing his shoulder before he came over to me. We both looked up at the monitors again.

"He's taken over the security room, so he must know you're here now," Geoff said, pointing to one of the screens. "The only demand he's made so far is to see you and no one will be harmed if you cooperate."

I shook my head, not believing it for one second. McCarthy was ruthless and uncompromising. His relationship with the crime families had always been tenuous. Russo and Mac didn't like each other, but they profited well together.

"Phone?"

Geoff handed me it. I dialled McCarthy's number.

"This better fuckin' be Knox," came his gruff voice.

"It is."

"Took your fuckin' time."

"I had things to do, which Geoff explained to you earlier. Now, I suggest you tell your men to stand down."

He laughed, making me clench my fist.

"Oh no, you don't get to call the shots here. You think you're so fuckin' tough, eh? Didn't take much for me to lock your place down now, did it?"

When this was over, none of his fucking gang would be allowed to set foot in here again.

"We'll meet you in the VIP area. Don't expect me to come alone. I'm not a fucking idiot."

I hung up, not caring what else he had to say. The idiot would soon learn he didn't have the upper hand.

"Let's go."

Xav and André followed me from the room. Geoff could take care of Eric whilst we dealt with McCarthy and his gangsters. We met André's men downstairs and went through to the VIP area. Mac was waiting for us with some of his men including Colm Moran. This would be interesting. Xav and I still had our guns from when we'd dealt with Julian and I was sure André and his men would have them too. They flanked me as we stopped a few feet away from Mac with Xav standing by my side.

Mac glared at me. He was a stout man with a thin grey moustache and a balding head. And I didn't care if he hated me. The man was about to get a fucking lesson he wouldn't quickly forget.

"This is one way to get my attention," I said before McCarthy could speak.

CHAPTER ELEVEN

Quinn

McCarthy took a step towards me. Not all of his men were here. I could fucking guarantee that, but at least we weren't outnumbered. I hoped I wouldn't have to use violence to diffuse this situation, but you never knew when it came to a man like Mac.

"You've been fuckin' with my business for too long," Mac practically growled. "Now I know who the fuck you are, you're done in this fuckin' city."

I stifled the urge to roll my eyes and kept my expression neutral instead.

"You mean you wish to be the one who brags about finally taking down *Il Diavolo*?"

"This is business, not fuckin' bragging rights."

It was always about bragging rights with a man like McCarthy. Didn't know why he bothered putting on an act. We both knew how this game worked.

"And what? Your poor little business is suffering because of me, is it? Are your profits down? Are you floundering in the dark?"

His expression hardened at my mocking tone before he stabbed a finger in my direction.

"Shut your fuckin' mouth."

"You're telling me what to do in *my* casino?"

"Yeah, you're fuckin' right I am."

I shook my head as I paced away, tucking both hands behind my back. Xav had my fucking back so I knew no one would try anything right that second. I noted some hands twitching at the sides of Mac's men. The only person who remained still with a smug smile on his face was Colm. He still fucking owed me and he knew it. The question was… did McCarthy?

"You know, Mac, it's never a good idea to come after someone who knows your secrets."

"You don't know shit, Knox."

I cocked my head to the side.

"Don't I? You think I could disrupt your supply chains, *repeatedly*, without knowing a thing or two about your operations? That's rather naïve of you."

Fucking with McCarthy meant I fucked with Russo. Wasn't hard to find someone willing to help me when they discovered who McCarthy was selling to. Mac McCarthy and Frank Russo had a well-known hatred of each other. Came as quite a shock to one of his men when he learnt the feud was all fake. From then on, all Mac's deals with Frank crumbled. Drugs and weapons went missing. Money wasn't transferred. Russo could afford to take the hit, but McCarthy couldn't.

Probably why he had it out for me now he knew who I really was. And likely why Frank had sent Mac here to find me. Perhaps he thought the man could gain the upper hand and get rid of me. Pity he was so very fucking wrong. Russo had no idea what I knew. How many secrets I'd uncovered in my quest to rid the world of the sick motherfucker. How much his daughter had told me about him and his friends. His rivals. Everyone in this sick fucked up criminal underworld.

"You're fuckin' bluffing. You know nothing about me."

"I'd be very careful of what you say to me, Mac. You wouldn't want all your dirty little secrets coming to light."

"Why should I care about threats from a man with a target on his back?"

I stopped next to Xav and gave him a look. He nodded once. We had this.

"If the target is so large, why am I not dead yet?"

I eyed Mac, who looked a little stumped at my question.

"It's only a matter of time."

"There's that naivety again. Don't forget, we're on my home turf here. You came to me, not the other way around. He's using you to get to me because he has no other way of doing so. He thinks this will scare me… None of you fucking scare me."

Mac's eyes darkened and his expression turned downright murderous.

The only thing which scared me was losing my family and Ash. That was it. Everything else? Who gave a fuck? We could rebuild. But I couldn't replace Xav, Eric, Rory and Ash. They were fucking priceless.

"Not here on anyone else's fuckin' orders by my own."

"That's what you want your men to think. Pity it's a lie."

"Fuck you, Knox. No fuckin' lies here."

I shook my head again. The man was as thick as two short planks. How he ran his gang without slipping up every five minutes was a miracle. Mac McCarthy was nothing but a thug who was too fucking big for his boots.

"You don't want them to know the truth, do you? You're afraid of what they'll say."

"Shut your fuckin' mouth."

I straightened my spine and stared him down.

"Afraid they won't follow you when they realise who you've been selling to. Who's funded your entire operation."

"Fuckin' shut up!"

"What's he talking about, Mac?" asked one of his henchmen.

"Nothing. Stay the fuck out of it."

I almost laughed. The entire thing was borderline comical. Time to even the field a little.

"What I'm talking about is his dealings with Frank Russo."

The room went deadly silent. Mac looked like he was about to blow a fuse, his skin all blotchy and red. All of his men stared at him in shock. Mac recovered pretty quickly, relaxing his stance and waving a hand at me.

"Can you believe this fucker? As if I'd ever work with that bastard."

"You've been having us sell to Russo?" Colm Moran ground out through his clenched jaw.

"No, no, lad, of course not."

"After all the shit you sprout about hating him, you're fuckin' selling to him?"

Mac looked panicked.

"I've never sold to Russo. He can go fuck himself."

Colm shook his head and looked at the other men in the room. Their expressions hardened.

"Hey, lads, I would never. Are you going to believe this idiot over me?"

I put my hands out.

"Unlike you, Mac, I have no reason to lie to them. Simply because I don't really give a shit what happens to you, only that you get the fuck out of my casino and never darken my door again. I'm giving you one opportunity to leave now or I'll have no other choice but to end you."

Mac puffed up his chest.

"And fuckin' what?"

Xav pulled the gun from his pocket, followed by André and his men. Last but not least, I untucked mine from behind me and ran my free hand across the barrel.

"The next bullet which leaves the chamber of this gun will have your name on it."

None of his men moved to take out their weapons. Mac looked around them.

"Can you believe this fucker? We're not leaving until you re-fuckin'-pay me everything I've lost, right lads?"

The expressions on the faces of his men hardened as they stared at him. I caught Colm's eye and gave him a nod. Mac continued to look around at his men, growing ever more agitated.

"Lads… come on. This fucker is lying to you… Lads…" His face fell and his mouth narrowed to a thin line. Then he whipped out his own gun and aimed it at me. "You fuckin' bastard."

He froze the next moment as the cold steel at the end of a barrel was shoved in the back of his head, the owner of which smiled at me from over Mac's shoulder.

"Put your fuckin' weapon down, Mac."

"What are you doing?"

"The only bastard in here is you. Say hello to your Ma for me, she was a nice lady. Shame about her fuckin' son."

The shot rang through the room as Colm pulled the trigger and bullet left the chamber, sinking into the back of Mac's head. He was dead before he pitched forward. Colm caught him, holding the man against his chest. One of the other men came forward, pulling a bag from his pocket and wrapping it around Mac's head, tying it off at the bottom. Then he took Mac's body from Colm with another man helping him.

"That cunt talked far too much," Colm said with a shrug as he slipped his gun back in the holster strapped beneath his jacket. "Don't worry, Knox, we'll take care of this fucker for you. Been itching for a reason to end him for a while now."

I grinned, sliding my gun back behind me as Xav did the same.

"Took you long enough."

Colm shrugged.

"Wanted to see if he'd fuckin' admit it or not, the cunt."

Colm might have not known I was *Il Diavolo* until I'd admitted it to the families, but he knew all about Mac's dealings with Russo. He was my man on the inside. Even though I hated the idiot and thought he was better off dead, he'd come in handy. Besides, I had far more shit on both him and Mac after Ash had dropped it into my lap. Getting him to do what I wanted was easy. My little girl had proved to be our secret weapon in this war. She would help us defeat them all.

"The back door is that way."

I pointed towards the door where we'd come from. The least I could do was to let them get the body out of here without drawing attention to it. I didn't need that kind of heat coming down on our casino.

A couple of Colm's men carried out Mac's body whilst the man himself stared at me.

"When you're ready to go after Russo, count me in."

Then he gave me a nod and took his other men towards the direction of the main casino floor, no doubt to call off everyone else. The only thing I cared about now was securing my members and employees and getting the fuck out of here. My family needed to recuperate in peace without this shit.

"Well, that was fucked up," Xav said.

"You're telling me." I turned to André. "Thank you for your help. Tell Viktor I appreciate it."

He gave me a nod and a slight smile before he turned to his men and spoke in Russian. They walked out a few minutes later.

"Let's get E home, eh?" I said to Xav, slapping him on the back.

"Did you know Moran would shoot that idiot?"

I shook my head.

"I hoped he might finally do Mac in, but I didn't know for sure. Colm is a cunt, but he's a useful cunt."

"The fucker did a good job for once in his life."

We got back up to the top floor and nodded at Geoff when we entered the office. I turned to Xav before we moved further into the room.

"Delete the footage… don't want any evidence of that shit."

"You sure?"

"I'm pretty fucking sure I don't want anyone sniffing around here and asking questions. When this shit with Russo is over, we're done, remember? The Syndicate needs to remain neutral ground."

Xav nodded and got Eric to get up from the desk chair so he could use the computer. Eric's head had a plaster on it now and he looked tired. I nudged his shoulder with my own.

"Going to get you back to our girl," I murmured.

"I hope she doesn't cry when she sees this shit." He pointed at his face. "I hate seeing her cry."

"Me too. You and Xav good?"

He nodded, shrugging a little.

"What can I say? I love him even though he's a dick."

I grinned at his words.

"No, he just thinks with his dick."

Eric snorted, rubbing his chin.

"Like only all the time."

At least those two could get their rocks off with each other. The closest I'd got to anything was rubbing up against Ash last night whilst my hand had been buried between her legs and with Eric's mouth was latched to her tits. When she was better, there'd be zero hesitation on my part, but whilst she was still in pain, I didn't want to hurt her any further. Patience was my only fucking friend right now and what a shit friend he was.

"Right, done," Xav said as he stood up. "Let's get the fuck out of here. I, for one, am fucking tired."

"We good?" I asked Geoff.

"Yeah, go ahead… I'll handle the fallout with the staff."

I gave him a nod. It's what I paid him the big bucks for.

Xav, Eric and I walked out of the office. It was time we got home to our girl. She'd be worried about us. She needed us. And we fucking well needed her.

CHAPTER TWELVE

Ash

The moment I heard the front door open, I was off the sofa and running towards the hallway. The first person through the door was Quinn and even though I was relieved to see him, I looked behind him as Eric and Xav walked in, the latter closing the door behind him. I skated around Quinn and reached Eric, spying his black eye and the plaster on his head. My heart cracked.

"E…" I choked out, pressing my hands to his face gently and checking him over.

His eyes softened and he wrapped a hand around the back of my head.

"I'm okay… just tired."

Pulling me closer, he pressed my head against his chest and I let him hold me there, listening to his heartbeat. The rise and fall of his chest with each breath. The relief I felt was palpable.

"Told you she'd be making sure you're good," Xav said.

I pulled away and glared at him.

"Am I not allowed to be worried about E and his well-being?"

Xav gave me a wink and a grin before waving at the two of us.

"You are… Go on, take him up to bed, we've got dinner and all that shit sorted."

I slid my fingers into Eric's hand and he gave me a tired smile. Before we left, I gave Quinn a kiss on the cheek followed by Xav. Then I took Eric upstairs to his bed and got him sat down on the edge. He let me strip him down to his boxers without complaint, watching my face the whole time.

"I'm sorry I was reluctant to tell you I got hurt. I don't like making you upset, Ash."

I stroked his face and smiled down at him.

"It's okay. I'm glad you're home and safe."

I encouraged him to get in bed. He looked at me expectantly as I was about to pull the covers over him.

"Aren't you staying?"

I bit my lip, hesitant for only a moment. Eric wanted me here so I'd give him exactly what he needed. Shucking my jeans and jumper, I crawled on top of him and pulled the covers over the both of us. He curled his arms around me as I rested my head against his chest, stroking my hair.

"What happened with Julian?"

His body stiffened below mine, but his hand didn't still.

"He tied me to a chair and sprouted a whole bunch of shit before hitting me in the face… but before he could do anything else, Xav and Quinn turned up. They subdued him and then here we are."

"Is that everything?"

He let out a long sigh.

"No, but I don't want to talk about what he said. He's sick in the head, that's all you need to know."

I could imagine he'd said some horrible things to both Eric and Xav. I didn't like the fact any of them had to deal with Julian. Especially not Xav. He didn't need any more shit. At least we knew Julian was back where he belonged. The police had released a statement not long after he was re-arrested, which Rory and I had watched on the news.

"Are you sure he didn't hurt you anywhere else?"

"I'm sure. My face fucking hurts, but otherwise, I'm good."

"Do you need me to get you anything?"

His arm around me tightened.

"No, I need you right here with me. That's it."

I stroked his arm, running my fingers over his muscles. The past few hours had been incredibly stressful for all of us. What with Julian taking him and then the shit at the casino. Rory and I had watched the entire thing together. I'd been scared out of my mind over Quinn and Xav getting hurt, but it turned out I didn't need to be worried about them at all. Quinn always managed to have something up his sleeve. He'd never let anything happen to any of us if he could help it. My strong, dominant man who led us into battle each and every time. Rory had assured me Quinn had it all under control even before they'd gone down to see Mac. I don't know what I would have done if I'd been at home alone without him. Probably gone out of my mind with worry about my men.

"I'm worried about Xav and the way he was when he realised Julian took you. He looked like he'd died on the inside."

"I'm worried too. He seemed to laugh a lot of this shit off, but Julian really got to him, you know?"

"Maybe I should get him. He shouldn't be alone."

"He's got Quinn and Rory, plus he'll make dinner and it'll keep him distracted. I promise, hellcat, Xav needs time to process what happened. He'll come find us when he's ready."

It'd been the same way when Xav found out about Eric's feelings towards him. He'd run off and dealt with his emotions on his own. Sometimes he needed us and sometimes he needed to work through it without anyone around. Eric knew Xav better than I did, so he knew when to leave Xav be. I trusted his judgement on this implicitly.

"Okay," I whispered, shifting a little on top of him to get more comfortable.

He stopped stroking my hair, his other hand tightening around my waist. When I moved a little more, he let out a breath. I realised why a moment later when he thickened between my legs. Whilst he and Quinn had got me off last night, I'd not been able to reciprocate as my chest hurt. Today, it'd eased off a lot and the painkillers helped immensely, but I hadn't mentioned it to the boys. And honestly? Being around my men and not being able to touch them intimately was frustrating as hell.

So I continued to shift against him as his hand ran down my back and cupped my behind.

"Ash," he panted. "Stop."

I pushed myself up slightly and stared at him.

"No."

I ground against his cock, making his eyes go wide.

"You're still hurt."

I leant down and captured his mouth so he'd stop talking. There was no hesitancy to kiss me back on his part. If anything, it made him drop all of his protestations. His hand tightened on my behind and his other hand drifted around my front and found my breast. His thumb ran over the nipple and he ground back against me.

"Fuck, Ash," he groaned against my lips. "Are you sure?"

"Yes, I've missed you."

I sat up and tugged off my t-shirt. I hadn't started wearing bras again yet because of my injuries. He stared up at me with heat simmering in those green depths. He'd promised me it was only his face that hurt. He didn't have bruises anywhere else I could see.

"You're so beautiful," he told me as his hands curled around my thighs. "I love you, hellcat."

I smiled and shifted so I could pull off the rest of our clothes. I rested back against him, rubbing myself along his rock hard cock, coating him in my wetness.

"Are you in pain?" he asked me, running his hands up and down my thighs.

"A little, but I'm okay. Just stay there and let me do this… please. I can't take it any longer. You're all treating me like I'm a delicate little flower and I'm tired of it. I need this. Need you."

"You have me. Always." His smile made my heart thump. "Just don't tell the others I got to fuck you first."

I grinned as I rose up on my knees and reached between us.

"Oh, you know we won't be able to hide it from them."

He bit his lip as I sunk down on his length. His hands splayed out across my hips, banding around them like they were his anchor.

"Fuck," he ground out through gritted teeth. "Being in you is sweet fucking ecstasy."

I placed my hands on his chest, staring down at my beautiful man with chestnut hair and the most stunning green eyes I'd ever born witness to. Eric was the gentlest out of the four of them so to me, being with him first after my accident felt right. He wouldn't push me to my limits. Not that I thought the others would do anything to hurt me, but I knew how they liked to fuck without restraint.

I rose and fell on him at a leisurely pace, revelling in finally being able to have sex after going without since the crash.

"I love you, E… so much." Leaning down, I kissed his lips, nibbling at the bottom one. "You make me whole again."

He smiled, his hands leaving my hips. One curled into my hair as the other cupped my cheek.

"You're everything to me."

We kissed again. His hand fell from my hair to my breast, cupping it as his thumb swiped across my nipple. I moaned in his mouth, increasing my pace as my hands fell on the bed, keeping me steady. Pulling back, I rested my forehead against his, watching him as we drove each other higher. The way his mouth parted and the little exhales he made each time I took him deep inside me. Even though my chest burnt slightly, I didn't care. Being with him like this made it all melt away. *I need this. Need him so fucking much.*

"E," I panted. "E… I need… I need you to fuck me."

He was gentle as he flipped us over. He didn't lean over me, instead stayed on his knees and gripped my hips. I held the covers below us as he drove into me with sharp thrusts, sending me ever higher.

"Like this?"

"Yes… don't stop, god, don't stop."

His eyes were almost black as he gave it to me, making me mewl and cry out his name.

"Touch yourself, Ash."

I complied immediately, my hand snaking between my legs. He watched me stroke myself into a frenzy, a deadly expression on his face. Eric was beautiful like this. He didn't fuck me too hard, but it was enough to send me flying over the edge. I cried and whimpered as my body bucked.

"Oh, sweet fuck."

The blissful feeling raked up my spine, splintering my soul whilst he put it back together with each thrust of his hips. I panted as I watched him throw back his head and grunt as he hammered into me.

"Jesus, fuck…" he groaned, spilling inside me as his cock pulsed.

Both of us collapsed on the bed next to each other, panting and gasping for breath. Our bodies were slick with sweat, but I don't think either of us cared one bit.

"Maybe I should get kidnapped more often."

"What?" I squeaked.

"I quite like your interpretation of taking care of me afterwards."

I shoved him gently and shook my head.

"Do not get kidnapped just so I'll have sex with you."

I looked over to find him grinning.

"No promises."

"Eric!"

He grabbed me by the waist and hauled me on top of him, pulling me down so he could kiss me. I melted against him instantly. This man was so cheeky when he wanted to be, but I adored that about him.

"No more kidnapping, hellcat."

"Good. I can't go through that again and I don't think Xav can either."

"What's this about me?"

Both of us turned our heads, finding Xav strolling in with a raised eyebrow.

"I said you can't go through him getting kidnapped again."

I didn't even feel embarrassed about him finding us naked together. We both knew the boys would find out, regardless.

Xav hopped onto the bed next to us and lay back against the headboard with his hands behind his head.

"No, don't get yourself fucking kidnapped again, E. I will kill you myself."

"That's a bit harsh," Eric said, stroking my hair and reaching a hand out for Xav who let him entwine their fingers together.

"I told you she'd give you some sweet relief if you asked for it."

"Excuse me, what?" I interjected.

"Ignore him," Eric muttered. "He's being Xav."

"He didn't ask, I gave…"

Xav winked at the two of us. The last time he'd found us in bed together hadn't gone down very well, but this time, there was none of that awkwardness.

"Man, I'm going to love seeing Quinn's face when he realises he wasn't first."

Eric grinned and I shook my head, sitting up and swatting Xav's side.

"Don't start. E is gentle, unlike you and Quinn."

"Don't forget wolf boy."

I rolled my eyes.

"Ror is in a different league to all of you. Don't even try to outmatch him."

"Wouldn't dream of it. Now, you need to convince him to join us all, then we can show you a good time."

I almost sighed. Having all of them at once would be hot, but I didn't count on it happening.

"You lot show me enough of a good time as it is. Now, if you excuse me for a moment, I'm sweaty and in need of a wash."

I slipped off Eric, but he got up with me, his hand on my lower back as he directed me into the bathroom.

"Me too," he threw over his shoulder at Xav who we could both hear laughing behind us.

"Don't be long, lovebirds. Dinner's almost ready!"

I wasn't planning on a repeat of what we'd been doing before Xav came in, but the look in Eric's eyes as he pushed me in the shower was quite the opposite. It seemed once I'd given him the go-ahead I was ready for sex again, he was going to make up for lost time. And I didn't have it in me to say otherwise. Not when being locked together with him gave me the sweetest damn high I'd had in days.

"I love you," he whispered in my ear as he had me up against the wall, my legs wrapped around his waist.

"Love you too, E. Always."

CHAPTER THIRTEEN

Ash

When I woke up, I found myself squished between two very warm bodies. My arm was wrapped around Xav's waist with Eric spooning me. The closer we all got with each other, the less the boys were bothered by our sleeping arrangements. It seemed they didn't care who else was in the bed as long as they were with me or maybe we'd grown close enough, it was no longer a big deal.

"*Tesoro*, wake up," I whispered at Xav who was facing me.

I rubbed his waist before stroking his hair. He grumbled and shifted, pressing closer to me. As much as I appreciated being with both of them, I was also too hot and wanted to get up to stretch out my sore muscles. Not to mention popping a few painkillers.

"Xav, please."

I shook him this time. He cracked an eye open, his expression turning sour.

"Shh, angel, I'm sleeping."

"Can you let me out?"

He let out a huff and shifted back, giving me a little room to wriggle out of the bed. I had to shove Eric's arm off me, but as he slept like the dead, he didn't wake up. Hence why I'd bothered Xav in the first place. I kissed both of them on the cheek before I jumped off the end and went into the bathroom to deal with my pressing urge. When I came out, Xav was cuddling Eric.

Those two are utterly adorable together.

I shook my head and slipped out of the room, padding down to the kitchen where I'd left my painkillers. I stretched out after I'd taken them and wandered around the ground floor in search of Quinn, who was nowhere to be found.

Is he not up yet?

I went back upstairs and crept into Quinn's room. He was laid out flat on his back, his face at complete peace. I took a minute to watch him, hesitant to disturb my slumbering king. Perhaps I'd go see if Rory was up yet instead. But no, I came to see Quinn and talk to him about our next move. I walked up to his bed and carefully pulled back to the covers, slipping in beside him. He didn't even stir as I laid my head on the pillow next to him and stroked his shoulder with my fingertips.

Can't remember the last time he slept this late.

Quinn was always an early riser. Perhaps everything had taken a toll on him. He got stressed easily, but he kept it all bottled up half the time. I'd been too busy taking care of Rory to notice what was going on with my man. The painful realisation I might have neglected Quinn when he needed me reared up inside me.

"I'm sorry I haven't been here," I whispered. "Everything has been so messed up. God, Quinn, this is hard… trying to find balance, but I suppose the circumstances we're in aren't normal."

Leaning over, I pressed a kiss to his bare chest before gently lifting his arm and curling up against his side. He shifted in his sleep, cuddling me to him. I stiffened, worried I'd woken him, but his breathing settled again. I hoped me being here would help him in some small way. He'd told me on more than one occasion he slept better when I was there.

"I promised I'll be a better girlfriend to you, sir."

I glanced towards the door, realising I'd forgot to close it behind me and noticed someone leaning on the frame. Rory looked tired and run down, which made my heart ache. I reached out a hand to him. He padded into the room and came around my side of the bed, taking a seat next to me. Turning slightly, I pulled back the covers and he took the hint, sliding in next to me and resting his splinted arm on my side as he curled himself around my back, trapping Quinn's arm between us.

"Did you need me to make you breakfast?" I whispered.

"No, not yet," he murmured.

"Why're you up and about? You're meant to be resting."

"Couldn't sleep anymore. I missed you."

My chest tightened. All my men needed me and I felt hard-pressed to give them enough of my time.

"E and Xav needed me last night."

"I know, little star." He leant over me and kissed my cheek. "You've done so much for me already."

It didn't feel like enough. It'd take time for his wrist to heal and he was still suffering a few after-effects from his mild concussion, but he was on the mend. I just had to be patient.

"I'm worried about Quinn."

"Why?"

"You know what time it is, right? Is he usually still asleep?"

Rory was silent. I stared up at Quinn's sleeping face, surprised our whispering hadn't disturbed him. My hand splayed out across his stomach, wondering if we should be in here when he was resting.

"Is that why you're with him now?"

"Yes… he doesn't like to show how stressed he is to anyone, but I can see it. He needs me and I haven't been there for him."

"Hey, little star, don't do that. You've been taking care of me so he doesn't have to, that's what he needs so he can look after business."

I sighed, hating how right Rory happened to be. It didn't make me feel any better.

"This is why I wonder if I'm enough for you all."

Rory shifted up on his elbow and looked down at me with a frown.

"You are always enough. Don't beat yourself up. You were in the same crash as me, he knows that. We all know that. You needed rest too."

Why did I feel so inadequate? They'd constantly reassured me how much they loved me and wanted me and yet here I was, still worrying.

"Why do I still feel like I'm not doing enough?"

"You were told that every day for years by Frank. It's hard to break out of that mindset, Ash… trust me, it's taken me years."

Rory's words rang true to me. Frank had fucked me up in ways I couldn't begin to fathom. He needed ending. My heart lurched. He still had my mother in his clutches. It's partly why I'd wanted to talk to Quinn, but now I felt as though it would be wrong to press him. Quinn didn't need any added pressure.

"I just want to take this all away for you boys."

He reached up with his injured hand and stroked my face with his fingers. The gentle touch soothed my aching soul.

"You already do, little star. Just by being you."

He dropped his hand back down and settled behind me again. I felt Quinn shift next to me. My eyes flicked up to him. His were open, questions simmering in them.

"Quinn," I breathed, reaching up to stroke his cheek. "We didn't mean to disturb you."

He said nothing, merely tucking his fingers under my chin and pressing my face up towards him. I let him kiss me, finding my anxiety melting under his touch.

"Why do I have you and Rory crowding my bed?" he murmured against my lips.

"Your invalids missed you."

He snorted as he pulled away.

"You, I can believe, but Rory? When hell freezes over maybe."

"That's because you're an interfering arse who never shuts up," Rory muttered from behind me.

Quinn chuckled, tangling his hand in my hair and stroking his thumb down my cheek.

"I see you're feeling better unless this is still grumpy Rory who wants us to go away and stop babying him?"

"Shut up."

"You can leave if you don't want me giving you shit."

"Boys! Cut it out. You're as bad as Xav and Eric," I complained.

I already had enough of those two bickering like a married couple.

"Our girl is worrying she's not doing enough for you," Rory put in, ignoring me.

"Ror!"

"You don't need to worry about that, little girl," Quinn said as his eyes clouded over.

I huffed, wanting to glare at Rory for dobbing me into Quinn. I couldn't though since he was right. My worries about Quinn's well-being had started to get to me.

"But you slept in."

"I was up late dealing with the fallout from yesterday, that's all."

I didn't know whether or not to believe him. Quinn always took all of our problems on his shoulders. I shifted up on my elbow and cupped his face.

"You can't stop me worrying about you. I know you get stressed and I haven't been here for you."

His eyes softened as his hand drifted from my hair down to my chin. His thumb ran along my bottom lip.

"You've been taking care of Rory for me, sweetheart. That's what I need."

"I told her that," Rory mumbled.

"Quinn—"

"No, Ash, stop it. I would tell you if I needed more from you. I know better than to keep shit from you, okay? All I want is for you and Rory to be healed and whole again. That's it. Do you understand?"

I nodded before falling on his chest and clutching him tightly.

"I am better… mostly. You can just ask E."

"Are you saying what I think you are?"

I squirmed against him as his hand ran down my back. Eric and I had stayed in his room for dinner so Quinn and Rory had no idea we'd had sex until now.

"Rory… unless you want to watch me strip this little girl off and have my way with her, I suggest you fuck off."

Next thing I knew, Quinn flipped me on my back and he was staring down at me with a wicked expression on his face. I glanced at Rory who was biting his lip and looked as if he was in two minds about leaving us be or not. He still wasn't better, but he'd been doing so well for the past couple of days with minimal activity. His headaches had lessened and he could read in short bursts.

"You have to be gentle, sir," I whispered, still watching Rory.

"I can do gentle, little girl," Quinn said, leaning down to kiss my neck. "I'll do whatever you want as long you let me have you."

"I'm yours."

Rory smiled at me before he slipped off the bed.

"I'll make you breakfast after this," I called after him.

"Take your time, little star. I'll be waiting."

And I did, letting Quinn take me under because hell, I'd missed this intimacy between us so much. I'd walk through fire to feel this close to him and the boys. They were my everything and I was beginning to believe I was their everything too.

CHAPTER FOURTEEN

Quinn

"We need to talk about my mother."

I'd known the topic of Isabella would come up sooner rather than later. The issue I had was by losing my eyes and ears in Frank's inner circle, I had no clue where he was keeping her. Fabio had been shut out. Russo was closing his net, his circle of trust. This meant we might have to take drastic measures to extract Isabella. I wasn't sure how to broach the subject with Ash.

"I know, little girl."

It wasn't the only issue we needed to talk about. I hadn't forgotten what she said in the car on the way back from the accident. We might have all told her we wanted a future together, but what might that future entail? It was a matter we all needed to get out in the open. I didn't know how I felt about it, in all honesty. Hadn't considered her having a desire for a family given she wanted to be with all of us. Nothing about it sat well with me for reasons I didn't know if I wanted to examine or not.

Perhaps it came down to never having wanted a family or to be with one person for the rest of my life. It hadn't been a goal. My only focus was on keeping the four of us alive. It had been this way for so long, the possibility of anything else had never been an option. Another path beyond finally destroying the man who'd ruined our lives felt unobtainable. Now it was in our grasp, I had to think further ahead, to what we would look like when this was all over.

Ash cocked her head to the side, watching me with those damning eyes of hers. We were sat in the kitchen, all five of us, having breakfast. Now was a better time than any to have this talk.

"We can't go storming Russo's compound to go after her," Xav said, waving his fork at me.

"We don't know where she is," Eric put in. "That's our first problem."

"Not to mention we're a man down."

Xav glanced at Rory who glared at him. We needed all of us at full health if we were ever going to end this shit once and for all. Hence my reluctance to make any plans. We still had weeks before Rory's wrist healed, not to mention how he'd have to get his strength back with it. His concussion improved daily so I wasn't as worried on that score.

"And a woman. Don't forget our little tigress here." Eric put a hand on Ash's shoulder, squeezing it.

Ash didn't say anything, just continued to watch me. Waiting for my thoughts on the matter.

"If Ash can fuck again, she can damn well help us go retrieve her mother."

Eric flicked Xav's ear, making him scowl as he rubbed it.

"No sex talk during business, you know the rules."

"A stupid rule if you ask me."

"You agreed to them."

"Yeah, okay, teacher's pet."

I rolled my eyes as I settled my elbows on the counter.

"Do you two ever stop arguing?" I asked.

"On occasion, usually when one of us has a mouth full of cock," Xav replied.

Rory snorted, looking away. Eric's ears went red and I ignored Xav's comment, preferring to get down to business.

"Our first task is to locate Isabella, only then can we devise a plan of action. So, how are we going to achieve this now we no longer have contact with Nate?"

All of them went silent. Xav, Eric and I had been trying to work this out for days but none of us had any good ideas. Well, ones that didn't involve risking our lives. I knew for a fact Ash wouldn't agree with those so there'd be no point bringing them up.

"I know where he'll be keeping her," Ash said. "Where he keeps all his prisoners."

I put out a hand, wanting her to elaborate.

"In the basement of his building. It's where he shot the video he sent us. I recognise the room. It's where he conducts his killings not to mention all the other shit he does."

She shuddered as if the memory of the place affected her deeply. We all had a good idea of the things Russo had subjected Ash to now. Reaching out, I stroked her arm, reassuring her we were here and she never had to go back there.

"It's almost impossible to infiltrate. It's safest to wait until he brings her back out in public again. He will at some point. He'll want to provoke us into making a move. It'll be a trap since he'll know we have no other choice."

"We don't want to be waiting around for him to make a move," I mused. "That gives him the upper hand rather than us."

Ash leant closer to me as if she needed my touch. I'd already had her earlier. It'd been gentle and sweet, but by fuck had I missed her. The little breathy moans, the way she panted my name and told me how much she loved me. And whilst I loved sex with her, it was those moments afterwards where we were wrapped in one another I cherished the most. I'd never admit it to anyone else, but having her pressed against me, listening to the soft rise and fall of her chest and her heart thumping soothed me more than anything else in this world. I loved this girl to fucking death and beyond. That's why I wanted to make sure I did everything in my power to give her a life away from the horrors she'd grown up with.

I wrapped an arm around her, pulling her against me and kissing the top of her head. My little girl. My world. My home. That's what she was.

"Then we need to get his attention… and I think I know how."

I glanced down at her with a raised eyebrow. Ash's eyes had grown dark and her expression grim.

"I told you before… Frank values family above everything else. We fuck with his family, he'll stop at nothing to come after us."

"And what exactly do you have in mind, little girl?"

She took my hand and traced her fingers across my palm.

"You're not going to like it."

What on earth did she have going on in that head of hers?

"Ash…"

"He took Isabella… so we take someone close to him."

The entire room went deadly quiet as her words settled over us. It's not like we hadn't kidnapped someone and held them against their will before. Ash was proof of that. Except she had become our girl rather than our captive.

Would this really get Russo to make a move against us?

"Who?"

"Carlo," she whispered.

There was a growl from across the room. My head whipped up finding Rory looking practically murderous at the very idea of her cousin, who'd tried to kill both of them, being in our house. I could hardly blame him. Hell, I wanted to end the motherfucker myself for hurting my girl and my best friend.

"I don't think that's a good idea."

Ash sat up, letting go of my hand and forcing me to drop my arm from around her.

"Do you have any better ideas? Only something drastic will force him out in the open."

"Why would he care if we take your cousin?"

"Gianni will force him to care. They didn't give a shit about you taking me since none of them wanted me as Frank's heir, but if we take Carlo, he won't have a choice. Besides, that idiot tried to kill me. I'd quite like to make him suffer."

My little girl was beginning to show her ruthless side. And I couldn't quite say I hated it. In fact, I found it hot. Seeing her worked up had always got me going.

"Okay, say we do take your cousin… What then?"

"We tell him if he wants to see Carlo alive again, he will return my mother. If he refuses, well… Carlo is expendable."

"Are you really telling me you'd kill your cousin?" Xav interjected.

Ash turned to him, putting her hand on Eric's shoulder as she leant closer.

"He's not my cousin and he tried to kill me and Ror. Do you think I have any ounce of sympathy left for him? I'm done letting that family get away with the shit they've done."

"She doesn't have to kill him. I will," Rory put in.

"Jesus Christ, no one is killing anyone right now," I said, wanting to get off the subject of murdering Carlo Russo. "We haven't even agreed we'll take him yet, so would you lot pipe down and let me think."

What Ash had proposed could work. It would certainly piss Russo off. And his brother would put pressure on Frank to get Carlo back. It would be naïve to think we could achieve any of this without bloodshed. We already knew one of us would have to take down Frank Russo.

"I'm not one for advocating kidnapping," Eric said. "However, if it's the only way we get Isabella back, then I'm voting for it."

Xav stared at Eric like he'd grown two heads.

"Wait up, hold up. *You* are agreeing to a kidnapping? Who are you and what have you done with the real Eric?"

Ash hid a smile and Eric shrugged like it was no big deal.

"I'm just saying we do what's necessary to get our girl's mother back. When this is all over, we never have do shit like this again."

Xav shook his head. Rory nodded and Ash leant her head on Eric's shoulder, making him reach up and stroke her face.

"It could work. We need to plan it carefully," I said. "Any objections to us going ahead with this?"

No one said anything.

"Good… that's settled one thing."

Ash looked over at me with a frown.

"What's the other thing?"

I took a breath, wondering if now really was the time to talk about this.

"The future… specifically the future we started talking about the day of your accident before everything went to hell."

CHAPTER FIFTEEN

RORY

I might have been seriously out of it when we were in the car on the way back from the car crash, but I knew what Quinn was alluding to. The little revelation our girl wanted a family in the future. The way Quinn was eying Ash told me everything I needed to know. He wasn't comfortable with the idea at all. A cursory glance at Xav and Eric had me realising this entire conversation would not go down well with anyone.

My feelings on the matter weren't complicated. I loved Ash. I wanted to give her anything she asked for. And when I'd come to the realisation she was the one, her wants and needs in life became mine. So if Ash wanted a family, I'd give her it even though it wasn't something I ever expected to have in life. Then again, I never thought I'd ever meet a woman who'd step into the darkness with me. Ash had opened my eyes to a world of possibilities and they all included me and her together. So having a baby with her didn't seem so… scary because it was with her. My home, heart and soul.

"We're going to do this now?" Xav asked, rubbing a hand across his face.

Ash looked down at her hands, her face paling a little. The urge to go to her laced my veins. My stunning girl didn't look at all comfortable with this line of conversation. Eric dropped his hand from her face and glanced at her with a frown.

"If you're going to complain about it, you can go first," Quinn replied with a wave of his hand.

"Fuck off, Quinn, you brought it up."

"Touchy subject?"

Xav glared at him.

"I never said that."

"Then why don't you want to share your feelings with the group, huh?"

Ash would've normally broken up an argument between us, but she'd paled further and her body went rigid. Eric wrapped an arm around her shoulders and tugged her closer as if sensing her discomfort. At least someone had paid attention to her rather than picking a fucking fight over this shit.

"Why don't you share your damn feelings?"

"Because I'm asking you."

"What the hell do you want me to say? Huh? That this is some kind of normal thing for the five of us to talk about? Because it fucking well isn't."

"Why the hell are you being so cagey?"

I stood up abruptly.

"Enough you two. Can't you see you're upsetting her?" I waved my uninjured hand at Ash. "Arguing over who talks about this first is pointless."

Quinn and Xav looked at Ash and Eric, eyes widening as they took in her demeanour.

"Little girl…"

"Angel…"

I sat back down, resting my splinted wrist on the counter.

Eric looked at the two of them, his eyes dark as Ash curled into him, wrapping her arm around his chest and burying her face in his shoulder.

"I'm with Rory, you two need to shut up and stop it." He turned back to Ash. "It's okay, beautiful. Ignore them, they're being idiots who really don't know how to tactfully bring up a subject which we all have differing opinions on."

"If you don't want kids, you can all just say so," Ash replied raising her head from Eric's shoulder. "I don't like it when you start fighting and avoiding conversations when they're hard to discuss. It's unnecessary. We promised each other honesty, so just fucking well give it to me straight, okay?"

No one spoke. Ash was right. We could tell her that easily. Only Quinn and Xav had decided to let their stupid egos do the talking instead. I looked at the boys and realised none of them wanted to go first. Not even Eric. So I decided for once in my life I was going to talk and not keep my thoughts to myself.

"If you want a family in the future, little star, then I'll give you that… I want it with you."

Ash's head whipped around to me, crystal blue eyes wide. I didn't look at the others, not giving a shit what their reactions were to my statement right then. The only person who mattered was my girl. She slipped out from under Eric's arm and off her chair, coming around to me. Her hands came up and rested on my shoulders as she stepped in between my legs.

"Really?" she whispered.

I wrapped my uninjured arm around her waist, pulling her closer.

"I want everything with you, Ash."

She stared into my eyes, the hope and happiness radiating off her. Seeing her like this made my heart thump and had me wishing I wasn't still feeling the aftermath of the fucking crash because I'd take her straight up to bed otherwise.

"Ror… I never imagined… I don't know what to say."

"Just tell me you love me as much as I love you and one day, when we're ready… we'll take that step."

She leant towards me, her hands coming up to cup my face. When her lips were inches from mine, she smiled.

"I love you forever."

I closed those last inches and kissed her, feeling her melt against me.

"Well, that's a fucking turn up for the books," Xav muttered from behind us.

I decided it would be better to ignore him and concentrate on her rather than get into another fight over this shit. I didn't care what he had to say about it. This wasn't simply about giving Ash what she wanted. It felt right. I wouldn't lie and say I wasn't fucking terrified about the prospect of being a father, but with Ash by my side and these idiots, I'd cope somehow. I'd try to be better than the fucked up parental figures I had. I'd never let any child of mine suffer.

Ash pulled away and stroked my cheek. I knew this was the right choice. Not because it made her happy, but it made me happy too. Happy to know I had something to look forward to with her.

She turned in my embrace, levelling her gaze on the others.

"I never expected my life to turn out like this… and I know none of you did either. I'm not asking anyone to change what they want out of life to make me happy. Just because I want a future that has the possibility of a family of my own, doesn't mean I won't accept it if you don't."

Eric rubbed the back of his neck before letting out a long sigh.

"I don't know how I feel about it in all honesty. It's not something I've ever considered… until now. And it's especially complicated given we're all together as a unit. It's not a no, beautiful, it's an 'I don't really know yet'."

He glanced at Xav, whose eyes were downcast. I wasn't sure if those two had ever really talked about what they wanted out of the future. None of us had other than wanting Frank Russo and his legacy gone.

"That's okay, E… you don't have to know now. I didn't want to press the subject with anyone, which is why I never brought it up again after the crash."

All eyes fell on Quinn, who blinked before folding his hands on the counter.

"I don't know if I want kids or not. The practicalities of such a thing are far more complicated than a usual relationship, don't you think? It's all very well us saying we want that, but have you stopped to think about how it would work. Do we take turns in giving you a child? Do we raise them with four fathers like we're one big happy family?" He shifted in his seat. "We can't act like we're in a normal relationship because we're not. It's not as simple as let's have a family when doing so affects not just two of us, but all five of us."

Quinn had a valid point. It wasn't simple, but for Ash, I'd do anything to make it work. Having spent so long trying to hide from what we were, I couldn't do it any longer. We had to face up to the challenges thrown at us and this would be just another one of those.

Ash leant back against me as if she needed my strength to hold her up.

"I don't know, Quinn. It's not as if I've considered the logistics… we've only been together for a few months and I'm only twenty-one. It's not like I want it right now or any time soon. This isn't me asking any of you to give me a family, it's simply me telling you how I feel. That's it. There's no pressure. We can revisit this at a later date when you've all had more time to think about it."

Quinn was about to open his mouth to respond when Xav got up, shoving his stool back and scowling at all of us.

"Fuck this," he muttered and stormed out of the room, leaving us all staring after him.

Quinn shifted and sat back, rubbing his chest.

"What the fuck is his problem?"

"I should go see him," Eric said.

"No… leave this to me," Ash told them, pulling away from me after squeezing my arm. "I have some idea of what might be bothering him. He wears his pain on his sleeve even if none of you notice it."

And with that, she walked out of the room. Eric glanced between us before his eyes landed solely on Quinn.

"I think what Julian said to him yesterday has got to him."

"He should've just let me kill him. That psycho deserves nothing less."

Eric shook his head.

"You know that's not what Xav wants… Julian has to pay for his crimes."

"Well, he's fucked himself over further. They're not going to let him out now and he's lost his leverage over Xav. There's no fucking way he'll be there for Julian's cancer treatment now."

Eric nodded and picked up his mug. Xav might have felt obligated before, but after what happened yesterday, which Quinn had explained to me, his obligation would be null and void.

"Let's hope our girl can calm him down."

"Oh, I'm in no doubt of that. She handles grumpy over there just fine. Unlike him, Xav's bark is far worse than his bite."

"Fuck off, Quinn," I muttered.

"See? Grumpy."

I stuck my finger up at him. Eric chuckled and leant toward Quinn.

"I think he's upset he can't indulge in his wolfish tendencies and pounce on Ash."

I glared at him even though he wasn't wrong. Every time Ash's skin was on show, I wanted to claim her all over again. Mark her to show she was mine. My inner beast was very unsettled with the current circumstances I'd found myself in.

"Careful, E, he's getting that feral look again."

"Oh, I'm so scared. One-armed Rory coming after me is terrifying."

"You two are cunts," I grunted.

"You love us really." Quinn grinned and winked.

"You fucking wish."

Quinn turned to Eric.

"You know, all this protesting he does makes me think he wants to show us love but doesn't know how."

"I think you're right… maybe he should take some tips from Ash."

I got up, irritated the two of them were giving me shit, and stalked from the room.

"We love you too, Rory!" called Quinn as I disappeared.

For fuck's sake!

I ducked my head back inside the kitchen door.

"If you two are so fucking insistent on hearing it, fine… I do love you, but don't fucking well ask me to repeat it again."

I left them staring at me with wide eyes, a smile gracing my lips as I walked towards my conservatory. They'd forgotten I could play them at their own fucking game.

Serves them fucking right.

CHAPTER SIXTEEN

Xavier

I paced the room, running my hands through my hair as emotion after emotion swirled inside, tearing up the pieces of my heart. The conversation had set me off and I had no idea how to express how I felt about it. About having a family with her. With them. I had too many thoughts running through my mind, especially after yesterday. There was only so much I could cope with at one time.

I stopped in front of the print of me we'd put up on the walls of her room. Not wanting the reminders of my life in my own room and knowing on some level she'd follow me, I'd come in here to work through my feelings.

The man in front of me had a bright and cheeky smile, like he'd just told a stupid joke. He looked far more alive than I felt right then. He hid behind his humour and avoided talking about anything real. Tangible. Solid. Falling in love had altered him on a fundamental level.

I was still that man, but I changed. I'd learnt a lot of things since Ash had come in our lives. Things about myself. Things about the others. I had to really look at what I wanted out of life. I'd never taken anything seriously until her. Never wanted to delve beneath the surface and see the man behind the wall I'd put up. See the reality of myself. And that was someone broken by what had happened to him as a teenager. Ruined by the man he'd put behind bars. I didn't like that version of myself, so I'd buried him. Now he'd surfaced and I couldn't deny him any longer.

Because he, ultimately, was me.

"*Tesoro*."

I felt her voice surrounding me. Her warmth. Her light.

My angel.

Every part of me felt the urge to go to her, but I'd got stuck staring up at myself instead. I couldn't look away. She came to me, wrapped her arms around my stomach and pressed her face into my back. My girl was so small against me, but her presence gave me strength. She gave me courage.

"Do you want to talk or do you want me to take your pain away?"

Such a simple question from her, as if she knew exactly what I needed.

"I feel broken," I whispered.

Her hold on me tightened.

"I know, *tesoro*. It hurts… the reminders."

How did she even know that? How could she sense this was about Julian and not our future together?

She knows you. She understands you. She sees you.

"Going back there forced me to live that day all over again. It forced me to see myself and I don't like it, angel. I hate every part of it."

"After Julian was sent away, did you ever feel like you really got closure for your mum and Katie's deaths?"

I stiffened, the realisation flooding through me at an alarming pace.

"No."

Not even after we'd had them cremated did I feel any sense of closing that chapter of my life. The wide gaping hole their deaths had left never disappeared. I'd never let it go. The hatred I felt towards Julian and the pain I felt at him ending their lives.

"I can't forgive him for it."

She stroked my stomach.

"No one is asking you to. It's not a question of forgiveness, Xav, it's a question of letting go of the past." She reached up and placed her hand on my heart. "They'll always live on here, but maybe it's time you let yourself grieve their loss so you can put them to rest."

When the hell did she get so smart about this stuff? For someone so young, she had seen so much death and violence in her life. It'd changed her on a fundamental level, allowing her to see the good in people even when they did terrible things.

I turned in her arms and stared down at her. Her eyes were full of compassion and it nearly killed me. The way she cared and understood. I couldn't replace that in my life.

"Come with me."

She dropped her arms from around me and I slid my fingers into her hand, tugging her from the room. We went downstairs and into Rory's conservatory. He was sitting in his usual seat, his eyes following us as I took Ash to the patio doors at the end. I didn't feel like telling him why we were going out into the garden. Opening the door, I pulled Ash out and shut it behind me.

We had someone tend to it every few weeks. I'm sure Ash never noticed our gardener coming and going as he always slipped in through the back gate. He also maintained Rory's plants in the conservatory. We paid him to be discreet.

Ash looked around, her eyes falling on everything. The wildflowers which dominated the space like a wild, untouched meadow in the countryside. Beyond that was a lawn with a small shed at the end. Flower beds bordered the grass on each side. We stood on the deck we'd had erected containing a seating area with a heat lamp for the winters. We hadn't used it much over the past year, but sometimes we'd come out here in the evenings, just the four of us, and drink the night away.

I took Ash through the cleared path at the side of the wild meadow and out onto the lawn. I directed her over to one of the flower beds which contained a plaque with a dedication to Mum and Katie on it. This is where we'd scattered their ashes and from them, the pink roses had grown. Those were Katie's favourites and I couldn't think of a better place to have them. Whilst I didn't come out here much, I knew they were here and it gave me a sense of peace.

Ash was right. I'd never had a sense of closure. Never really grieved them in the way most people did. I'd been too wrapped up in my pain over Julian and the sense of betrayal I felt when he'd murdered the two people I'd loved more than life itself.

I crouched down and ran my hand over the plaque.

Erin and Katie Scott
Two sparks of light in the darkness.
You remind me every day to always fill my life with laughter.
I'll cherish you forever.
Love Xavier

I wasn't exactly poetic or shit like that. It just seemed right. Mum had always told me a life without laughter was no life at all. She never failed to make me smile.

"I kept their ashes in two urns after the funeral for the longest time. It was only when we moved here and had this spot created in the garden I decided to scatter them. This way I'll always have them close, you know… it just felt right."

Ash crouched down next to me, wrapping her arm around my shoulder as she read the plaque.

"I wish I'd let myself feel their loss all those years ago," I continued. "Instead I fell into a pit of depression which only Eric finally managed to pull me out of… then I filled the void with endless men and women. None of them made me feel. Not like you do."

She looked over at me, her eyes filling with tears.

"You made me realise what love really means, angel. What it means to care for someone so deeply and want to give them the whole fucking world."

"Xav…" she whispered, reaching up with her free hand and cupping my face.

"Mum and Katie would've liked you… a lot. They'd have seen what I do. A ray of sunshine in a world filled with horrors, violence, manipulation and death. You're the world to me, Ash. You're the whole fucking world. I love you and

I'm so grateful you're in my life. Every single day I remind myself how lucky I am to have met you. To know you. To love you."

I turned my head again, staring down at the plaque. Tears blurred my vision and I didn't care when they fell down my cheeks.

"I miss you," I whispered, planting my hand on the ground below the plaque. "I miss you every single fucking day. You wouldn't want me to live like this. To be filled with pain and regrets. So I'm going to do something I never thought I could… I'm going to forgive myself for being unable to save you from your fate. I know it wasn't my fault and I have to stop beating myself up over it."

Ash stroked my face as my tears fell over her fingers. Having her right there gave me the will to do this. She made me realise I had to for myself so I could move on. So I could live. So I could be happy. So I could love the family I'd found without living with regrets and wallowing in the misery of my past failures.

"I wish you could see us now… me and the boys… how we've grown, how we've all learnt to love without restraint or conditions. I hope you're proud of us, Mum."

Ash moved towards me, leaning her face against mine. I wrapped my free arm around her, holding her close.

"She always used to tell us we were four misfits who should never have been friends, but somehow we all worked together. I think she loved them as much as me, you know. She was the only one out of all our parents who actually gave a shit about us… So when Julian took her away from me, he took her away from them too. I guess I took on that loss more than I should've."

None of us had grown up with much love in our lives. Probably why it was so devastating to lose her and Katie. And why the four of us had clung to each other. Why we'd forged our own family. One we'd never give up. One we'd fight for till our last breath.

"You four were already a family before you lost yours… you always have been," Ash whispered. "As an outsider, I could see that. The bond you all share. It's a beautiful thing, you know."

I turned into her, wrapping my other arm around her small frame and burying my face in her hair. Her hand fell from my face and clutched my shoulder.

"You're our family now too, angel. You're our missing piece. You make us whole."

"I think your mum would be proud of you, of the man you've become."

My heart lurched at her words. I believed them. Mum would be proud of me for letting love into my life. She'd be happy I'd finally realised who was staring me in the face this whole time. And it was only because of Ash I'd been able to open myself up to the possibility. The idea of me and Eric. She'd taught me to cherish those around me. Especially the one person who'd loved me since the day we'd met.

"Thank you, angel… you have no idea how much you've done for me. I love you so much."

"I love you too, *tesoro*."

I pulled her away from my chest and held her face in my hands. Her blue eyes were intent on mine, showing me how much she loved and cared for me.

"I want our family to grow in the future. I want that with you so much. I don't care if it's hard to navigate or whatever other bullshit Quinn says. We can do this together. So fucking what if our kids have four dads? They'll have five parents who love them with every inch of their souls. A beautiful mother who'd do anything for them. We'll give them the life we never got to have. One away from heartache and pain. One they fucking deserve."

Ash's bottom lip trembled. She was our guiding fucking light in all of this. So taking those steps with her in the future would be no brainer. I'd always wanted kids, even if I didn't think it'd ever happen given how we'd grown up and the battles we'd faced.

"I want that too. We can do it together when the time comes… the five of us… if Quinn and Eric get on board with it."

"Oh, trust me, angel, they'll come around, eventually. When all this shit with Russo is over."

Her eyes clouded over.

"I'm technically still a Russo… even if it's only in name."

I stroked her cheek.

"Do you want to change that?"

She nodded.

"Then why don't you? You're an adult, you can change your name to whatever you want."

Her hands came up and rested on my chest.

"Is it strange I want to take Viktor's name?"

My lips curled up into a smile.

"No, angel, it's not. If you want to be Ash Bykov, then I'll support you. I know how much he means to you. Hell, I'll even help you fill out the forms to do it."

"I want to talk to him about it first before I take that step. We're still getting to know each other."

I got to my feet, pulling her up with me and taking her hand. I felt lighter than I had done in a long time and there was only one way I wanted to celebrate this.

"I'm sure he'll be happy you want to take his name."

It reminded me I still had to book in an appointment with my tattoo artist. Now more than ever I wanted to get my tattoo for Ash and Eric. Something which symbolised our love for each other.

"You think?"

"I don't think, angel, I know. He loves you even if he's never said it. I think you make him proud to be your father."

She blushed as I led her back in the house. We walked by Rory again, who raised an eyebrow at me. I gave him a smile and a wink before dragging Ash into the hallway and upstairs.

"What are we doing?" she asked when I took her in her room and closed the door behind us.

My smile widened.

"You are taking your clothes off and getting on the bed. And I am going to make you scream."

CHAPTER SEVENTEEN

Ash

I eyed Xav for a long moment. His piercing blue eyes were full of life and his smile absolutely wicked.

"You still have to be gentle with me."

He wrapped a hand around my waist and leant down, nuzzling my nose with his.

"I won't hurt you, angel. I promise."

I could see an enormous burden had been lifted from him. As if realising he'd been carrying the weight of his grief around for twelve years and it was finally time to let go of it. He wasn't out of the woods yet. There'd still be bad days to come, but at least he'd recognised it as a problem he could solve. He didn't have to live life in perpetual grief and sadness deep down inside.

So I backed away towards my bed, pulling off my clothes as I went. His eyes darkened as he took me in, his fingers flexing at his sides, waiting for the moment to strike. The anticipation of his hands on me had my skin tingling. I loved this man so much and his admission he wanted a family with me, with all of us, warmed my entire soul.

Quinn forcing the subject on us hadn't exactly been pleasant, but getting our feelings out in the open would always be the way forward. Honesty, trust and acceptance were the foundations upon which we built our quintet. I had to make sure we stuck to them so we'd survive. Not only our battle with Frank, but our future together. Now more than ever we needed to present a united front. We had to stick together. Take care of each other. And grow with one another.

"Fuck, angel, I've missed you."

I smiled, shimming out of my knickers and getting on the bed.

"Lay down on your front for me."

I did as he asked, trusting he'd stick to his word and be gentle with me. I felt rather than saw him approach. He carefully straddled my legs as he got up on the bed and ran his hands down my back. Leaning over, he grabbed something from one of my bedside table drawers. I'd let them put whatever they wanted in terms of supplies in there.

When his hands next came down on my back, they were coated in something oily. His hands slid over my muscles, kneading them slightly with his fingers. Then he began to work on my shoulders, his fingers gentle as he worked out the kinks in them. I groaned, loving the feel of his hands on my skin and knowing I needed this. He'd turn all my limbs to jelly before he had his way with me.

"Like that, angel?"

"Mmm."

He chuckled, working his hands up my back and massaging the muscles there after he'd moved my hair out of the way.

"How's your chest now?"

"I still get twinges and I'm really stiff when I first wake up, but I'm getting there. Just need to keep moving, it's what Alekhin said anyway."

I tried to stay as active as I could. Taking painkillers regularly helped.

Xav worked his way down my back. His hands remained soothing, relaxing me further.

"I think you've proved once and for all how good you are with your hands."

"Knew I'd have you singing my praises one day."

I snorted and turned my head up so I could look at him. His smirk made me roll my eyes.

"Don't make me retract my statement."

He leant down and kissed my cheek.

"Never."

Straightening, he pulled off his t-shirt, followed by the rest of his clothes. I watched the way his muscles flexed and his tattoos shifted. Xav had always made my mouth water.

"Like what you see, angel?"

"Maybe."

His eyes twinkled as he spread my legs, running his hands over my behind.

"I've definitely missed this view."

I squirmed as his fingers sought out my pussy, stroking their way down to my clit.

"Someone's a little excited."

I whined when he slid two fingers inside me, stretching me out as he worked me. He pulled me up onto my knees with his other hand. My chest protested mildly, but I ignored it. His fingers in me felt so good, but they weren't enough.

"Xav, please."

His hand left my hip and landed in his lap. Gripping his cock, he stroked his hand up and down at a leisurely pace. I couldn't take my eyes off it. Off him.

"Please."

He didn't move though. Just continued fucking me with his fingers and stroking himself. I wriggled against him, wanting more. So much more.

"Xavier, please fuck me."

"Mmm, angel, I love my name on your lips."

His fingers disappeared, then he gently turned me over on my back. Crawling over me, he stroked a hand down my face, his eyes full of heat and love at the same time.

"My precious angel."

My heart went wild. I wrapped my hands around his shoulders, pulling him closer. And when he finally slid inside me, I felt the sense of fullness he always gave me. The sense of belonging and home.

"I missed you," I breathed.

He smiled, leaning down to kiss me as his hips thrust forward, impaling me on his length. I rose mine to meet him, wanting every inch he had to give me.

"You feel like home," he murmured against my lips.

He took my hands and entwined our fingers together. Raising himself slightly, he watched me as he fucked me with slow, measured thrusts. Out of his eyes poured all of his love and longing. Every part slammed into me, cocooning me in his affection and adoration. No words were needed. We spoke without them. Our bodies danced together, playing the sweet music of our lovemaking.

I could get lost in him. In this. In us. Xav kept me safe. My protector. My treasure. I wanted to be the same for him. In those moments, I knew I was the girl he needed to stand by his side. To help him through the hard times. And love through the good. He'd always been the one I could turn to when I needed affection. When I needed to be held until the world melted away and it was just me and him together.

I couldn't stop watching him. The way his lip curled up at the side. The concentration on his face. The ecstasy and joy we shared in those moments our bodies were one.

"I love you," I whispered. "*Tesoro mio*."

In response, he moved faster, driving me closer to the edge. I wrapped a leg around him, keeping him pinned to me, loving the way he thrust inside me. Each press of his hips against mine. Each exhale and gasp. The tightening of his fingers as he held my hands against the covers.

"Angel," he ground out. "Come with me."

My other leg wrapped around his, shifting the angle so he brushed against me with each stroke. My heart overflowed as the stirrings built inside my core. And the shattering happened the next moment. We both groaned, me crying his name as his eyes rolled back. The blissful feeling carried me over and dragged me under. The air seemed to disappear from my lungs, ripped from me with the sensations rushing up my spine.

And then it was over. Both of us panting from the exertion.

Xav rested his forehead against mine, staring at me with sated eyes. It hadn't been lust which drove us but a deep-seated need to chase the high together. To show our love and devotion in the one way we knew worked so fucking well. Bringing us so close together, we were practically one.

"Precious angel, I love you with every inch of my heart and soul."

I smiled. My bones felt jellified after his massage and our lovemaking. I didn't want to get up out of bed or do anything else. After having two of them make love to me today, I was already tired. Perhaps I needed to take it easy. They needed me back at full health.

He rolled off me and laid flat on his back, his hand resting on his chest.

"Do you really think Quinn and Eric will come around to the idea?"

"If they don't, Rory and I will give you all the babies you want, angel."

I snorted. I didn't want more than one with each of them.

"We'd have to repurpose some of the rooms downstairs."

"We won't need the shit we have down there when all of this is over and we're free to live our lives."

"Well, I'm in no rush. I want to keep the four of you to myself for now."

I turned, finding him grinning.

"Greedy girl."

I shoved his arm.

"Just because I want to have uninterrupted access to earth shattering sex doesn't make me greedy."

He laughed, the deep sound of it turning my already jellified bones to liquid. I loved the sound of his merriment. Always had. He shifted up on his side and ran his hand down my chest.

"Having experienced restricted access to this hot little pussy, I'm certainly not complaining about having as much time with you as possible."

"Perv."

"Always."

I curled a hand around his neck and pulled him closer, letting him kiss me as his hand ran lower.

"Xav…" I mumbled against his lips, unsure if I could take another round.

"Shh, angel, I just want to touch you."

I probably shouldn't have let him or even believed it would only remain touching because knowing Xav, he'd be between my legs without hesitation. But being with him like this made me happy. My heart was full and my body completely on board with his ministrations. Intimacy with my men was something I craved. So I allowed him to carry me away on a sea of pleasure because life would get very complicated soon and I was going to take my wins where I could.

CHAPTER EIGHTEEN

Xavier

Even with a man down, it didn't stop us calculating this next move with ruthless efficiency. Planning every last detail down to the wire. It'd taken a week of surveillance and a further two days to bring us to this evening. I, for one, could not fucking wait to get this over and done with.

I sat in a club, surrounded by women and a few men, blending into the background with dark clothing and a lazy smile on my face. I might look as though I was laid back and relaxed. Inside, I was anything but. Every part of me was on high alert, eyes slowly taking the room.

Watching. Waiting. Biding my time. Patience.

I tapped my fingers against my thigh, a whisky tumbler in my other hand which was resting on the back of the booth. The woman next to me slid a hand up my shirt underneath my jacket. I ignored her. Nothing about her touch did a thing for me. Perhaps in the past, I'd have been all over that, but not now. Not when I was working. And especially not when my loyalties and love lay with Ash and Eric.

Ash was out with Quinn, the two of them having dinner together in public. We'd deliberately tipped off the press to create a distraction. One which would provoke Russo. It's exactly what we wanted. Push a man too hard and he'd start to make mistakes. We'd capitalise on those. It would be his downfall. His ultimate demise. And I was fucking well looking forward to it.

"*He's heading in,*" came the crackle of the tiny earpiece I wore. "*Ready when you are.*"

I didn't respond, not wanting to draw attention to myself. I had to maintain the façade until the time came to strike. Instead, I tapped my thigh again, signalling to the tiny little camera in my lapel I was prepared.

"*Also, on a personal note, that woman better keep her claws off your chest. It's mine.*"

I smirked. Eric had nothing to worry about on that score, but to reassure him I leant over to the handsy girl next to me, "Sorry, sweetheart, but I don't get down with the ladies if you catch my drift."

I heard the snort of laughter in my ear and smiled wider. I did very much get down with pussy, but there was only one I wanted clenching around my cock and it was my girlfriend's. The boys had been right about one thing. Ash really did have the magic unicorn pussy we all searched for. It was more than that though. It was her laughter, her smile and the way she never took any shit off me. She loved fiercely. Her capacity for it astounded me at times. She took care of us in ways I never imagined possible. Simply put… Ash was our angel. Our everything. Our house. Our home. Our world. Our one.

"The disappointment on her face is enough to make my evening."

The girl was pouting hard and turned away from me, focusing her attention on another guy. I brought my tumbler up to my lips but didn't sip the liquid. Maintaining a clear head tonight would be paramount.

"You're welcome," I said quietly.

Carlo Russo walked in with his entourage. The man had black hair and dark eyes like his father and most of the Russo family, their Italian roots showing through. It made me wonder how Isabella had ever managed to pass off Ash as Russo's daughter. She looked nothing like them. Perhaps Russo was so desperate for an heir, he didn't care. It wouldn't surprise me knowing what kind of man he was.

My eyes tracked Carlo's movements towards the VIP area near the back. They all slid into a booth. It wasn't long until they were served drinks, a bucket of champagne placed at the table along with several glasses.

"I'm looking forward to wiping that smug smile off his self-righteous face."

None of us were big fans of Carlo after he'd tried to kill Ash and Rory. The fucker would have a wake-up call tonight.

"I'm going to kill the smug piece of shit," came Rory's voice.

"For fuck's sake, stay off the comms, Rory. You're not part of the damn operation."

I snorted. Quinn had insisted we bring Rory with us so Eric could keep an eye on him. The two of them were in the car outside waiting for me to bring Carlo to them.

"What? Not like anything is happening."

"Not the point. You're here because Quinn is making us babysit you."

I could hear Rory's grumbling, but my eyes were still on Carlo and his entourage.

"Quinn is an overbearing dick."

"True, but he's just worried about you, so suck it up and be quiet."

I almost shook my head. Those two needed to both shut up and be patient. All I had to do was bide my time. The opportunity to take Carlo would present itself, eventually. At least when we'd taken Ash, there hadn't been a room full of people to account for. We couldn't take Carlo from his house due to it being guarded, so we'd got creative. Ash told us he frequented his club on Friday nights. Personally, I thought this place was a bit of a shithole full of sleazy men and desperate women, but whatever. I wasn't here to have fun.

"Quinn's texted, wanted to know our status," Eric said, keeping me appraised of the situation after I'd been watching Carlo and his people for at least ten minutes if not more. *"Told him we're working on it. Hope he's actually paying attention to Ash; after all, it is the first time any of us have taken her out for real."*

"Quinn wouldn't know how to do romance if it slapped him in the face," Rory replied.

"As if you know any better."

These two really needed to shut up.

"I know more than Quinn."

"Right, what's your idea of romance? Tying her up and showering her with a pearl necklace."

I held in my laughter. Eric definitely didn't mean the jewellery. Ash did let us come all over her tits if we wanted it.

Seeing her skin painted with our mutual pleasure was fucking hot.

"*No, I've already given her romance I'll have you know. I ran her a bath with candles, rose petals, essential oils and music when I took her away before that cunt tried to kill us.*"

I almost choked in surprise. Rory doing romance? That was practically unheard of.

"*Well, shit… I bet she liked that. She was all over me when I gave her a candlelit picnic.*"

"*She certainly showed her appreciation.*"

I shook my head. I could well imagine she had. If these two were going to start doing over the top romantic gestures for her, I was going to have to up my game. Then I remembered the appointment I'd had whilst we'd been planning to kidnap Carlo. What was more romantic than getting a tattoo declaring my love? Eric had gotten all teary-eyed over it, but I hadn't shown Ash yet. Soon she'd see how much she meant to me. It was my idea of a romantic gesture.

"*You know, we all have to take her out for a day out together when all of this is over. She'd like that.*"

"*I don't like going out.*"

"*You say that, but I know you'll do anything for Ash.*"

"*I hate how you all keep using that against me.*"

Carlo stood up, his eyes darting around the room as he slipped out from the booth. One of his men stood with him, but Carlo waved him off. I watched him walk towards the toilets at the back. It was my cue. I got up, placing my tumbler on the table in front of me and strolled along to the toilets casually.

"You two really need to shut up now, I'm following my mark," I said in a low voice.

"*You agree though, don't you, Xavi? We need to do things together outside the house.*"

"For fuck's sake, yes, I agree," I hissed. "Now, zip it."

I glanced back at Carlo's table, but none of them saw me slip into the toilets behind the man. Looking around, I found he'd gone into a cubicle. There was another guy at the urinals, but otherwise, the place was deserted. I strolled over to the urinals and went about my business. I didn't want this guy getting the wrong idea. When he left, I went over to the sinks and started washing my hands.

Carlo came out of the cubicle a minute later. He looked at me in the mirror as he washed his hands but said nothing. The idiot had no idea who I was. Ash had told me her cousin didn't have too many brain cells. I dried my hands and slid the gun from my waistband out. He didn't have time to do a thing as I walked up behind him and pressed it into his back.

"Hello, Carlo."

His eyes widened and his mouth went slack.

"Here's what's going to happen. You're going to keep your mouth shut or I'll blow your brains out all over this nice counter here, got it?"

He nodded. I almost laughed. He hadn't put up a fight at all. Probably knew he was fucked.

Should've let your man come in with you.

"Good. Now, weapons?"

"In my pocket."

I frisked him all over, making sure he had nothing else other than the small handgun in his pocket. I slid it into mine and then moved him towards the door.

"You're going to come down the back with me. If any of your men try to talk to you, you're going to get them to go away, do you understand? I don't play nice, Carlo, so you better not give me any shit."

"I get it, Jesus."

"Act natural," I hissed as we walked out of the toilets with the gun still pressed to his back to hide it from view.

His idiot men hadn't even been paying any attention, so none of them even looked our way as we strolled out. Several people were hiding us from their table anyway. I shoved him towards the back of the club, having already paid off the staff to let us through. Didn't need anyone stopping us now I had him.

This was proving to be easier than I thought. Probably because Carlo was too stupid to even tie his own shoelaces. I had to be quick about it though. Didn't need them noticing straight away he hadn't reappeared at their table.

"I've acquired the package," I said as I led Carlo down the dark hallway at the back of the club.

"*We're at the end of the alley, got the car running,*" came Eric's response through the earpiece.

I shoved open the fire escape at the back, knowing the owner had disabled the alarm and pushed Carlo outside. I raised the gun from his back to his head, directing him down the alley. Didn't need the fucker bolting at the last moment. This part would be precarious. I had to get him in the car without anyone noticing he was being held at gunpoint.

"What is this about?" he asked as he walked without complaint.

"You'll find out soon enough."

"Do you want money? I've got money."

"Not about fucking money, man. Just shut up and keep walking."

What a fucking idiot.

I didn't need his or his family's dirty money. We had more than enough of our own. Carlo didn't realise how expendable he was. I might have baulked at the idea of killing this guy in cold blood when Ash had first brought it up, but he'd tried to kill her and Rory. So, to be honest, he didn't deserve our mercy. He deserved nothing.

We got to the end of the alley and I lowered the gun to his back again, holding his shoulder so he didn't move whilst I checked the street. A few people were loitering outside in the smoking area at the side of the club on the pavement behind a roped-off area. The Range Rover sat idling in front of us.

"Here's what's going to happen, you're going to get in the back of the car in front of us. No funny business, you hear me?"

"Yes," he gritted out.

I shoved him out into the street towards the car, trying to look as normal as possible when holding a gun to someone's back and trying to get them to come peacefully. Carlo, to his credit, didn't even try to escape. I wouldn't fucking hesitate to shoot him in the back if he did. He opened the back door when we reached it and climbed in. I started to get in behind him when I realised he'd scrambled across the seat to try open the door on the other side.

I rolled my eyes, hopping in and putting a hand on his shoulder, pulling him back and shoving him into the seat.

"Wrong fucking move," I growled, closing the door and I heard the locks clicking the next moment.

Eric and Rory both looked back at us from the front seats. Rory looked downright murderous whilst Eric grinned.

"What the fuck is this?" Carlo asked, straining against my hand.

"This is called a mother fucking kidnapping, dipshit. Now… it's time for you to take a nap."

I put my hand out and Eric slapped a syringe into it. Carlo strained harder, but I ignored him as I jabbed the needle into his neck and sunk the plunger down. Pulling it out when I was done, I dropped it back into Eric's awaiting hand and patted Carlo on the shoulder before leaning across and strapping him into the seat.

"What the fuck?" he grunted, putting a hand over his neck.

Eric pulled away from the curb and started off home. Operation Kidnap Carlo was complete.

"Well, that was far fucking easier than expected," I said, watching Carlo as his eyes began to droop.

"You mean easier than when we last had to kidnap someone?" Eric asked.

"Just a bit. His idiot men didn't even notice he'd not arrived back at their table. I'm sure they will soon."

Carlo's head dropped on his shoulder. He was out cold. Next time the fucker awoke, he'd be locked away, unable to escape. Served him right.

"Let Quinn know, eh?"

I pulled out my phone and fired off a text to him, hoping he'd be happy we'd accomplished our goal. It's not like any of us wanted to kidnap this idiot and hold him hostage, but Ash was right. We had to play Russo at his own game. Make him angry. Then he'd play right into our hands rather than us playing into his. Russo gaining the upper hand again would fuck us over royally and none of us wanted to be in that situation again.

"Let's get home before the cunt wakes up."

"On it."

Time for some fucking fun.

This fucker didn't know what was about to hit him. When he found out who'd taken him, I was pretty sure he'd be chilled to the god damn fucking bone.

CHAPTER NINETEEN

Quinn

I looked down at the text from Xav, a slow smile spreading across my face. Everything had gone to plan so far. When we were meticulous, our plans usually went off without a hitch. It's why I'd made sure we'd taken the time to get everything in place before we attempted this rather than diving right in.

"What is it?" Ash asked, putting her hand on mine to get my attention.

"They're on their way home with the package secured."

"Oh good… Does that mean you'll stop staring at your phone and actually pay attention to me?"

I slid my phone back in my pocket after firing off a response and levelled my gaze on my girl. She looked stunning, a little red cocktail dress hugging her figure and her blonde hair around her shoulders in loose waves.

"Have I told you how beautiful you look this evening?"

Her cheeks went pink.

"No… if that's supposed to make up for you ignoring me then you're going to have to try harder."

I grinned and leant closer. The twinkle in her eye told me she was messing with me. I'd been paying attention to her whilst we waited for the boys to execute our plan. Eric assured me Rory was staying out of trouble in the car next to him. Rory might hate it, but I still had concerns about his recovery. Some days he was good and some days not so much. Alekhin had said it would take time for him to go back to normal.

"You have my full, undivided attention, little girl. And you'll have it again later when we're alone too. I plan on doing some very depraved things to you."

"Lucky for you I like your depravity."

Her fingers stroked over mine. It struck me all over again how lucky I was to have her. Despite how we'd begun, Ash had become the single most important person in my life outside of the boys. She's made my world go around. We had all grown so much over the past months since we'd taken her. We still had so many challenges to face and overcome, but I took a moment to appreciate what the five of us had. Our quintet. Even if they gave me shit for the term, I didn't care. It's what we were.

I was just about to tell her so when I glanced up and felt a little ill at the sight of who'd walked in the restaurant. It might have been years since I'd last laid eyes on her, but she was definitely the one woman I never wanted to see again. She had a man with her who must be her husband. Of all the fucking restaurants, she had to walk into this one where I was taking out the love of my life for the very first time.

For fuck's sake.

"Quinn… are you okay?"

My eyes landed back on Ash. Clearly, my composure was shot or maybe she'd learnt to notice every small detail about me. Ash had become rather adept at reading my moods and adapting to them. It's one of the reasons I loved her so much.

"Yes and no."

She cocked her head to the side as if asking me to elaborate as her fingers continued stroking across my hand. I turned my palm over and gripped her hand tight, needing her to anchor me. My skin prickled with discomfort and I soon realised why. The damn woman was making a beeline for us along with her husband in tow, giving me no opportunity to tell Ash exactly who was about to descend on our table.

"Quinn Marotta. It's you, isn't it? I'd recognise that face anywhere," came the nasal tones of my one and only previous girlfriend.

"Hello, Leah," I said with an ease I didn't entirely feel in those moments.

Our relationship had been the biggest disaster. Not only was Leah Devine a pain in the arse, but she also hated Xav, Eric and Rory for no reason other than I cared more about them than I ever did her. We were terrible for each other, constantly fighting with our teenage hormones running rampant. The boys had been glad when I'd called it quits for good.

"What a coincidence, it's been an absolute age." She put her hand on the arm of the man next to her. "This is my darling husband, Jimmy. This is Quinn, remember I told you about him?"

Why she'd ever think to bring me up to anyone was a mystery to me but who the fuck cared. I wanted her gone from the table as soon as possible.

"Nice to meet you," Jimmy said with a frown.

Clearly, it's not. I'm certainly not happy to meet you either.

Leah's eyes fell on Ash who was staring at the newcomers with a blank expression on her face. It concerned me. Leah's eyebrow twitched in that way it always had when she was pissed but didn't want to show it. We hadn't ended on amicable terms and I'm sure she didn't like me dating someone who was clearly quite a few years younger than me. But Ash and I weren't just dating. We were in it for the long haul. So who cared if we had a nine-year age gap.

"This is my girlfriend, Ash," I indicated her with my head, "Ash, this is Leah. We knew each other when we were teenagers."

Leah laughed. The sound grated on my ears.

"Oh come now, Quinn, it was a little more than just *knowing* each other, wouldn't you say?"

"Oh?" Ash asked politely but I could see by the fire in her eyes, she was pissed off at Leah's appearance.

"We were childhood sweethearts."

I almost choked.

Is she fucking kidding me?

I'd hardly define our toxic relationship where we constantly argued and broke up every second week as being childhood sweethearts. Leah had cheated on me more times than I could count. There was zero love involved on my part. The first person I'd ever loved was Ash and it would remain that way.

Ash's eyes narrowed to slits. I could feel the tension radiating off her.

"That's nice. I'm sure *Quinn* will tell me all about it later."

Well, I'm in the shit now. Great.

"I'm sure he will," Leah responded with another laugh.

I wanted to slap her stupid smile off her face.

"Well, you enjoy your evening now."

"You too," I said with a fake smile plastered on my face.

The two of them thankfully left as the hostess came up to lead them over to their table. I watched them, making sure it was far away from ours before turning back to Ash.

"Childhood sweethearts, huh? What happened to 'you're the only girl I've ever given my heart to'?"

She tried to tug her hand out of mine, but I didn't let her. This wasn't how I wanted the evening to go at all.

"I wasn't lying to you when I said that."

"Then what the fuck was that?"

"That was Leah fucking Devine making up shit because she's crazy."

Ash snorted and ripped her hand away from me, scowling.

"Yes, blame the woman for being crazy, Quinn, because it's always the woman's fault, isn't it?"

I almost rubbed my face out of sheer frustration.

"That's not what I meant and you know it."

"No, I don't think I do."

"Little girl…"

"Don't you little girl me!"

Our main meals hadn't arrived yet, but I was ready to get out of this stupid restaurant now. Rather than do that or have it out with her in front of people, I got up and took her hand, pulling her up out of her chair and tugging her away towards the toilets.

"What the hell, Quinn? What are you doing?" she hissed, trying to discreetly pull her hand out of mine.

"Be quiet."

I felt her stiffen at my tone and stop her attempts to escape me. Glancing around, I pulled her into the ladies' toilets. There were two women by the sinks whose eyebrows shot up when they saw us, but I ignored them, dragging Ash into a cubicle and locking the door behind us. I kicked the seat closed and turned to her.

"Now, you listen to me," I started in a low voice as I grabbed her arm and tugged her closer before tipping her face up with my other hand so she'd look at me. "It has only ever been you. It will only ever be you. Anyone who says anything different is lying. Are you going to stand there and tell me you believe a woman you've never even met before this evening over me?"

Her bottom lip trembled and she shook her head. Ash knew better. She knew how much I adored her. How she'd become my entire universe.

"Leah and I had the worst fucking relationship imaginable. You can ask the boys who will confirm it for you. They hated her. She would constantly try to get me to ditch them because she didn't like how close we were. She was crazy, cheated on me and gave me hell all the time. The only reason I still went back time and time again is because I was bored. It was wrong of me, but it's the truth. We ended for good when she gave me an ultimatum, her or the boys. As you know full well, I chose Xav, Eric and Rory. That's the end of it. Whatever she said just now, she did it to make you jealous because she's vindictive and clearly hasn't changed in the past thirteen years since we broke up. So, tell me, little girl, are you still angry with me or are you going to calm the fuck down?"

Her blue eyes clouded over. Maybe I was an idiot, but I wanted to kiss away the frown on her face. Ash drove me absolutely nuts, but I still loved her for it. I needed everything about her in my life. Our love was volatile, but there was tenderness and affection between us at the same time.

"Quinn…"

"Yes?"

"I love you."

"Well good. I love you too."

"Good."

We stared at each other for a moment longer before my mouth crashed against hers and she wrapped her arms around my neck, pressing as close as she possibly could to me.

"Little girl," I almost moaned against her mouth, shoving her backwards into the wall.

The need to be inside her pounded in my veins.

"We're in a restaurant," she murmured against my lips.

I hadn't forgotten. Pulling away, I stroked her face, eying her lips and wanting to kiss them all over again.

"Punishment comes when we get home…"

"Don't we have to deal with you know who first?"

I almost slapped my hand over my head. We did have to deal with him first depending on what dosage Xav gave Carlo to knock him out.

"For fuck's sake, you're right. Fine, we deal with him then punishment, understood?"

She nodded, running her fingers along my neck.

"Good, now let's go have a nice dinner together since I have no idea when I'll be able to take out you like this again."

Ash smiled up at me, her eyes twinkling.

"Yes, sir."

I groaned as I unlocked the cubicle door and tugged her out. Thankfully, there were no women in the toilets this time.

Nothing surprised me when it came to me and Ash any longer. We fought. We taunted each other. And yet we still loved hard. Our push and pull kept us grounded. It's how we worked. Nothing would keep me from my little girl. Nothing at all. So fighting with her over shit? Didn't matter much in the grand scheme of things. I'd still punish her before worshipping her the only way I knew how later on when we were alone. Then we'd fall asleep in each other's arms, content and satisfied.

Ash stared up at me as I lead her back out into the restaurant, her eyes betraying her love and affection. I'd fight with her to hell and back if she kept looking at me like that. Just like that. As if I was her heart and soul. Her fucking king.

She was my queen. And soon, she'd been the queen of ashes when we destroyed Frank Russo for good. With Ash by my side, I could accomplish anything. First, we would deal with Carlo and send Russo a message.

We're coming for you, Frank. We're coming. And you should be fucking scared out of your fucking mind.

CHAPTER TWENTY

Ash

The moment we got in the front door, I heard a voice which sounded distinctly like Xav singing, "The lovebirds are home!"

I rolled my eyes and Quinn huffed.

"Does he ever switch off?" I muttered.

"No. Never."

All three of the others popped their heads around the living room door.

"Did you two have fun?" Eric asked as they filed out of the room the next minute.

"Apart from Quinn's ex-girlfriend turning up, yes we did."

I hung my coat up, ignoring their stares, which were mostly directed at Quinn.

"Hold up, Leah was at the same restaurant as you?" Xav asked, incredulity dripping from his tone.

"Yes, fucking Leah," Quinn grunted, walking by them and looking distinctly pissed off.

I honestly couldn't blame him. We had got into a bit of an argument over it until I realised I was simply acting irrational and jealous after he explained the circumstances of their relationship. Quinn was mine and only mine. He'd opened up to me, given me his love, trust and affection. Besides, he'd had to deal with my ex and the first guy I'd been intimate with so I had to suck it up. We both had pasts. What we had now was the most important thing. And it was each other.

"Oh shit, bet that was so much fun."

"She called them childhood sweethearts," I replied, following Quinn down the hallway towards the cell.

The peal of laughter coming from behind me had me glancing over my shoulder. It wasn't just Xav, Eric and Rory had joined in too. If I hadn't believed Quinn before, I certainly did now seeing their reactions to it.

"Oh man, that's fucking rich. She made our lives hell, not to mention whenever they broke up the three of us kept betting how many other people they'd fuck before getting back together."

I raised an eyebrow. Quinn hadn't mentioned that part.

"Oh really now?"

"I never cheated on her," Quinn said as we all arrived outside the cell door. "Now instead of reminiscing on my past failures, can we please deal with this shit?" He waved at the door. "I, for one, don't want to waste any more time."

Xav looked between us then smirked.

"I see how it is, you just want to take Ash to bed."

Quinn smirked.

"And?"

I rolled my eyes and shoved Xav's arm before waving at the door myself.

"Can we please get on?"

"Is he awake yet?" Quinn asked, pressing a hand on the door.

"No, we've been monitoring him, but nothing yet," Eric said.

Quinn pushed the door open and walked in followed by the rest of us. He glanced back at Rory giving him a warning stare. We all knew how much Rory wanted to get rid of Carlo for good. He stayed back by the wall as the rest of us walked up to the prone figure on the floor who had a shackle wrapped around his wrist. The one they'd put on me when they brought me here. I didn't like the memory or the reminders of that time.

"Okay, angel?" Xav murmured to me.

I shook my head. Being in here bothered me far more than I expected. I wanted them to get rid of this cell. He reached up and squeezed my shoulder. I turned into him and he wrapped an arm around me, giving me the comfort I needed.

"How much did you give him?" Quinn asked, nudging Carlo with his foot.

"Enough to knock him out, but not so much he'll be out as long as Ash was when we took her. I know what I'm doing."

It should've made me feel uncomfortable, them talking about me like that, but it didn't.

"Okay, I have to know. Who exactly injected me?" I asked.

The boys looked between them before Quinn pointed at Eric who flushed.

"He did, then Xav carried you out into the hallway, along to the lift and down to the carpark. We hacked the cameras so they went blank before we took you. That way, Russo wasn't able to find out who took you. He didn't even know we were there. We brought you home and put you in here and you know what happened next."

I wasn't sure how I felt about it. There wasn't exactly any way we could go back in time and erase that part. I couldn't hate them for it. They'd set me free. And we'd forged an unconventional kind of relationship together.

A groan came from the floor and all of us looked down. Carlo shifted and rolled onto his back. When he opened his eyes, he blinked rapidly. Then he was looking around frantically as he took in his surroundings and the fact he was chained up before his eyes finally rested on us.

"What… what the fuck?" he croaked.

"It's nice to see you're awake," Quinn said with a deadly expression on his face.

"Who are…" he faltered when his eyes found mine. "Ash? What did you do?"

I stepped out of Xav's arm and stared directly down at Carlo.

"I told you I'd come for you, Carlo. It seems you haven't got any smarter since the last time we saw each other."

"Why am I still alive?"

I smirked before squatting down so we were eye level.

"We're going to send Frank a little message. He thinks he's untouchable. Pity really. He's always underestimated me. And he's definitely underestimated my men."

Fear bled out of Carlo. His skin was clammy, his brow beading with sweat and he looked like he was about to piss himself.

"Shit, Ash… I'm sorry I tried to kill you, okay? I don't… I don't want to die."

I shook my head.

"Who said anything about dying? None of us are planning to kill you… yet."

The last word hung in the air. He didn't need to know we didn't intend to kill him. Only if Frank decided not to cooperate with us, would we consider disposing of Carlo as an option.

"You're merely a hostage, but don't mistake this for mercy. None of us has any for you."

I rose to my feet and looked at the boys. I'd made sure they'd given him a blanket and pillow along with a glass of water which sat beside the little cot.

Carlo said nothing, merely looked between us with abject misery on his face. I didn't feel sorry for him.

"I'll see you in the morning."

I turned and walked out, not wishing to stay in the cell for another minute. When I got outside, I pressed myself up against the wall and took a deep breath, stuffing down the anxiety flaring inside me. Rory joined me. When he saw me, he immediately came to my side and pressed his uninjured hand to my face, stroking a thumb down my cheek.

"Little star," he whispered. "It's okay."

"Ror," I choked out.

"Shh, shh, come here."

He wrapped his injured arm around me and pulled me against his chest. Fingers tangled in my hair, stroking down my scalp in a soothing manner.

"I don't like being in there… I hate that room."

"I know. You don't have to go back in. The others will deal with it, okay?"

I nodded against his chest. His warmth seeped into me, calming me down. I reached up and ran my fingers along his face.

"I love you, Ror," I whispered, needing to say those words to him. "I'm so sorry you got hurt because of that idiot."

He clutched me tighter.

"You don't have to apologise, little star. Not your fault. You've done nothing but take care of me."

"Is it selfish of me to want you better because I miss us so much?"

He let out a little chuckle.

"No… I want that too. You, me, no clothes and my bed sounds like heaven."

I wished he was better. It wasn't even about sex. I really missed the way we were together. It felt like our time got cut so short. He'd only just opened up to me finally and then the fucking car crash happened, derailing everything. Carlo robbed me of my Rory. I was still fucking pissed about it. When my beautiful broken man recovered fully, I'd give him anything he needed. I craved our violent version of making love.

"I promised Quinn tonight, but I'm yours tomorrow. Even if we can't… you know… I just want to be close to you."

He breathed out a sigh. I didn't want to ruin his recovery by going too fast.

"I'd like that."

I smiled into his chest. We could do whatever he wanted as long as I got to be close to him like this. He didn't recoil at my touch any longer. He accepted it so readily, wanting everything with me. The way he'd come out of himself and grown to love me as much as I loved him still had me in awe some days.

We pulled away from each other when we heard voices and the boys filed out, Quinn shutting the door behind them. He reached out a hand to me. I went up on my tiptoes and kissed Rory gently before slipping my hand into Quinn's and letting him lead me away upstairs.

"Is everything okay with Carlo?" I asked as we reached his bedroom door.

"Yes. We'll record a video for Russo in the morning and set everything in motion."

"I don't like being in the cell… I want it gone."

Quinn glanced down at me as we walked into his bedroom, a frown apparent on his face.

"You want it gone?"

"Yes." I turned so he could unzip my dress. "I want it and the other rooms on that side of the house to be converted into bedrooms."

His hands came up, unzipping my dress and carefully pulling it off me. I took it from his hands and folded it across the back of a chair. I'd hang it up in my wardrobe tomorrow. Next, I slid out of my shoes and padded into Quinn's bathroom before setting about getting myself ready for bed. I kept stuff in each of the boy's bathrooms now so I didn't have to keep moving my shit around. It was more practical that way. Quinn came in with me, his eyes on me the whole time but he said nothing as he prepared for bed too.

I crawled into bed when I was done having discarded my bra in exchange for one of Quinn's t-shirts. All my energy left me. My eyes felt heavy. I burrowed myself under the covers and got comfortable. I didn't even raise my head to watch him undress like I usually enjoyed doing when I heard him moving about the room. The lights went out and the bed shifted behind me. The warmth of his body seared into me as he wrapped himself around my back. His fingers stroked my hair back from my face.

"Tired?" he asked quietly.

"Mmm."

He kissed my shoulder and then settled himself down, his breath dusting across the back of my neck as he held me close. It occurred to me a minute later he'd promised punishment and sex in the restaurant. I felt bad immediately. We'd had such a romantic evening apart from our argument and here I was too tired to give him more than just a cuddle.

"Don't you want to…?"

"Not if you're tired."

"And what about what I said just now?"

He was silent for so long, I didn't think he'd answer me. I needed Quinn to be on board with it since this was technically his house. His hand dipped under my t-shirt, splaying out over my stomach.

"It reminds you of us taking you."

I nodded. Whilst I could never forget how our relationship started, I'd moved past it. So having a stark reminder of it? It didn't help me at all.

"When this is over… we'll talk about getting rid of it."

"Thank you."

"I want you to feel like this is your home too, little girl."

I felt more at home with the boys than I'd ever done anywhere else. It wasn't the house but being with them. They were my safety. They all owned pieces of my heart and soul.

"It is."

He kissed the back of my neck, nuzzling my hair and stroking his fingers across my stomach.

"We could be anywhere, Quinn, as long as I have you and the boys, it'll always be home."

"You're our home too."

My heart tightened. Despite my exhaustion, I turned around in his embrace, tangled my hands in his hair and tugged him closer, allowing our lips to meld together. It wasn't an all-consuming kiss, but a reminder of how much we meant to one another. It spoke of our love without words.

When we pulled apart, Quinn rolled on his back, pulling me with him. I settled my head on his chest, stroking my hand down his bare skin. And that's how I fell asleep, tucked up against my man in the way he loved, dreaming of a future where the five of us were free from the tyranny of the man who'd raised me.

CHAPTER TWENTY ONE

Rory

Ash seemed subdued this morning when she came down to breakfast with Quinn. Even when Xav tried to engage her in conversation, her answers were short and her demeanour was completely off. It concerned me, more so when none of the others seemed to notice. Eric had taken Carlo breakfast. I'd had a word with him and Xav about making sure Ash didn't have to go in the cell any more than necessary before Quinn and Ash came down, which they'd both agreed with.

We all filed out of the kitchen and walked to the cell. I caught up with Ash, putting my uninjured hand on her lower back. She leant into my touch, which put a smile on my face. I'd help ground her after the filming had taken place. She'd need me.

"How's your wrist?" she asked, looking up at me as we came to a stop outside the cell.

"Okay, I guess. Doesn't hurt too much and I can finally hold cutlery, just about anyway."

The splint bugged the hell out of me, especially when the skin underneath it got itchy. The urge to scratch could be maddening. I daren't take it off though, knowing the only way my wrist would heal was by keeping it in place. Ash had been helping me wash, which I kind of hated but put up with. Letting her take care of me seemed to make her happy. I'd do anything to see her smile and laugh, her crystal blue eyes twinkling with mirth.

Ash made me so fucking happy. My light in the darkness. My little northern star. She got me on a level the boys never had. She knew exactly what I needed and when, like she'd become completely in-tune with my emotions and moods.

"Ready to spend the day with me?"

I nodded. An entire day with Ash. I'd savour every moment.

Quinn unlocked the door and walked in, followed by Eric and Xav. Ash hesitated by my side before visibly steeling herself. We strolled in together, finding the boys already dragging Carlo up off the bed and sitting him down in the metal chair in the middle of the room.

"Stay," Quinn said before stuffing a gag in Carlo's mouth and giving him a hard stare.

Carlo did nothing but look at him with disgust. I'd quite happily wipe it off his face if the others let me. Nothing would please me more than to see this fucker dead and gone. He'd hurt me and Ash.

Xav fiddled with the camera and I pushed Ash closer to Quinn. Her hands shook at her sides. She hated this room and I could hardly blame her. The memories she associated with it weren't exactly the best. She was trying not to show it, but I could read her all too well. Quinn squeezed her shoulder with one hand when she arrived next to him. Eric and I stood behind Xav, who'd got the tripod set up and gave Quinn a nod.

"Ready, little girl?"

Ash nodded and turned to the camera. Her eyes grew determined and her stance relaxed a little. I kept my eyes on Carlo because I didn't trust the man at all. He looked like he wanted to strangle Ash and that couldn't be a good sign at all.

"Okay, recording… now," Xav said, giving them a thumbs up.

Ash shifted on her feet before staring at the camera.

"Hello, Papa… I got your message loud and clear. You say you're going to find me, but I've been sitting right under your nose for months. So I ask myself… you and what army? I'm waiting. We're all waiting. I guess we got a little bored because as you can see… I have Carlo here." She waved at Carlo with one hand. "You took my mother so I thought I'd repay the favour."

Quinn moved forward, coming to stand next to Ash. His eyes were dark as he stared at the camera too.

"Our demand is simple. Return Isabella to us and we will set Carlo free. If you do not… well… we're not above disposing of him."

"He's expendable, Papa. After all, he tried to kill me."

It was at that exact moment I realised in hindsight we should have tied Carlo to the chair. He launched himself out of it, his hands extended, and barrelled into Ash. She crashed onto the floor with him on top of her. We were all so shocked, no one else moved as Carlo gripped Ash around the neck and started trying to strangle her.

Quinn was the first to move, grabbing Carlo by the shoulders and trying to haul him off Ash.

"Let go of her," he ground out.

Eric was moving next, slamming down on his knees and grabbing Carlo's hands, ripping them off Ash's neck. Quinn pulled Carlo back, shoving him against the chair. I couldn't see his expression, but I imagined he was furious. Ash put her hands to her neck, trying to breathe in deeply as Eric pulled her head into his lap and stroked her hair back.

"Shh, beautiful, I've got you… just breathe," he murmured.

I didn't give a shit if I'd been told not to go near Carlo or hurt him. He'd tried to strangle our girl. Before Xav had a chance to stop me, I strode forward, grabbed Carlo by the head with both hands and kneed him in the face. The crunching sound of his nose shattering rang through the room. I got dragged back by Xav, who shoved me up against the wall and held me there.

"What the fuck?" Carlo moaned, putting his hands to his face as blood dripped down from his nose.

"Well, it's no less than you fucking deserve," Quinn stated through gritted teeth as he hauled Carlo up and sat him back in the chair. "You fucking touch Ash again, it'll be more than breaking your nose, you hear?"

Carlo didn't even acknowledge Quinn, merely groaning at the pain.

"Let me go," I hissed at Xav who raised an eyebrow at me.

"Are you going to attack him again?"

"No… I want to go to Ash."

"E's got her covered, man."

I glared at him. Ash was curled up in Eric's lap now, breathing in and out whilst he stroked her hair and held her.

"Let me go to her."

"Get him out of here, Xav," Quinn said without looking at the two of us. "And her too, E. I'll deal with this mess."

Xav pulled me out of the room and I didn't fight him. He let go when we were in the hallway, his eyes on me, checking to make sure I wouldn't do anything stupid.

"What the fuck was that?"

"He tried to kill her."

"And you just kneed him in the face? Since when did you stop caring about human contact?"

It occurred to me I hadn't even hesitated, acting on instinct. The instinct to protect my girl at all costs. So I hadn't exactly given a shit about touching him. All I'd wanted to do was hurt the fucker.

Eric came out the next moment, carrying Ash in his arms. She had her face buried in his neck, her arms wrapped around him. I was about to open my mouth when he shook his head and walked away towards the living room. Xav and I followed after him. I needed to know if she was okay or not. My beautiful girl who I never wanted to see hurt again. She had to be okay.

Eric sat down with her on the sofa. She refused to let go of him and he didn't try to pry her off. I sat next to them and stroked a hand down her back.

"Little star."

Eric looked up at Xav.

"You should get Quinn the first-aid kit."

He shrugged but ambled out of the room. That fucker, Carlo, didn't deserve to be tended to. I hoped he was in pain. I hoped he fucking regretted trying to kill Ash again. If I had my way, he'd be dead so he could never get his hands on her.

"Ash, you need to give us a sign you're okay," Eric murmured in her ear.

One of her hands lowered from his neck and found its way into his hand, squeezing it. Both Eric and I let out a breath.

"Do you just need a minute?"

She nodded against his neck.

"Okay, beautiful, take all the time you need."

He kissed the top of her head, tangling his free hand in her hair. Then he turned to me, his green eyes searching.

"That was a rather dramatic response from you."

I shrugged. Ash brought out things in me I never knew I possessed, such as the need to protect her at all costs. And exact revenge on anyone who harmed her.

"I love her," I muttered.

"Oh, trust me, I can see that."

He grinned. I scowled in response. This lot pissed me off with their taunting over my feelings for Ash. I might have come out of my shell and changed since she'd been in our lives, but to me, it was all for the better. She made me a better man. I could only be grateful to her for her patience and understanding. She never once made me feel inadequate or broken for the way I was.

"Leave him be, E," came Ash's voice.

We both stared at her. Ash had a habit of defending me when the boys were giving me too much shit.

"Little star…"

She lifted her head and turned to me. Thankfully, there weren't any marks on her neck as Eric and Quinn had gotten Carlo off her pretty quickly.

"I'm okay."

I reached out and stroked her cheek. She gave me a tight smile. A need to have her close pounded within my veins. I wanted her pressed against my chest, my arms around her. She must've seen it in my eyes because she shifted off Eric's lap and crawled into mine, cupping my face with both her hands.

"Thank you," she whispered before pressing her mouth against mine.

I hadn't kissed Ash in front of the boys, but I got so distracted by her body against mine, it barely concerned me.

"Well, I was going to check to see if you were okay, but I can see you are," came Quinn's voice from behind us.

Ash pulled away and looked up at him over my head.

"I am… What are we going to do about the video?"

"Xav thinks he can use what we recorded, cutting it before Carlo attacked you."

I glanced back, finding Quinn right behind us, looking over Ash with a concerned expression on his face.

"Oh… that's good, I don't want to go in the cell again."

He reached down and stroked her hair.

"You don't have to, little girl. We'll take care of it from here, okay?"

She nodded then shifted down, resting her head on my chest with her hands on my shoulders. I wrapped an arm around her.

"Would you like me to read to you?" I whispered.

She nodded again. She'd done it enough times for me and now I was feeling a hell of a lot better than I had been since the accident, I could do it for her. Pulling out my phone from my pocket, I set about looking for a book.

Eric got up and he and Quinn retreated from the room, leaving Ash and me alone together. I could take care of her whilst they dealt with everything else.

"I feel so stupid… here I am, trying to be strong, and yet I fall apart whenever something goes wrong."

"Carlo just tried to kill you, little star. None of us are expecting you to bounce back from that straight away."

"You and the boys always seem to have to take care of me though."

"It's what we're here for… we love you so all of us will do anything in our power to make you happy."

She stroked my neck with one hand.

"I don't know where I'd be without you."

"You never have to find out."

We both got a little more comfortable on the sofa. I laid out across it and she curled herself up against my side, resting her head on my chest as I started to read to her. Books, comics and graphic novels were our thing. So getting to show my little star my appreciation for her looking after me all this time? I'd do it in a fucking heartbeat.

"I love you, Ror," she whispered at a pause in the story.

I kissed the top of her head.

"Love you too, little star."

CHAPTER TWENTY TWO

Eric

Xav was busy working on the video at the desk whilst Quinn paced his office like a caged wild animal.

"How's our prisoner's nose?" I asked, taking a seat in a chair opposite the desk and eying Xav. The little furrow of concentration in his brow was so fucking cute. I wanted to kiss it away, but not sure Quinn would appreciate me getting all handsy with Xav right now when he was in a mood.

"Fine or as fine as it can be after Rory decided to break it."

"You sure about that?"

"Yes, I can set a fucking broken nose, E, I'm not that inept. He screamed fucking bloody murder about it, but hey, he's properly secured now and feeling very sorry for himself."

Quinn glared at me. Being used to his moods, I merely grinned at him, which I don't think helped matters.

"Can you blame Rory for doing it?"

"No, I can't. I'm not mad. Cunt tried to kill him and Ash, so he deserves what's coming to him."

I raised an eyebrow.

"And what is coming to him?"

Quinn merely dragged his finger across his throat.

"Hey, man, we did not agree on the killing him part," Xav interjected.

"You think there won't be a shit ton of bloodshed before this over? We're going to kill Frank. People are going to fucking die so we can get to him."

Quinn had a point and I'd resigned myself to it. None of us relished the prospect of murder, but we'd all done it. For our own survival and for each other. So us having to get rid of Carlo seemed a small price to pay in the grand scheme of things.

"I know that, but if we kill him, Russo will retaliate and it'll get worse."

"It's going to get much worse before it gets better, Xav. This shit is a gamble and it could backfire. He might kill Isabella and where will we be then, huh?"

Xav rubbed the back of his neck before concentrating on the screen again.

"Ash might break completely if that happens."

We all knew it had to be a possibility, but none of us wanted to bring it up to Ash. The last thing we wanted was for Isabella to die, no matter how we felt about her. It was also a little too obvious. I didn't think Frank would dispose of his wife. He'd want to draw it out, torture Ash for as long as possible. The thought of it made my fists clench. It didn't matter so much he wanted me dead, but the fact he'd kill me with the explicit reason of torturing the girl he thought was his daughter sickened me to my very core.

"We don't need that happening. I'd rather our girl be healthy and whole instead of a shell of herself. We need her if we're going to win this fucking fight."

Where would we even be without Ash now? All of us might have gone through a shit ton of emotional turmoil with her, but she completed us in a way nothing else had. Having her made us more focused. We had a future to fight for and one that looked bright rather than dark and depressing. Before Ash had come along, none of us cared if we lived or died, only that we got rid of Frank Russo. We had meaning again. So we owed it to her to save her mother.

"Do you think she's okay out there with Rory?" I asked, rubbing my chin.

"If you haven't noticed how much he dotes on that girl, you must be blind. She's fine. Those two are like two fucking peas in a pod sometimes… and to think, I wasn't sure she could handle him… turns out I was very fucking wrong. He's changed and, in my opinion, for the better."

Quinn admitting he was wrong about anything was a turn up for the books.

"Hold on, did you just admit to being wrong about something?" Xav asked, his head whipping around to Quinn and his eyes wide.

Quinn shrugged in a manner that could only be described as nonchalant.

"Yes… and?"

"Excuse me whilst I savour this moment in time… it may never happen again."

Quinn stuck his middle finger up at Xav.

"And there we go, the real Quinn emerges from his cave of darkness."

"Oh… just shut the fuck up and get that damn video done."

I snorted. Those two would never change.

"It is done, I was working on something else."

I saw the glint in Xav's eyes. He was blatantly saying it to wind Quinn up further. And unsurprisingly, Quinn's expression turned murderous.

"Are you serious right now?"

Xav winked and went back to fiddling with the computer.

"No, but it was worth it to see your face. It's still rendering so be patient."

"Asking Quinn to be patient is like buying a lottery ticket, the chances of you winning are slim to none," I said with a smirk.

"You two can both fuck right off," Quinn muttered, giving us evils.

"You're right, Xavi… totally worth it."

If Quinn stormed out of the room, it would hardly surprise me. He paced away again, crossing his arms over his chest and huffing noisily.

"When I'm done, we can go spy on Ash and Rory."

"For what purpose?"

"Those two are cute as fuck when they think no one is watching. They get all cuddly and shit. Seeing Rory actually give a shit about another human being is seriously like the most fascinating thing happening in this household."

I rolled my eyes. I had no idea what his obsession with Rory and Ash was. It was kind of cute how he got all protective over her, but I was no way near as invested in creeping on them like Xav. Sometimes I wondered about my boyfriend and his quirks.

"You are seriously fucking weird," Quinn muttered before throwing himself down in a chair next to me.

"Are you grumpy because Ash didn't put out last night?"

"What? How do you know that?"

Xav smirked.

"Lucky guess."

"She was tired."

"And this morning?"

"Fuck off."

Xav waved a hand at him.

"You get moody when you don't get to stick your dick in her."

Quinn got extremely irritable if he didn't get laid regularly. We'd all noticed it.

"Can we not talk about my dick right now?"

"Why not? Not like I haven't seen it enough times already."

"Jesus Christ, is that what gets you off, huh? Staring at my cock?"

"Nah, man, only E's does it for me."

I couldn't help it. These two were killing me. The peal of laughter erupting from my lips had the two of them looking at me. Xav with amusement and Quinn with a scowl.

"Look what you did to him!" Quinn waved a hand at me.

"Me? It was you going on about me wanting to stare at your dick… I won't lie, you have a nice one, but I've told you enough times I don't want to have sex with you."

"I don't want to have sex with you either."

"You two need to stop," I choked out through my laughter. "I'm dying."

After all the tension from earlier, I needed this. When Carlo had his hands around my girl's neck, all I'd thought about was saving her and making sure she was good. The way she'd clung to me as if reassuring herself she was still alive almost damn near broke my heart.

"Glad someone finds it amusing," Quinn muttered, still glaring at me.

"Right, it's done. I'll just pop this over to Geoff and we're good to go," Xav said with a grin.

"Finally."

"Hey, man, this shit takes time. Jesus, you really need to get laid."

They set me off again. I clutched my chest as it started to hurt from all the laughing.

"For fuck's sake, you're breaking Eric."

"You… two… are… too… much," I said as I struggled to breathe.

Xav got up off the desk chair and came around before grabbing my head and placing a kiss on my forehead.

"That's my man."

Quinn rolled his eyes.

"Get a room."

"All right, Mr Prude, that was nothing… if you want a proper show, then I'm more than willing to oblige."

Before Quinn could say a thing, Xav planted his mouth on mine, stopping my laughter in its tracks. I didn't even protest considering it was the first time Xav had actually kissed me without restraint outside the bedroom. Usually, we tried to keep our PDA on the down-low.

Xav pulled away grinning at me before turning to Quinn who blinked at us.

"Do you think we rendered him speechless?"

"Maybe we did," I replied, smiling back at him. "Would be a first."

Quinn's phone went off. He dug it out of his pocket and sent a few messages back and forth before showing it to me and Xav.

GEOFF: You seriously want me to send him that?

QUINN: Do it.

GEOFF: Your funeral.

QUINN: Trust me, the only funeral happening any time soon is Russo's.

GEOFF: I really hope you're right.

"He's only worried about his own safety," Xav said with a shrug.

"He knows the risks. Besides, Colm has granted us the use of his men so I had him stick a few on Geoff and his family."

"Well, the Irish cunt is good for something, I suppose."

Quinn grinned.

"Geoff has been loyal for years, it's the least I could do for him."

Geoff had been with us for a long time, helping us with the families and our investments. He was as loyal as they came and none of us wanted him to be taken out. He played a very important role. Thankfully, he wasn't too unhappy with our plans to scale back and retire the *Il Diavolo* name when all of this was over.

"The guy is solid as fuck."

Quinn's phone went off again and he frowned when he read it.

"What?"

He handed me the phone.

GEOFF: His response was to tell you if you think he will meet your demand, you're more deluded than he first thought. Be prepared for the backlash.

"We are prepared, aren't we?" I asked.

Quinn gave me a look.

"What do you think?"

I rolled my eyes, shoved his phone back at him and got up.

"You're lucky he has no idea where we live, Quinn, because if he did, we'd be fucked."

The house wasn't in any of our real names for good reason. We didn't want to be found, especially not by men like Frank Russo. This place was our sanctuary. Our home away from everything else in the world. It's where we belonged.

"It's the only saving grace we have right now."

And didn't I fucking well know it? If this all backfired, all of us would be in for a huge wake-up call. It scared me, but I wouldn't admit it to the boys. Right now, we needed to present a united front. For all our sakes.

CHAPTER TWENTY THREE

RORY

I stared up at the ceiling, eying the star consolations I'd had painted on it and trying to stop myself from thinking too much. Ash was sound asleep next to me, her blonde hair splayed out over the pillow. She looked so fucking peaceful and serene, like she didn't have a care in the world. Like we didn't have a man chained up in our cell downstairs and we hadn't all just put bigger targets on our backs. Frank Russo was coming for us. No question about that.

I looked over at my girl, wanting so much to protect her from all of this. I clenched my uninjured hand into a fist. The more I thought about it, the more having Carlo here unsettled me. Made me angry. In fact, it made me fucking furious. He'd tried to kill me once and Ash, twice. Having him here was like a fucking kick in the teeth.

I hadn't thought about it much during the day since my focus had been on keeping Ash occupied. We'd spent all day on the sofa together, reading for a while, then watching a film. My headaches had completely disappeared, which pleased me no end. Now I had to wait for my wrist to heal up. Then we could go after Frank once and for all. We were biding our time. Waiting to strike.

I felt completely on edge. The house was deadly silent considering it was the middle of the night. The urge to rid the fucking world of the scumbag downstairs drove through me. It clawed at me, making me feel completely unhinged. I needed it to end.

Reaching over, I stroked the fingers of my injured hand down Ash's face. How was it possible to love someone as much as I did her? It's as if she was permanently etched on my heart, a tattoo banding around it over and over. She was starlight. She was beauty. She was the epitome of everything I'd ever wanted in life. Ever needed.

"Little star," I whispered into the still air. "You make me want to be better… but I fear I might disappoint you one day."

I leant forward and kissed her cheek. She stirred a little, letting out a small sigh as she snuggled deeper into the covers. Everything about her made me happy, but she couldn't stop this. No one could. The only way to quiet the dark, twisted part of me would be to act on the desire coursing through me.

I slipped out of bed, careful not to wake her, knowing if I did, she'd know what I had planned. My muscles were coiled tight in anticipation. No doubt the boys would be fucking livid. I no longer cared. The only person who mattered to me in those moments was Ash. Protecting Ash. Keeping her out of harm's way. And that meant ending all threats against her.

There was one huge fucking threat in our house right now. So for me, there was only one course of action.

I moved with precision, keeping my footsteps light as I made my way downstairs. With my hand being injured, I couldn't use a gun like I wanted to. There were other ways to kill a man. Other methods I could resort to. If I was at full capacity, I might have made it hurt. Tortured him. He deserved no fucking less. I didn't have time for that. The only thing I had time for was a silent death so I wouldn't wake the others. So they wouldn't know until the morning. By then, it'd be far too late.

I slipped into the office to acquire the key for the cell from Quinn's office. He kept a spare there. He should've hidden it better. Walking out of the room, I padded along to the cell and unlocked the door. I pushed it open and stepped in. The prone figure on the cot lay sleeping soundly.

Time for you to meet your fucking maker, you cunt.

Walking over, I stopped at the side of the cot and stared at Carlo. His face was swollen with a bandage across his nose. Quinn had done his best to set it. Didn't matter. Carlo wouldn't be alive very much longer. This fucker was done for. Now and forever.

I climbed onto the cot, towering over him and carefully removed the pillow from behind his head, throwing it away. Moving swiftly, I sat on his arms, pinning them to his sides. Before I'd gone into the office, I'd got a plastic bag from the kitchen. Lifting his head, I pulled the bag over it and tied it off around his neck. Then I held my hand over his mouth and nose.

It took a minute for his body to realise he couldn't breathe. He jerked awake and then he was struggling against me. I could hear him trying to talk behind my hand. The bag muffled his words. I tightened it around his neck. As his body struggled for oxygen, his movements became jerky and weaker. I held on until he went limp and even then, I waited until I couldn't feel his chest moving below me any longer.

I let go of his mouth and checked his pulse. There wasn't one. He was dead. A sense of satisfaction and calm washed over me. I untied the bag from his head and got off him. Then I replaced the pillow underneath him and walked out. After locking the door, I placed the key in Quinn's hiding place back in his office and put the plastic bag in the bin in the kitchen.

I walked upstairs and along the hallway until I reached my bedroom. Shutting the door behind me, I crawled back into bed and settled the covers over me. It had been quick, silent and easy. No fuss. Nothing. I didn't regret it. I didn't even feel bad for doing it. I felt nothing but peace.

Carlo was dead.

I'd got rid of him for Ash so he could never hurt her again.

My beautiful little star who was awake and staring at me.

"Did you end it?" she whispered.

I tensed up, not knowing what her reaction would be to the news Carlo was dead.

"Yes."

Lying to her about it would be worse.

"Thank you, Ror."

She moved, tucking herself under my arm and wrapping her own around my bare chest, splaying out her hand over my heart which was beating steadily.

"You're welcome, little star."

Her reaction surprised me, but then again, Ash never ceased to do the complete opposite of what we thought she would.

"He deserved it, but the boys won't see it that way."

"No… they won't."

She shifted higher and kissed me, cupping my face with one hand. A need for her pounded in my veins, spreading down my chest and causing me to harden.

"Ash," I groaned against her soft lips.

"You want me?" she whispered.

"Always."

Next thing I knew, she'd shifted over me, rubbing herself against my length and driving me crazy. It's not like I could fuck her in quite the way I wanted with my injured hand. It'd be the first time we'd been intimate since the crash. The first time I felt well enough to be with her like this.

"You killed a man for me," she whispered against my mouth, her lips brushing across mine. "I never thought I'd ever want that from someone after the way Frank brutalised and murdered men in front of me." Her hand stroked across my face. "I didn't know I needed it from you." Her other hand tugged at my boxers, pulling them down and wrapping her fingers around my cock. "Let me reward you… let me make you feel good."

"Please."

She stroked me, making me jerk in her hand. I wanted inside her, feeling her tight, slick heat encasing me.

"Don't fucking tease me, little star. I need you now."

I wrapped a hand around her thigh, gripping tightly, showing her I was still in charge of the situation. She would do as I said.

"What part of me?"

We weren't going to play this fucking game.

"Your tight little pussy. Take your clothes off and sit on my cock."

Ash sat up, letting go of my cock before pulling off her camisole. She rose up on her knees and tugged down her lacy panties, tossing them away. I stared at her naked body, growing uncomfortably hard at the sight of her tits and the blonde curls between her legs.

"Now, little star," I almost outright growled.

I couldn't wait any longer. The moment my cock met her heat, I almost fucking died on the spot. I groaned, feeling her tightness encase me as she sunk down on my dick. The most perfect pussy I'd ever been inside.

"Ror," she moaned. "I've missed you."

The way she took me was like being welcomed with open arms. Every inch made me twitch. Ash was so fucking stunning like this. Her body bowing backwards as she sunk deeper until she'd taken all of me. Her pussy pulsed around my cock, stretching to accommodate me. She let out a little pant, leaning forwards and planting her hands on my chest.

"You want me to fuck you? Want me to impale myself on your cock over and over?"

"Fuck yes… show me how dirty you can be."

She smirked and began to rise and fall, building a steady rhythm within minutes. I gripped her thigh tighter, staring up at this beautiful girl. The one who was all fucking mine. Her tits bounced on her chest as she rode me. I wanted to bite those hard nipples. Have her cry out in pleasure and pain.

My hand left her thigh and gripped her arm, tugging her down roughly until her tits were level with my face. I cupped one before indulging myself in them. My lips enclosed around the stiff peak. Her cry when I bit down echoed in my ears.

"Yes, fuck, Ror."

"So fucking needy, aren't you?" I murmured. "I swear when I'm better, I'm going to ravage every part of you. Make you scream so fucking loud, the boys get fucking scared of what I'm doing to you."

She moaned in response, still riding me hard as I continued to play with her tits until her nipples were dark from my ministrations. Seeing her marked again fed me. Made the beast sigh in contentment even as he told me to take more.

My hand brushed down her stomach and between her legs, finding her little bud and stroking it. It'd been too long and I was so fucking close already. The way she rode me, the breathy moans she let out. All of it fuelled the fire.

"Ror," she cried out, shaking and trembling above me as she came violently.

It set off a chain reaction in me. My body tensed up and then released. My cock pulsed inside her. Waves of pleasure washed over me, making my eyes almost roll back in my head. Never before had I let a woman ride me like this. It didn't even occur to me to stop her from doing it. Any type of sex with Ash was like fucking heaven and I revelled in it. The beast no longer controlled me like it had before. I just needed her. Nothing else mattered.

She lay on top of me, her head on my chest when she was spent and I caught my breath.

"I love you, little star," I whispered.

She kissed my chest. I never wanted her to leave this bed. I wanted us just like this, locked together after passion and ecstasy. And she stayed for the longest time. Eventually, she slid off me, going into the bathroom for a few minutes. When she returned, she curled up against me, stroking my side and soothing me.

"Sleep, Ror… tomorrow we'll deal with everything."

I closed my eyes. My mind was finally quiet and still after all the turmoil of before. No matter what the boys said when they found out I'd killed Carlo, I knew I'd done the right thing. Frank Russo wasn't going to listen to reason. But he would listen to this. He would see we weren't fucking around. He would truly know who he was up against.

The five of us would destroy him. Taking Carlo's life was only the beginning. Soon… it would be the end. The only end. And that was Frank dead in a pool of his own blood with my little star standing over him.

Xav might call Ash an angel, but really, she was something very different.

A girl who'd had enough of the shit she'd been dealt with.

My girl was wild.

My girl was free.

My girl was the harbinger of death.

CHAPTER TWENTY FOUR

Quinn

Something felt off this morning when I woke up. I couldn't shake the feeling as I went downstairs to get breakfast. The atmosphere in the house was almost too still. I glanced down the hallway before I turned to go to the kitchen, finding the cell door open and wondered why. My skin prickled all over as I stalked towards it. Xav and Eric were inside, standing over the cot. Neither of them seemed to be moving or talking.

"What's wrong?"

Eric almost jumped and Xav's body jerked. He swung his head around to me, a grave expression visible on his face.

"He's dead."

"What?"

"Carlo is dead, Quinn."

I walked in and came to a standstill next to them, staring at the body on the cot. No question about it. His chest was absolutely still. There were faint ligature marks around his neck. My blood went cold. I only had one explanation for his death and I should have fucking well known this would happen.

"Why did neither of you come get me?"

"We only just got here… I mean, shit, man, I didn't expect to walk in here and find a fucking dead body you know."

"I think I'm going to be sick," Eric ground out, putting a hand to his mouth before backing out of the room.

Xav and I stared after him before turning back to each other. Eric wasn't normally so squeamish. Maybe it had less to do with Carlo being dead and more the result of knowing who had killed him. Hell, even I felt a little ill.

"For fuck's sake." I rubbed the back of my neck. "I don't even know what the hell to say right now."

"What do you want me to do with him? We can't keep him in here, he's going to start stinking up the entire fucking house."

"It's fucking daylight, how do you propose we move a dead body without the neighbours seeing?"

Xav looked a little put out, but I had no clue right now. It's not as if I expected to deal with a dead Carlo when I woke up this morning. We knew how to get rid of one. The way we went about it would have a significant impact, so I had to think carefully.

"I don't really want to stand around here with him if you're not going to decide right now."

I turned and walked out, not wanting to stay in the room with Carlo either. Xav followed me, stopping outside and leaning against the wall.

"I'm going to go deal with the culprit, you should go check on E."

I started towards the stairs not knowing how I would deal with this shit. Not what I needed first thing in the morning.

"Rory's got balls, I'll give him that," Xav called after me. He wasn't under any illusions about who'd done this, and neither was I.

I sighed, striding up the stairs and along the corridor to his room. Not bothering to knock, I opened the door, walked in and came to a stop by his bed. Ash and Rory were tucked up in each other's arms, both looking so fucking peaceful it gave me pause. I hadn't seen Rory look so at ease in years. I wanted to give him hell for what he'd done, but I couldn't. Watching the two of them made my chest ache. Seeing my best friend, the man who was like a brother to me, so happy… I wasn't prepared for the relief and sense of contentment it gave me. For so long all Rory had known in life was pain. For him to finally open up his heart to someone and give her his love, affection and care was quite something.

So instead of waking them up, I backed out of the room and closed the door, resting my forehead and hands against the frame.

"Fuck," I whispered.

Normally I would've berated the shit out of him for it, but just as having Ash in his life had set Rory on a different path, so had she done to me too. I always thought before I acted, it's just now I thought before I reacted to things too. I didn't go in all guns fucking blazing when it came to the delicate nature of our family unit. Our quintet.

I almost laughed. Was I growing soft? Maybe I knew I had to be a better person. To make up for all the shit I'd put Ash through. I hadn't remotely been good to her in the beginning.

Done a lot of shit I wasn't proud of. Now I was going to do the two things in my power which would bring the horrific chapter of her life she'd lived through so far to a close. I would return her mother to her and give Ash the means to destroy the man who raised her. Who ruined all of our lives. I understood more than ever why it had to be her who wielded the axe, cutting off the head of the snake. Brought down by the one he raised to be his heir. Such poetic justice.

For now, I had to work out what to do with Carlo's body. It's not as if we hadn't told Russo we'd kill his nephew if he didn't comply with our demand he return Isabella to us. I'd planned to give him more time and cross that bridge if it came to it.

Think, Quinn, fucking think!

Shoving off the doorframe, I walked away knowing I needed to remain focused. Just because Carlo was dead didn't mean I couldn't use this to my advantage. We'd have to play this carefully. Very fucking carefully.

I reached the kitchen, finding Xav and Eric sat at the counter. They weren't speaking, just staring down into their mugs.

"You two look fucking miserable."

Eric raised his head.

"Where's Rory?"

"Sleeping."

Xav raised an eyebrow.

"And you didn't wake him up?"

I shook my head as I walked further in and started making myself a coffee.

"What the fuck, Quinn? Shouldn't you be going off on one right now?" Xav continued when I didn't answer.

"What's that going to achieve? Carlo is dead. We need to work out what we're going to do with him rather than bickering amongst ourselves."

Out of the corner of my eye, I watched Eric lean into Xav.

"Has Quinn been replaced by an android? I feel like we're in *Blade Runner* right now."

"I'm beginning to think so."

I rolled my eyes, pouring coffee into my mug before putting in a dash of milk. I took it over to the counter and sat down on one of the stools.

"I can be calm and reasonable when necessary."

Both of them looked at each other before levelling their gazes back on me.

"Robot Quinn is in the house," Xav replied. "Do I need to fix your CPU? I think it malfunctioned."

"Fuck off, Xav."

He clapped his hands together.

"Phew, I was beginning to think I'd have to reprogram you."

"Jesus Christ," I muttered, rubbing my face.

Xav really did not have an off switch.

"Quinn's right," Eric said. "We do need to work out what to do with the body… maybe we should wait for Rory and Ash to get up though."

I'd completely forgotten about what her reaction could be to this.

Well, fuck.

"We might as well use it to our advantage now he's dead." Xav waved his hand around. "It'd be a hell of a way to get Russo's attention."

"What are you suggesting?"

"His nephew turns up dead. He'll know we did it after yesterday's video. Gianni will be livid no doubt. All hell breaks loose in the Russo compound… Perfect time for us to strike and take him down."

"Did you forget Rory can't fucking hold a gun right now?" I interjected.

Xav rolled his eyes.

"He's more than proven he can kill a man without a gun, Quinn. He suffocated Carlo with his wrist in a fucking splint."

I didn't want to think too hard about how Rory had done it. It was very clear it'd been carried out with brutal efficiency since there didn't seem to be signs of a struggle on Carlo's part. Rory had always been dark as fuck in the recesses of his mind, so for him to carry this out without batting an eyelid? Yeah, it didn't fucking surprise me in the slightest.

"Xav has a point," Eric said before taking a sip of coffee.

"Okay, so we dump Carlo's body for Russo to find. Then what? We storm his compound? I don't think so."

"We infiltrate his compound, storming it will get us killed," came a feminine voice from behind us.

Xav, Eric and I all turned and found Ash and Rory standing the doorway, their fingers entwined. Rory didn't look remotely perturbed or ruffled. So he didn't regret what he'd done.

Fucking typical.

"Well, that would be great if we knew how to get in without setting off any alarms."

Ash pulled Rory further into the room, determination written all over her face.

"Did you conveniently forget you have a secret weapon?" She pointed at her chest. "I grew up in that place. I can draw you a layout, give you the locations of all the cameras and where he places his security. I can even give you the guard rotations if he hasn't changed them."

"Why didn't you tell us before, little girl?"

She put her hand on her hip.

"Did you even think to ask me? I gave you the information you might need to take him down, but this is different. What you're proposing is not only dangerous, it's pretty much a suicide mission."

"Ride or die, right, angel?" Xav said with a huge grin on his face.

She gave him a nod and a smile.

"Are we going to talk about the elephant in the room?" Eric interjected before Ash could reply.

We all turned to Rory except for Ash, who was still clutching his hand tightly and watching Xav.

"I did what I had to," he said as if it was a valid explanation.

"I'm going to need more than that," I said, trying not to raise my voice, knowing it wouldn't help matters.

Ash looked between us before realisation dawned on her face. She glanced up at Rory before returning her gaze to me.

"He did it to protect me."

"Hold on, you know what he did?"

"Yes."

"You seem very calm about it."

Ash flicked her hair back over her shoulder with her free hand.

"Carlo deserved it… Now, can we move on and decide our next moves?"

I stared at her like she'd grown an extra head. Ash might have grown up in this world but she seemed more than a little traumatised by Russo killing people in front of her. Yet, Rory had killed the man she'd thought was her cousin her entire life for her and here she was acting like it meant nothing.

"We need to get rid of the body," Rory said, glancing at her.

"Xav's suggestion is to leave it somewhere Russo can find it," Eric said. "To send a message we aren't going to be fucked with."

Ash looked thoughtful for a moment.

"Oh, that's easy… leave it in Gianni's family restaurant. Then he's guaranteed to have a huge go at Frank. If you want to spread chaos in the ranks, that's how."

"Our girl is proving to be quite the strategist," Xav grinned, waving a hand at her.

She shrugged, pulling Rory over to the stools and making him sit down, then she walked over to the kettle and started on making tea.

"You have Frank to thank for that," she muttered, pulling mugs out of the cupboard.

She'd proven she knew more than she originally let on, showing Frank had groomed her to become the head of the Russo family. Ash may not be Russo blood, but she'd been raised in the kingdom of corruption and greed. The one which dealt in death and destruction. She knew what was expected and how to play the game.

"It has to be tonight, he will start decomposing and it's going to reek."

I shook myself.

"Okay so we leave Carlo for Gianni to find, but we need a plan to get his body to the restaurant and not get caught."

"There's an alley out back you can drive the car in. I'm sure Xav can trip out the security cameras. Dump him in the walk-in freezer in the kitchen and that gets rid of the serious decomposing problem."

"Should we leave a note?"

"No, when Gianni goes to Frank, he'll know it was us. You should expect some kind of retaliation. I doubt he'll do anything to my mother, but he will do something to send a message. Are your people safe?"

Frank had already tried coming after us in the casino by sending Mac, who was now dead. His body had turned up in one of the canals. Police were investigating it as a serious crime related murder, but they had very little to go on. Colm Moran had done his job well. He'd taken over the gang swiftly and efficiently. As much as I thought he was a cunt, he'd become a useful ally in this war. We'd cut ties with the criminal underground the moment Frank died.

"Yes, or as safe as they can be right now."

She nodded slowly, pouring the now boiled water into mugs for her and Rory.

"Okay, then we need to strike against him. We can't wait too long or we'll lose our advantage. I'm all for infiltrating his compound, but it won't be easy. We'll have to be coordinated." She turned and eyed us steadily. "Two primary objectives. We find my mother and we kill Frank. When we've had breakfast, I'll draw up everything for you, then we can plan. Any objections?"

No one said a word.

"Good… now let's not talk about murder over breakfast again. Makes me lose my appetite, you know."

The way she'd so casually addressed this like it was an everyday occurrence where we planned to dump a body and then murder the man she thought was her father made me very aware of the ruthless streak she possessed. It shouldn't make me love her more, but it did.

A thrill of excitement ran through me. The end of this war drew closer. We were almost there. I could feel it. Fucking taste it. After this, we'd be free from his fucking legacy. His tyranny. We'd have finally exacted revenge for everything his empire had done to our families. If we could pull this off, it'd be a fucking miracle.

Ash was right. This was a suicide mission. It was us or him. Either we came back alive and Frank drowned in his own blood or none of us lived to see the next day. If I had to go out, it'd be with my family and the woman I loved.

For once in his life, Xav had made a very accurate statement.

It really was ride or die.

And I intended to ride all the way into this war, guns blazing, and destroy everything Russo stood for.

CHAPTER TWENTY FIVE

Eric

I pulled up the car just inside the back alley. The three of us got out and walked around to the boot. Quinn opened it, wrinkling his nose in disgust. Right now, I was glad Ash had suggested leaving Carlo in the freezer since he was beginning to smell. I wanted to get this over with quickly so we could get back to the house and go to bed.

"This is worse than when we offed Rory's family… just saying," Xav complained as the three of us pulled gloves on.

"Really?" Quinn replied, frowning.

"At least they were fresh bodies and didn't stink to high fucking hell."

The smell was getting to me as well. I'd never been a fan of being around dead bodies, nor did I want reminders of the night when we'd done unspeakable things either. As fucked up as it had been, it gave Rory a sense of justice which he sorely needed after everything he'd been through.

"Come on, we need to get this done."

We'd wrapped Carlo in a sheet and some plastic after scrubbing any evidence of our involvement thoroughly from his skin. In case the Russos went to the police. We doubted they would, but you couldn't take any chances. We didn't need that on top of the shit we were already dealing with.

All of us glanced around, making sure no one was in the alley or walking by. Xav and Quinn hauled Carlo's body out of the back and I shut the boot. They grunted as they carried him over to the back door of the restaurant. I set to work picking the lock. Before opening the door, I tugged out the little piece of paper Ash had given me, checking the numbers. She'd explained the layout of the restaurant in detail so we could get in and out without too much trouble.

I opened the door and the sound of the alarm tripping blared. Walking to the right, I opened a cupboard and found the security panel. Bashing in the numbers, the alarm stopped. I grinned. Our girl had come through for us.

Quinn and Xav hauled Carlo in. We walked down the corridor together until we came to the kitchen. The place was eerily silent. It was the dead of night, so hardly surprising, but it made me uneasy all the same. I walked over to the walk-in fridges and freezers, opening the left-hand one like Ash had told us to. A chill seeped out of the door, the air thick with a frosty vapour. Xav and Quinn carried the body in, dumping it on the floor right in front of the door.

"Let's get the fuck out of here," Xav said, his expression grim.

"You have to wipe the security footage first," I replied with a shrug.

We shut the door of the freezer. Quinn looked around, his eyes dark and expression concerned.

"Something about this doesn't feel right."

"This is the right place, Ash wouldn't have led us wrong."

He rubbed the back of his neck.

"It's not that. I just don't like this… there's something off about this place."

I didn't know how to explain it, but I agreed with Quinn. Something felt wrong. An air of death surrounded us and it wasn't because we'd dumped Carlo's body in the freezer.

"What are you suggesting? You want look around?" Xav asked.

Quinn pointed at a door with a padlock on it on the other side of the room.

"No, I'm suggesting we open that."

Xav stared at the padlocked door for a moment and then back at Quinn.

"We should not be getting involved in whatever shit Gianni's got going on here, Quinn. We came to leave Carlo's body and that's it."

I didn't know whether to agree with Xav or Quinn. Curiosity plagued me. I wanted to know what was behind the locked door and I think Quinn did too. It would be the only way we'd find out why there was such a stench in this place. As if it was seeping out of its pores and permeating the air.

"I can't leave without looking."

I shrugged helplessly.

"Yeah, sorry, Xavi, but neither can I."

Xav huffed and crossed his arms over his chest. I didn't blame him for not wanting to go in there. We were all on edge at the moment. Anything could happen in this battle against Russo.

"Fine, but it's on your fucking heads."

Quinn stalked towards the door like a lion prowling in the bush. He fingered the padlock.

"You reckon you can pick this?"

I followed him over and looked at it. Should be relatively simple. I squatted down and pulled out my kit again.

"Ash never mentioned this room," Xav said.

"She only told us the relevant details we needed to dump the body," Quinn replied. "Did you expect her to give us everything when we didn't need it?"

"Well no… but you'd think she'd have noticed a padlocked room if she's been here as much as she says she has. I mean, shit, she knows the fucking alarm code."

I had to turn the pick a little more and we should be in. These two needed to shut up though, I was trying to concentrate.

"What are you accusing her of?"

"Nothing! I'm just saying."

"Did you think maybe this wasn't locked when she's been here before?"

I looked over to find Xav's expression a little contrite and Quinn rolling his eyes. The lock clicked and I tugged it off the door.

"Fine, you have a point."

"We can ask her when we get home, okay?"

"And wake her up at this time? Yeah, I'm out. Our girl needs her sleep."

I rose to my full height and dropped the padlock on the counter next to the door. Taking a breath, I pushed it open. The smell immediately assaulted my nose. I raised my arm to my face, covering it. It was like death and rot all rolled into one. I had a hard time not throwing up.

"Jesus Christ," I choked out.

"What the fuck?" Xav said, pulling his jumper up to cover his mouth and nose.

Quinn looked like he wanted to be sick too, covering his nose with his arm like me.

"Are you sure you want to go in there?"

"Yes," Quinn ground out. "We need to know."

Now I was thoroughly regretting agreeing with Quinn, but there was no going back now. I stepped in, searching for the light switch. The lights flickered on when I found it. It seemed to be some kind of pantry or storage room with shelves upon shelves of stacked goods.

"Stay here," Quinn said to Xav. "Someone has to keep watch."

I glanced back, finding Quinn walking in and Xav pulling out a gun, taking a stand right in front of the door. Quinn and I looked at each other before he gave me a nod and we ventured further in. I walked down one side of the shelves on the right and he took the left path. The closer I got to the end, the worse the smell got.

"Fuck me, this is the worst thing I've ever smelt in my life."

"You're fucking telling me," I heard Quinn call back.

I stopped dead when I got to the end of the shelving unit. Bile rose up in the back of my throat. I pressed my arm harder against my nose and mouth, wanting to back away but knowing I couldn't.

"Uh, Quinn…"

A huge pile of rotting animal carcasses sat in the middle of the floor. It explained the smell but not the padlock. I noticed something beyond them a moment later. A hook was suspended from the ceiling and a man was strung up by his hands, his feet just about touching the floor. There was blood all over him so I couldn't make out who it was.

"Well shit," came Quinn's voice next to me. I almost jumped out of my own skin.

"Fuck, don't sneak up on me."

"You seeing what I'm seeing?"

"Yeah… I don't even know what the fuck to say about this shit."

He walked forward and skirted around the carcasses. I followed him, both approaching the hanging man together.

"Do you think he's alive?" I asked.

"Fuck knows."

I moved closer and reached up, checking his pulse. It was very faint, but definitely there.

"Help me get him down, I think he's still breathing."

Quinn came over and we both managed to get him down from the hook, untying his hands. His face was almost brutalised beyond recognition, but something about him was very familiar. I looked closer before rearing back and putting my hand over my mouth.

"What is it?"

Quinn stared at the man with confusion.

"It's… it's Nate."

"What?"

"It's fucking Nate, Quinn."

It took a few seconds then recognition filled his features.

"Shit. Shit! This is why we couldn't get a hold of him… Fuck. What the hell do we do?"

He was unconscious, but his chest rose and fell in a shallow motion.

"What do you mean what do we do? We take him to a hospital. He won't fucking survive if we leave him here. Help me get him out."

Quinn seemed to move on automatic as we both held him between us and walked towards the entrance but I could see the cogs turning in his brain.

"Jesus Christ, what the fuck?" Xav said as we approached.

"We found our missing contact," I replied.

"What? Wait… that's Nate?"

I nodded as he moved aside to let me and Quinn out.

"Is that why it smells so fucking bad in there?"

"No, that'd be a bunch of rotting dead animals. Fuck knows why they have them in there."

I didn't really care. Xav shut the door and replaced the padlock. None of us spoke any further as Quinn and I carried Nate out to the car and got him in the backseat.

"Go deal with the security cameras, Xav," Quinn said. "We need to get out of here as fast as fucking possible."

"On it."

Xav disappeared back into the restaurant. I eyed Quinn as the two of us pulled off the gloves we'd been wearing and stuck them in our pockets.

"What are you thinking?"

"We can't drop him at some random hospital. When they find out he's gone, they'll come looking for him. I don't like the cunt, but I never wanted this for him."

Shit, he's right. We can't do that.

"Then what do we do? He needs medical attention."

He rubbed his chin.

"We do the only thing we can."

Pulling out his phone, dialling a number before pressing it to his ear. I had no idea what he meant, but I had to trust in Quinn.

"Hello… Yes, sorry to wake you, we have a situation… Got someone in need of a hospital, he's been fucked up pretty badly, but he needs protection or they'll come after him when they find we took him… Sure, okay, thank you… Right, meet you there."

He hung up and sighed.

"Who was that?"

"André. He'll arrange shit at the private hospital where they treated Rory and protection, no questions asked."

"It's fucking lucky we're in with Viktor."

Quinn grimaced.

"As much as I hate it, you're right. Ash being his daughter works in our favour… Fuck. This will really set Russo off. Not only have we killed his nephew, we've extracted his traitor."

"You know we owe Nate this much."

He nodded. No matter our personal feelings, Nate had done a lot for us. Putting his life on the line to infiltrate Russo's inner circle. Pity he'd been discovered. That could be the only reason he'd been beaten within an inch of his life.

"Why were they holding him here and not at the compound?" I asked as it suddenly occurred to me this was a little odd.

"I don't know. Russo is doing all sorts of shit right now and I don't have the energy to second guess him. Maybe he gave him to Gianni to handle? He no longer has an heir so likely he's named his brother for the role. We've left him with no other options."

Xav came out of the restaurant, having finished up in there and walked towards us, ripping the gloves off his hands.

"What's happening?"

"We're taking him to hospital and then we're going home." Quinn swiped his hand across his face. "I need a shower and I'm fucking done with this shit today."

"Right you are, let's get the fuck out of here then."

Xav hopped into the driver's side, Quinn got in the front and me in the back. I checked on Nate, making sure he hadn't died on us yet. Who knew how bad his condition really was. His hair was matted with blood and dirt as were his clothes. He'd likely been in there for days and days. I shuddered. The thought of being left with all those dead, rotting animals after being beaten made me feel sick. No matter what he'd done, he didn't deserve that.

"This is shit," Xav muttered.

"You're fucking right it is… This is going to seriously fuck with our plans. We need to hurry. We have no other choice. If he's done this shit to Nate, there's no telling what he might do to Isabella. I'm not letting our girl go through that. She needs her mother."

"Then what? We move up the timescale?"

We'd spent all day planning our attack. It'd been exhausting going through everything repeatedly to make sure we'd thought of everything. Usually, we had a lot more time, but now we'd run out of it. We had to act now. Topple the empire by taking out Frank.

"Yes… we have to. Tomorrow, we call in all our favours and then we go to war."

Xav looked at me through the rearview mirror. I gave him a nod.

"We go to war," I agreed.

"Ride or fucking die," Xav joined in.

And I was in no doubt this war would be brutal and bloody.

Time to end this shit for good.

CHAPTER TWENTY SIX

Ash

Vaguely I heard noises coming from the room, but sleep dragged hard at my senses. Quinn had told me not to wait up whilst he, Xav and Eric dealt with Carlo's body. I'd tucked myself up in Quinn's bed after Rory had fallen asleep. I think I wore him out after he'd dragged me to his bed whilst the others were downstairs still planning the night's events. He'd pinned me down on the bed, tore off my clothes and drove into me at a brutal pace. His mouth had been planted against my ear, whispering all sorts of dirty things. It'd been like the accident had never happened. He'd mastered my body even with his broken wrist and I gave in completely.

The sound of running water pierced through my ears, but still, I didn't move or open my eyes. The warmth of the covers and the smell of Quinn made me want to curl up in a ball and never leave. My home was right here in his bed even without him.

The next time I was dragged out of my groggy state, a body wrapped around me, its hand diving beneath my t-shirt and touching my bare skin.

"Little girl," came a whispered voice, drifting across my shoulder.

"Mmm."

"Wake up."

I shoved at the body holding me, not wanting to be pulled from my sleep. Why was this person disturbing me?

"I need you."

I blinked.

"Quinn?" I asked, my voice full of sleep.

He kissed my shoulder, his hand drifting higher and cupping my breast. His skin felt a little damp and I wasn't sure why.

"Turn over, sweetheart."

He moved and I rolled onto my back on command. Quinn shifted over me, his hands tugging at my clothes, pulling them off me and leaving me bare below him.

"What's going on?"

He leant down and his mouth latched onto my nipple. My hands went to his hair instinctively.

"Quinn, why is your hair wet?"

"Shower," he murmured before continuing to lavish my nipple, his fingers brushing over the other one.

I let out a gasp, desire flooding my veins even in my confused, sleepy state. Quinn always knew exactly how to master me. I noticed he wasn't wearing anything either. He did say he'd just had a shower. But why? Wasn't it the middle of the night? The room was still very much dark.

"Little girl," he groaned, his mouth travelling lower, dancing across my stomach. "So soft… so pliant… all mine."

It registered with me finally. Quinn, Xav and Eric had been out and they'd clearly only just got back. What time was it? How long had they been gone? And why did his voice sound so desperate?

"Quinn, what happened? Did everything go okay at the restaurant?"

He stilled, his body stiffening.

"Yes and no."

I sat up on my elbows and stared down at him.

"What's that supposed to mean?"

His hands banded around my thighs, pulling my legs apart before his nose traced down my stomach and lower.

"It means I don't want to talk about it right now."

"Quinn…"

He let out a long sigh.

"We dumped Carlo in the freezer without issues… but we didn't leave straight away. There was a padlocked room just off the kitchen, some kind of pantry, we broke in and found…"

He laid his head against my thigh, taking a deep breath.

"You found what?"

I knew about that pantry. They stored the dry goods in there as far as I knew and there'd definitely been no padlocks on the door when I'd visited the place.

"We found rotting animals, the smell was awful… like death… and then we found Nate hanging from a hook, brutalised almost beyond recognition. So we got him down and took him to the private hospital after I called André. He's in surgery right now and I don't fucking know how I feel about it all… so I just want you to let me make love to you, little girl. Can you do that?"

My heart wrenched painfully. As much as I hated Nate, I didn't want him dead or beaten up. It's not as if he really deserved that even after he'd tricked me into a relationship with him and lied to me for two years.

The sadness in Quinn's voice almost damn near killed me. He sounded so weary and downtrodden.

"I can do that," I whispered.

I'd do anything to make him feel better. Anything at all. Seeing Quinn like this broke me.

He kissed my inner thigh before burying his face between my legs. My fingers tangled in his hair, listening to him groan in satisfaction as he devoured me with his tongue. Out of all the boys, Quinn loved going down on me the most. I didn't even have to ask. He went all out and I drowned in him.

My back arched off the bed. My climax built so quickly, almost as if he was determined to send me soaring. I cried out his name as I shook beneath him, the sensations rushing across my body and making me limber. I was utterly at his mercy, his touch and his needs.

He crawled up my body, a smirk on those beautiful lips, but there was still despair in his eyes. I reached for him, pulling him towards me, making him cover my body with his. He fit so perfectly to me, our bodies moulding together as if they were made to entwine like this. He stared down at the place where we joined, watching himself sink deep inside me. He let out a little agonising pant like this was everything he needed.

"I love you," I whispered, getting his attention.

Quinn stared down at me, his eyes dark with emotion. I cupped his cheek, stroking my fingers down the rough stubble there. His body shuddered with the touch. Swaying closer to me, he pressed a kiss to my forehead.

"Little girl," he breathed. "I'm so sorry for everything I did to you in the beginning. I'm sorry we ever went through that. I'm sorry we started so wrong." His hand tangled in my hair. "I'm sorry for all of it… but I don't regret you. I don't regret this… us… the boys… everything. I might not have found it easy to accept in the beginning, but now I understand. Now, I know it's right. You fit us in a way no one else ever could. You are our home."

A tear leaked down my cheek and he brushed it away, leaning his forehead against mine.

"I… I want to have what I never had when I was a kid. I want us to be a family… A real family. You… Me… The boys… and a brood of little ones running around. I want all of that with you and them. I want forever with you."

My words got caught in my throat. Quinn wanted a family with me and the boys. Could I love him any more than I already did? This man had fought through so much. So strong and determined. But he was vulnerable too. Only with me and the boys. He showed me all of him and gave his heart to me for safekeeping. I'd never let him go. I appreciated him in ways he probably would never understand.

"You really want that?"

He nodded, pressing his forehead harder against mine.

"I have one stipulation."

I had a feeling I knew what it was, but I asked the question anyway.

"And that is?"

"I get to impregnate you first."

I snorted, unable to help myself. It's exactly what I thought he would say. My king wanted first place and I couldn't really blame him for it. It was just so typically Quinn.

"You can fight that one out with the boys. I'm so not getting in the middle."

"I plan on it."

He pulled his hips back and thrust inside me, causing a moan to spill from my lips. I gripped his back, holding him close, feeling his heart hammering against my chest in tandem with mine.

"You'll let me though, won't you, little girl?"

"You know it."

He smiled such a boyish grin, my heart melted on the spot. Quinn was rarely in this kind of carefree mood where he was fully open. When he let me past his walls, I felt on top of the world. But my joy was tempered by the fact he was sad over what he'd dealt with tonight.

We said no more as we watched each other. He found a leisurely rhythm, driving us higher in small increments as if he wanted to draw this out as long as possible. Be lost with me in this so he didn't have to think. He wanted to forget. I gave him what he asked for. Being in the moment with him fully with nothing else intruding on us.

I felt the shift in him when he couldn't hold back any longer. He thrust harder and deeper, shoving my legs up against my chest so he could have the exact angle he wanted. I gasped, the friction between us pushing me closer to the edge.

"Quinn, fuck, please."

"That's it, little girl… I want to feel you."

His words were the spark, lighting the fuse and it burnt bright. I snapped. I shattered. And I cried out his name on repeat, practically singing my praise to him. His eyes were dark with satisfaction and desire. When I fell back to earth, he pulled my legs around his waist and drove into me harder. My hair wrapped around his fist as he held it tight.

"Little girl," he grunted. "Fuck, little girl. Fuck, I need you. Jesus, fuck!"

He bit down on his lip as his body tensed up and he erupted inside me. Watching him come apart, all his worries and cares leaving him for those moments his body shuddered above me gave me heart palpitations. He was like a beautiful fallen angel. Exactly the devil he'd told me he was in the beginning. Except my devil was sweet, kind and caring when he chose to be. He took care of me. Kept me safe. He loved me deeply. He was my king.

He leant his forehead against mine, holding himself above me as if he didn't want to leave my body for anything.

"I love you, little girl. Now and forever," he whispered.

And then he kissed me, stealing my breath, locking away any words I had to say. Quinn didn't want to talk anymore and I didn't push him. I let him kiss me and after we cleaned up, I let him hold me close until he fell asleep. I lay there watching him for the longest time, making sure he was still calm. My beautiful devil who'd shown me how much he needed me tonight.

"I'll always take care of you, Quinn," I whispered into the still night air. "You need that even if you don't think you do."

I stroked his hair back from his face and kissed his cheek. "I'll be here for you forever. Never forget that."

CHAPTER TWENTY SEVEN

Ash

We got word Nate had made it through his surgery and was in the ICU recovering this morning. All the boys except Rory got up late, but it was unsurprising given they'd been out half the night. They'd been busy calling in all their favours and shifting up the timescale of our attack on Frank. I'd helped them as far as I could, but there was another pressing matter I had to attend to. Tomorrow, we might not be here any longer. I didn't want any unfinished business hanging around. So whilst the boys continued to talk in the dining room, I went to answer the front door. Viktor stood with a tense smile on his face. He knew we were in the final stages before we took down Russo. He knew we might not survive it. And I knew he hated it.

"*Kotik*."

"Dad, come in."

I shut the door behind him after he walked in. We embraced, his warmth enveloping me and reminding me I had someone who loved and respected me in a way I'd never had from a parental figure before. That's why I took his hand as I led him into the living room. It felt right.

"Would you like a drink?" I asked as he sat down on the sofa.

"Vodka, please."

I grinned and padded out through the dining room to the kitchen, rubbing Quinn's back on my way. He gave me a kiss on my way back with Viktor's drink. Next time, I'd get Viktor a vodka without asking. Quinn had brought a specific brand we knew he liked so I was hoping Viktor would appreciate it. I set it down on the coffee table for him before taking a seat.

"How have you been?"

"Well enough, *kotik*. I heard about your… ex."

I looked at my hands. We had no idea if Nate would recover completely from the multiple beatings he must've taken. His spleen ruptured and he had some internal bleeding, hence why he needed surgery. They'd told André if the boys hadn't got him to the hospital when they did, he definitely would have died. I couldn't abide by the thought of it. And it only made me hate Frank even more than I already did.

"Yeah… He doesn't deserve what happened. I just hope he's safe from Frank now."

Viktor patted my hand.

"He is under mafia protection now."

I tried not to flinch. I knew very well where most of Viktor's resources in terms of men came from even if he wasn't fully affiliated with them. The Russian Bratva. I should be grateful he was doing all of this for us, but I couldn't help my feelings about the Bratva. They were dangerous. I guess it was a good thing my father would protect me from all that shit.

"That's not what I wanted to talk to you about."

He reached over and took a sip of his drink, leaning back against the sofa.

"Is something wrong?"

I shook my head.

"No… well other than the obvious."

I'd spoken to the boys about this over breakfast. Xav's acceptance of it when I'd told him about it gave me the courage to explain it to the rest of them. Thankfully, they'd all understood. Xav had helped me order the paperwork already and it'd arrived this morning.

"I've been thinking a lot. Even though our future is uncertain right now, there are a few things I know for sure I want to do."

Viktor eyed me with wariness in his expression.

"I'm not a Russo by blood, only in name. And I no longer wish to associate myself with that identity. So I wanted… I wanted to know if you would accept it if I changed my last name to Bykov and… and if you'd help me get my birth certificate changed to reflect you're my biological father rather than Frank. I don't want anything to do with him after this is over. I just want a fresh start and this will help me with that. Besides, you are my real father and I want… I want us to be a family. You mean a lot to me, Dad… I love you."

He was silent for a long time. Leaning forward, he placed his glass back on the coffee table and took my hands in his. His blue eyes were full of unspoken emotions. Each of them hit me in the chest one by one.

"Nothing would make me happier." Reaching up, he stroked my hair back behind my ear and brushed his fingers across my cheek. "I would be honoured and proud to publicly call you my daughter. To show the world you are my flesh and blood."

A stray tear slipped from my eye, but I didn't dare dash it away. The way he spoke with such reverence had me vibrating with joy. After everything I'd been through, I had a father who loved and cared for me, who wanted me the way I was without trying to change me.

"Won't it cause some kind of scandal for you?"

He smiled wider and shook his head.

"As if I care about such frivolous gossip. When Frank is gone, you will be free, *kotik*. You can be whoever you choose. I will support you regardless. And I love you too."

I couldn't hold back any longer. Tears fell freely and I pressed closer. He let go of my face so he could wrap his arms around me.

"I do hope those are happy tears, Ash."

"They are," I choked out.

He held me until I stopped crying. When I pulled away, I noticed the boys eying us from the dining room, all with expressions of concern on their faces. My boys were nothing if not protective over me.

"Excuse me a minute."

Viktor gave me a nod. I stood and walked into the dining room, wiping my face on my sleeve. Xav was closest and he rubbed my shoulder.

"Angel, is everything okay?"

I nodded.

"Happy tears."

He drew me closer, kissing the top of my head.

"I told you he'd be happy about it."

I'd believed Xav, but a part of me still worried Viktor wouldn't want me to take his last name. Stupid really since he'd supported me from the moment we'd met.

"Didn't make me any less scared," I whispered.

I knew I didn't have to impress Viktor or anything, but to have him be proud of me meant more than I could express in words.

"Angel…" his voice was so soft as he pulled me into his arms and held me tight.

"I'm okay, I promise."

"I can still hug you."

I smiled into his chest. Xav was my big teddy bear even when he was being incredibly annoying and winding me up with stupid shit. I loved that about him though. He brought joy and laughter into my life.

Next thing I knew, I had further bodies surrounding me. When I looked up, I found not only Eric but Quinn and Rory there too. I blinked. Why were they all hugging me at the same time? It felt significant. Like we'd really come full circle and were finally one big unit.

"What's happening?" I whispered.

"You're getting loved on, angel."

"I see that, but since when is this a thing?"

"Since we love you."

I snorted but didn't say another word, letting them all comfort me for a long minute before we all pulled away from each other slowly. They looked away with awkward expressions on their faces. I bit my lip.

"You guys don't need to feel weird about hugging me together, you know."

Quinn turned back to the table where they had papers laid out.

"I know," he muttered, fiddling with the end of a page.

Eric and Xav glanced at each other with a grin. Rory leant down and kissed my cheek before walking away to stand by Quinn. I rubbed my cheek before walking back into the living room. Viktor was observing me with a neutral expression and I knew he'd probably seen what just happened. Thankfully, he didn't comment on it as I sat back down.

Leaning forward, I pulled the paperwork I'd left on the table towards me.

"I filled out the form to change my name by Deed Poll, but I need this statutory declaration thing so I was thinking of asking Fabi as he meets the criteria. Witnesses are easy, the boys can do that."

Viktor smiled.

"I'm sure he'd be more than happy to."

"Getting my birth certificate changed is harder, but we can fix that after we've dealt with… Frank."

He nodded, his expression growing solemn. I swallowed the lump in my throat at the thought of us not surviving the war with Frank. It terrified me in all honesty. To lose everything when we were so close to winning would be devastating.

Viktor reached over and took my hand, squeezing it tightly.

"I'm scared of losing everyone I love," I whispered, the truth falling out of my lips without my say so.

"It's okay to be scared, *kotik*. It's not a weakness. Use your fear to remind you of what you have to live for."

I nodded. There would be no other way to do this. I had to take down Frank. And I knew I could do it. Take his life. It was the thought of losing my boys and my mother that had me in knots.

"Will you show me what you have planned? I may be able to help and perhaps alleviate your fears a little."

How on earth did I get so lucky to have a man like him as my father?

"Yes… I'm sure the boys would be happy to show you."

We both rose from the sofa. Viktor brought his glass into the dining room with him, saying hello to the four boys in turn.

"He'd like to see what we're planning," I said to Quinn, putting a hand on his arm.

Quinn nodded.

"Welcome to the war room."

Xav snorted.

"Nah, it's the ride or die room. We go hard or we go home."

"Would you take this seriously for one minute?"

Xav winked at me and I grinned. He was messing with Quinn as usual. It surprised me Quinn hadn't strangled him in the twenty-two-years they'd known each other. Those two were always bugging the hell out of each other.

Viktor leant over to me.

"I like him," he whispered.

"Why? Because he winds Quinn up all the time?"

"Yes."

I stifled my laughter by putting a hand over my mouth. Quinn glared at me and I immediately straightened, trying to keep my amusement in check.

"Shall I then?" Quinn asked, putting his hand out over the table to indicate the papers.

"By all means," Viktor replied.

I hoped my dad approved of what we intended to do. This really was a suicide mission and one we'd enlisted a fair few people to help us with. In order to win the war, we'd incite chaos. And in that chaos, the boys would rescue my mother whilst I destroyed Frank.

If this worked, we'd never have to deal with him ever again.

If it didn't… I couldn't think about that.

We had to win because the alternative would destroy everything. If it meant I had blood on my hands, so be it.

I was ready to take down Frank Russo.

I was ready to destroy the man who raised me.

I was ready to murder him in cold blood.

CHAPTER TWENTY EIGHT

Ash

Viktor ended up staying for dinner and the six of us used the time to talk, laugh and forget tomorrow everything could go to hell. It worried me we'd had no retaliation from Frank yet, but I couldn't think about it. Tomorrow I would focus on that. Tonight, I wanted to forget we might not survive the war.

When Viktor left, hugging me tight and telling me how much he loved me, I tried not to cry. The thought of not seeing him again upset me because of how much I'd grown to love him in the brief time we'd known each other. I felt so emotionally distraught, I didn't even go back into the living room with the boys. How could I choose who to spend the night with? It didn't seem fair to just have one when I wanted them all. It could be our last night. My heart had never felt so tight.

So even though I wanted to be with the boys, I went upstairs to my room instead. I pulled off all my clothes and tugged on a short silk robe. I sat at my dressing table and stared at my reflection, almost not recognising the woman I'd become. The months I'd been with the boys had changed me, shaped me into a new person. Or perhaps this was the woman I'd always been inside. Perhaps I needed the little extra push in the right direction from the four men who'd become so intrinsic to my life, they were a part of my soul.

I cleaned my face with a wipe, dumping it in the bin beside the table when I was done. Sometimes I wore makeup to make myself appear older than I was because I'd always looked younger than my twenty-one years. Right now, I felt as though I'd aged a thousand times over. My eyes held a certain darkness in them which hadn't been there before. I'd seen things and done things I never expected. And before this war was over, I would have blood on my hands. It didn't scare me as much as it should.

I'd been raised to be the queen of corruption. It's time I took on that role. To kill a king, bathe in his blood and wear his crown.

Picking up my hairbrush, I sat there for several minutes, taming my tangled mess of waves. The motion calmed me. Soothed my warring mind. Kept me focused. I watched the woman in the mirror. She looked tired but resolute. Her determination shone through. She would be the one to cut down the man who'd terrorised her. She'd win this for her men. She'd protect them with her life. Even if it meant she forfeited it in the process.

I was willing to die for them if it came to it. I wanted to set them free. They deserved more than the shitty lot they had in life. They deserved everything. And I'd give it to them. I'd show them how strong their woman was. Prove to them I would do anything to make them happy and keep them whole.

"Little girl."

Quinn appeared in the mirror's reflection followed by Xav, Eric and Rory. I placed the brush down and turned around on my stool, facing them. They all looked like they wanted to say something but were holding back. So many emotions radiated off them. I fought to keep calm and composed under the onslaught. We were all feeling the strain of knowing what would come tomorrow.

"I can't choose between you tonight. Please don't ask me to… It's not fair. None of this is fair," the words were out of my mouth before I could stop them. "I won't do it. I won't choose."

They didn't even look at each other. Quinn merely put his hand out to me, beckoning me over. I rose slowly from my stool, wondering what he wanted. What they wanted. The room became charged with tension. Whether or not it was of a sexual nature, I wasn't sure.

I crossed the room and stood in front of Quinn, staring up at him, hesitant to ask what was happening right now. He raised his hand and cupped my face, brushing his thumb across my bottom lip.

"We're not asking you to choose."

It took a second for his words to register, but I didn't have time to process it as his lips met mine in a soft kiss. It's only when I felt the others move closer, their presence surrounding me, lips touching my neck and hands on my body, I realised what was going on. What they wanted. What they intended to happen. And none of me wanted to question it even though I probably should. Instead, I surrendered to each touch. Each kiss. Each caress. Hands fell to the belt of my robe, untying the bow before more hands pulled it off my shoulders, allowing it to flutter to the floor.

"What are you doing?" I whispered as Quinn pulled back slightly, his eyes inky pools of black.

"We're making love to you."

I looked around, finding Xav behind me, Eric to my left and Rory to my right. Swallowing hard, I looked back up at Quinn as I stood there completely bare in front of them whilst they all remained clothed.

"All four of you… at once?"

Xav's hands banded around my waist and his breath was hot against my ear.

"Yes, angel… Everything might go to hell tomorrow. Tonight we want our woman."

I had no idea what to say. No idea what to even think. This seemed crazy, but everything in our lives was. We'd never had a normal beginning. It seemed fitting for us not to have a normal ending. Because tonight could be our ending. It could be our demise.

"Okay."

I felt the rumble of Xav's approval at my back.

"But I have some requests."

Quinn stroked my cheek as if urging me to go on.

"One, I need you all to look me in the eye and tell me you're okay with this. Two, I get to undress you one by one because I want to savour you… And three, you all have to promise whatever happens tonight, it won't get weird between us afterwards."

Quinn looked over the top of my head at the others, silently communicating with them for a long moment. He turned his eyes back to me.

"I want this, little girl."

My heart thumped once.

Eric turned me to him.

"I want to do this, hellcat."

My heart thumped twice.

I turned to Xav.

"I want all of it, angel."

My heart thumped three times.

Rory put a hand on my shoulder and twisted me around to him.

"I want this with you and them, little star."

My heart thumped four times.

All of my emotions got tangled up inside. I couldn't think let alone speak. Their expressions had been so open. So full of honesty. This wasn't something we had to do, but something we needed with each other. To show our love and devotion to this quintet in a moment where we forgot all the other shit weighing down on us.

"I love you." I twisted around, taking each of them in. "All of you. I love you all so much."

Not wanting to wait any longer or talk about it any further, I turned back to Quinn and reached up, flicking open the top button of his shirt. His eyes darkened further as I undid each one, pulling his shirt out of his trousers and off his shoulders. I dragged my nails down his chest, leaving faint red lines in my wake as if marking him as mine. His jaw clenched as if he was trying to hold back. I'd make him lose himself in this… in me… in us.

Leaning towards him, I kissed my way down his chest as my hands went to his belt, undoing it and pulling it out of the belt loops. I ran my tongue over his nipple, making him choke out a groan. His hands flexed at his sides, holding back from grabbing me. They could ravage me later. We were going to do this part on my terms.

I unbuttoned his fly and tugged his remaining clothes off his hips, leaving them pooled at his feet. My eyes fell between us. My hand wrapped around his length, stroking slowly. Quinn was ready for this judging by how hard he was.

"Little girl," he panted out as his hand curled around my waist.

"Patience, sir."

Going up on my tiptoes, I kissed him, my free hand wrapping around the back of his neck. When I released him, taking a step back, his eyes were so dark and the heat in them whipped my skin, setting it alight. I smiled before turning around and taking the few steps to close the distance between me and Xav. His piercing blue eyes bored their way into mine as I reached for his t-shirt, tugging it off him and dropping it to the floor. I ran my fingers down his arms and then I stared at his chest, my breath catching in my throat.

"When did you get this?"

He looked down at the heart with the letters A and E entwined together he'd had tattooed right over his heart. It looked very new and had scabbed over.

"Last week… and he cried over it," Xav replied, pointing at Eric.

"Shut up, Xavi."

Xav grinned and winked at Eric before looking at me again.

"Do you like it, angel?"

I nodded. It meant the whole damn world to me. I stroked my fingers down his chest, careful to avoid the fresh tattoo. He didn't need to tell me he'd done it to show his devotion to me and Eric.

"It's perfect," I whispered, leaning forward and placing a gentle kiss to it.

I stripped the rest of his clothes off his body, revelling in the sight of my beautiful tattooed king staring down at me with a smirk on his lips. I kissed him, stroking his cock because I couldn't help myself. I wanted all of them so fucking much.

Then I turned to Eric who was eying both of us, his face flushed which made me smile. He blushed at everything and I found it incredibly endearing.

"Hey," I whispered as I tangled my fingers in his chestnut hair.

"Hey, beautiful."

I kissed him, my hands dropping from his hair and running down the length of his body, feeling him shudder under my touch. I took my time undressing him, touching his bare skin before dragging my nails down his back in the way I knew he liked. Leaning down, I ran my tongue up the length of his cock before straightening, winking at him and turning around to my last man. I heard the groan from behind me and bit my lip as I stepped up to Rory.

His hazel eyes were intent on mine, the heat and desire simmering in them almost burning me to a crisp. I reached up and cupped his face, searching his gaze to make sure he wasn't going to disappear on me. As much as Rory loved me, I knew his issues still held him back in so many ways. So him doing this with me and the boys meant a whole great big deal of things.

"Ror…"

"Take what you need, little star… you have all of me," he whispered, taking my hand from his cheek and pressing it to his heart.

I held it there for a long moment before dropping it to the bottom of his t-shirt. He raised his arms to let me pull it off him. I stroked my fingers down his chest, running one down the length of the scar on his abdomen. He watched me silently as I knew he would. Next, I unbuttoned his jeans and tugged those from his hips before stroking my hand up the length of him. His eyes darkened at my bold touch. I ran my fingers along the waistband of his boxers, the last item of clothing between me and him. Between all of us.

"Do it," he murmured, his voice having that commanding note to it.

I obeyed, pulling them off him and leaving him bare before me. It took me a few seconds to stop staring at how beautiful he was in all his glory before I reached up and kissed him, pressing my body against his. His fingers stroked down my back, leaving my skin tingling.

I pulled away and turned back to Quinn. None of them seemed to have an issue with us all being bare together. It felt right. All of it.

"Where do you want me?"

"On the bed."

I stepped out of the circle and walked towards the bed, crawling onto it and sitting up in the middle. Quinn stalked towards me first, grabbing both my legs and pulling me down so they were dangling off the end. Then he was on his knees, kissing his way up my inner thigh. The others joined me on the bed. Rory fit himself behind me, kissing my neck whilst Xav and Eric were beside me, sharing my breasts between them. I moaned, getting lost in the sensations of four mouths on me.

I raised my hands, tangling them in Rory's hair behind me as I turned my face so I could kiss him. Our lips met, tongues tangling together in a wild mess. His cock dug into my back as he devoured my mouth whole. I wanted so badly to taste him. I wanted to taste them all. To feel them in ways I'd never done so before.

One of my hands fell to Quinn's head, digging into his hair as his tongue flicked over my clit, teasing me and driving me wild. The boys I was between were alternating between kissing each other and wrapping their mouths around my nipples. The sensations of their hands and mouths on me was unlike anything else.

"Ror," I panted. "I want you."

He bit down on my earlobe.

"You want to choke on it, little star."

I moaned in agreement. It wasn't a question but a statement. He knew I liked it when he took control and made me do what he wanted.

"Please… please, fuck me."

"So needy."

"You heard our girl," came Xav's voice. "Fuck her."

It wasn't only Rory who moved from behind me, but Quinn's mouth left me too. Next thing I knew, he'd fit himself between my legs and was pressing inside me. I whimpered, staring up at him and his dark eyes watching me intently. I wasn't allowed more time to look at Quinn. Rory's hands were turning me towards him. He'd stood up so my mouth was level with his cock. I licked my bottom lip. He pulled my jaw open and fed me it. I stared up into his hazel eyes, watching him sink deeper and the expression of pure satisfaction on his face.

The feeling of having him thrusting into my mouth whilst Quinn fucked me, made my insides clench. I moaned around Rory's cock, wanting more. More of this. More of them. More of our connection with each other. Reaching out blindly with both hands, they landed on Xav and Eric. They seemed to understand what I wanted as Xav guided it down to his cock and Eric kissed my fingertips before tracing them down his chest. It should have made me feel wanton and dirty touching all of them at once like this, but it didn't. Nothing about this felt dirty. It felt as though we were showing each other how much we loved one another. How much we all meant to each other.

"Look at our girl, not wanting to leave anyone out," came Quinn's voice, his hands banded around my thighs as he thrust harder. "Don't worry, little girl… Everyone will get their turn inside you."

I trembled at his words. The thought of them all spilling inside me heating my body up further. I couldn't talk because

I still had a mouthful of cock. I moaned around Rory's length again, indicating I was on board with it.

Quinn's thumb landed on my clit, stroking me towards an explosive ending. I was already sensitive everywhere from their ministrations so it really didn't take much. My eyes were on Rory as I came, clenching and releasing around Quinn like I couldn't get enough.

"Fuck," he grunted, then he tugged at my face with his hand. Rory's cock popped free and was replaced by Quinn's mouth, kissing me as his body shuddered. I felt him pulse inside me, emptying himself deep. Pulling back, he rested his forehead against mine, holding my face and staring at me with an intense expression on his face.

"I love you."

He kissed me one more time before pulling out of me entirely and standing up. He smiled and stepped back. My attention was torn away as Xav pulled my face to him, kissing me with unrestrained passion. A moment later, I felt hands cleaning me up below, but I was too wrapped up in my mouth being devoured whilst another mouth was at my breasts, licking and tasting my nipples.

Someone tugged me up the bed and turned me over, finding myself facing Eric. He smiled, his verdant green eyes twinkling as he pulled me over him. My hands landed on his shoulders. He gripped my hip and pressed me down on his cock, making me groan. It wasn't long before I felt a body behind me and I knew it was Xav by the way he exhaled as he ran his hands down my back. His hands went to my behind, spreading me before his fingers were there, coated in lube. I moaned at the stretch whilst I continued to fuck Eric who was staring at me with absolute adoration on his face. To his right sat Quinn, watching us with hooded eyes and to his left was Rory, whose hand landed on my thigh and was stroking it in a possessive motion in tandem with his hand around his still hard cock.

Once Xav was satisfied he'd opened me up enough, he entered me from behind, making me cry out at the fullness. Rory's hand on my thigh tightened whilst Eric stroked my face and brought me closer so he could kiss me. It made me feel sexy having Quinn and Rory watch me get fucked by Xav and Eric. Not one of them made me feel wrong about this. It was as if all of us had lost our inhibitions and were acting on pure animal instinct mixed in with our love for each other.

I arched back into Xav, pulling away from Eric so I could turn my head to kiss him.

"So fucking tight," he murmured against my mouth. "You're so beautiful, angel. I love you so much."

I felt beautiful and wanted, needed by them all. My gaze turned to Quinn who was still watching me with heat and desire. He leant forward, wrapping a hand around the back of my head before running his nose up my cheek.

"That's it, little girl. Show them how much you love them… make them come."

The way he said it made me shiver. I had to obey his command. Do as he said because my sir had told me to. He released me and settled back down. I was pulled to the other side by Rory. His mouth latched onto my neck, pressing kisses down my skin.

"Please," I whimpered.

His mouth landed below my collarbone and he bit down, making me cry out with the intense pleasure and pain whilst my boys continued to thrust inside me in tandem. And it didn't take long for me to come again when Xav reached around and stroked my clit. I detonated on them, which made both Xav and Eric curse loudly. Eric's hands gripped my hips tightly as if he was trying to hold back, but I didn't want that. I wanted him to lose control.

"I want… I want your cum," I gasped out whilst my climax rocked through me, my fingers digging into Eric's shoulders.

"You can fucking have it, angel."

Xav groaned in my ear as I felt him pulse and twitch inside me. I think it set Eric off too because he was cursing and moaning my name too.

"Fuck, Ash, fuck… fuck, I love you."

I felt so high, I wasn't sure I could come down.

Xav pulled out of me first, kissing my shoulder before he moved away. I rose off Eric who slid out from under me. I was about to turn over when Rory's hand on my shoulder stopped me.

"Stay," he almost outright growled.

Not wanting to disobey I stilled and waited for his next instruction. One of the boys, I wasn't sure which one, cleaned me up again and then hands were on my hips, pulling them up so I was on my hands and knees. Then I felt Rory's body covering me, his hand came around my neck as he thrust inside me.

"Little star," he whispered in my ear. "You looked so sexy getting fucked by them… made me so hard. I can't be gentle with you."

"Don't be."

I wasn't sure what the others would think, but I guessed at this point it didn't matter. We weren't judging each other. This was about coming together, the five of us as one.

Rory's free hand banded around my hip as he went to town on my pussy, making me clench around him over and over. Quinn's face came into view before his mouth covered mine, kissing me whilst Rory brutally thrust into me from behind. I moaned in Quinn's mouth, loving every moment, never wanting it to end.

"Such a good little girl," Quinn murmured.

"Thank you, sir."

He pulled away and smiled at me. Rory's hand around my neck tightened, making me buck against him. I turned my head, finding Xav and Eric curled up together at the head of the bed, watching Rory fuck me with rapt attention. Something about having the boys watching each other take turns with me set my body on fire. It went one step further than when they'd punished me together. Now we felt as one, like this was always how we were meant to come together.

"Ror… harder, please."

He let go of my neck, both of his hands circled my hips. I didn't care about how the splint around his wrist dug into me, all I wanted was Rory. He drove into me over and over, fucking me with no restraint. My fingers dug into the covers. Curses flew out of my mouth, but it was heaven. All of it. I felt complete. Like the last piece of the puzzle had slipped into place. So when I felt fingers at my clit, coaxing and stroking me, I exploded around Rory's cock and practically screamed.

The wild intensity drove me higher until I was almost crying with the release.

"Fuck, little star," Rory grunted as he climaxed hard, giving me everything he had.

When he pulled out of me, I collapsed on the bed, utterly spent and unable to move. For several minutes, I lay there just breathing until I felt a hand stroking my hair back from my face. I opened my eyes and blinked before rolling over. All the boys were still on my bed, watching me quietly.

"Little girl?"

My heart tightened. As much as I'd loved every moment of our lovemaking, I realised I didn't want any of them to go. I wanted them all here so we could have our last night together as a group. As a family.

"Don't leave me."

"Um, I hate to be the bearer of bad news, but this bed isn't big enough for the five of us," Xav said, frowning.

He was right. We could just about fit three of us in here at night but sleeping without two of them didn't sit right with me.

"We'll make it work," Quinn said. "You go get cleaned up, little girl and we'll sort it out between us."

I nodded, smiling at him. Quinn was trying to give me what I needed. In all honesty, I think we all needed this. I slid off the bed and padded out of the room, going into the bathroom and went about my business. I was a little sore, but thoroughly satisfied.

By the time I came out, I found the boys had dragged the mattress off the bed and dumped it on the floor. They'd also got another mattress from one of their rooms and placed it beside mine. The nest they'd made was complete with duvets and pillows. I put my hand over my mouth, shocked they'd actually gone to the effort.

"Boys… this is… Thank you."

I didn't have any other words. They'd all pulled on boxers so I found a t-shirt for myself. Then the five of us got tucked up together after one of them turned out the light. Xav and Eric got comfy on one mattress whilst I was laid out between Rory and Quinn.

"We're going to win this, aren't we?" I whispered.

"We're going to damn well try, little girl."

I snuggled closer to Quinn as Rory wrapped himself around me from behind.

"I love you."

My words were met with a chorus of "we love you too," from the boys.

I wanted to stay awake longer to savour these moments with them, but exhaustion dragged me away into a deep, dreamless sleep.

Tonight had been everything and more. And tomorrow could be the end of it all.

I hoped deep down in my heart, we'd come out of the war alive. And we'd come out with each other so the future we all wanted could be mapped out in front of us. All I wanted was a life with my boys. I'd have it if we pulled this off. If we took down Frank Russo.

We'd have forever. And we'd have it… together.

CHAPTER TWENTY NINE

Quinn

I'd lain awake for a long time last night watching Ash sleep. For once, she didn't look peaceful. The weight of the world was on her shoulders. My strong little girl was trying so hard to put on a brave face for us. I knew deep down she was terrified of what would happen when we made our move on Frank Russo.

The boys and I had agreed we all needed a distraction. One night where we forgot about the coming storm and did something for ourselves. Seeing how much pleasure she'd received from the four of us made my heart fucking soar. She'd been so happy and free the entire time we'd made love to her. If any of us had any doubts left about our relationship, they were completely gone. We'd set them free. Making love to her with them had meant the fucking world to me.

Waking up this morning had been difficult for all five of us. I'd come to first, glancing around at the others. Xav and Eric were wrapped around each other next to me. I had Ash sandwiched between me and Rory. He clutched her like she was his lifeline. Before all of this happened, I would've never guessed I'd be perfectly happy to sleep next to my best friends, but hell, it made me feel safe last night in some strange way.

I didn't disturb the rest of them when I got up, kissing Ash's forehead and stumbling out of the room to take a shower. Standing under the spray, I breathed deeply with my hands pressed up against the wall. So much was riding on today going to plan even though no doubt it wouldn't. There were too many things we couldn't account for. And we were relying heavily on Ash to play her part. Out of everything, that scared me the most. She wanted to cut down Frank, but would she be able to go through with it? Would she falter?

I believed in her, but killing a man was no easy task for anyone. I struggled with the act even though I was technically already a killer. Those deaths were necessary. The blood on my hands had never been without reason. Without motivation.

Ash had the biggest motivation of all when it came to Frank. He'd been the reason she'd felt so broken before she came to be with us. He'd traumatised her. With us, she'd been free of his influence. His corruption. His greed. She'd grown into such a strong woman and my pride knew no bounds when it came to her.

I shut the shower off and dried myself before getting dressed. When I got downstairs, I found Eric cooking up a storm. A full English with all the trimmings. It made me smile. He knew we needed the fuel for later when we made our move.

"Morning," I said as I took a seat. "Is everyone else awake?"

"Yeah, they're showering and getting dressed."

I noticed his hair was wet so he must have got up right after me. Admittedly, I'd taken my time in the shower, consumed by my thoughts. Once we'd wrapped up breakfast, it'd be game on. We had a lot to achieve today and none of it would be pretty.

"How did Ash seem?"

He glanced over his shoulder at me from the stove.

"Quiet I guess, and very reluctant to get up. Said we wore her out last night."

I smirked. We certainly had. I wondered if we got through this would we ever indulge in that way with each other again. I couldn't say I'd be averse to it. Perhaps on special occasions.

"I hope she wasn't complaining."

He turned back to the stove but not before I saw the glint in his eyes.

"No, not complaining, more like glowing. Maybe we should do it again… to make her happy, you know, if we get through this shit."

I blinked.

"You'd want to?"

He lifted a shoulder as if to say, maybe.

"I enjoyed it, more than I thought I would."

"Me too."

I didn't feel weird admitting it. My inhibitions when it came to me, the boys and Ash were well and truly gone. Crossing that last hurdle felt necessary because now… there was well and truly no going back.

A squealing noise came from down the hallway. Both Eric and I whipped our heads around to find Xav chasing after

Ash. She dashed into the kitchen with him on her tail, screaming with laughter. He made a grab for her but she ducked out of the way and ran towards me, squeezing herself between me and the kitchen counter.

"Stop it," she yelled at him through her laughter.

"Um, may I ask what's going on?" I said as I wrapped an arm around her.

Rory walked in shaking his head and rolling his eyes.

"He's trying to get me back for tickling him, threatened to put me over his knee and everything."

I raised an eyebrow at Xav who'd stopped next to us and was giving Ash a look of utter disapproval for going to me to protect her.

"What? She needs to stop being such a bad girl."

I snorted.

"You like the fact Ash is a bad girl."

He grinned and shrugged.

"Only when she's being bad in the bedroom… like last night."

Ash blushed heavily before burying her face against my chest. She'd been a naughty girl for us last night. Letting us take her whatever way we wished.

"He was winding me up about my dad," she whispered. "He deserved it."

"Don't tell me you were calling Viktor, Daddy V yet again."

Xav's grin widened.

"She loves it really."

I shoved him away from us and he thankfully retreated towards Eric.

"He's gone, happy now, sweetheart?"

She nodded against my chest, wrapping her arms around my neck. I stroked her hair before she raised her head, blue eyes twinkling. Next thing I knew, she'd kissed me, her tongue parting my lips and delving inside my mouth. What followed was probably far more PDA than the boys needed to see this morning, but Ash didn't seem to give a shit.

When she pulled away, her smile made it all worthwhile. The way her eyes lit up and her body relaxed into me showed me how much she needed our affection right now. To remind her who she belonged to. Who she had to rely on.

The only thing which didn't make it worthwhile was the uncomfortable stirring it gave me. I swear to god I had no control when it came to her pressed against me.

"Are we all getting kissed like that this morning or is Quinn getting a special treat?" Xav asked, leaning against the counter as he helped Eric with breakfast.

He was pouting which made me smirk. Ash squeezed out from between me and the counter and skipped over to him. She stood there with her hands on her hips.

"Jealous?"

"Very."

He grabbed her and she let him kiss her with as much passion as she'd kissed me. His hands were all over her, squeezing her behind and making her wriggle against him. When he let her go she glanced at Eric. He leant down and kissed her forehead.

"After I've finished this, beautiful."

She smiled and took the mugs from Xav who'd made tea and coffee, placing them at our respective places on the counter. She proceeded to set out knives and forks for us all and stacking a load of plates next to Eric. Then she slipped into a stool next to Rory, glancing up at him with a shy smile. He put a hand on her knee, squeezing it but didn't move to do anything further. She simply rested her head on his shoulder, running her fingers down his arm and fiddling with his splint.

"Only another week until this should come off."

"Thank fuck," he muttered. "It's itchy as hell."

"Aww, Ror. I know, but you'll be better and then we can…"

His eyes darkened and his mouth curled up at the side.

"*We* can what, little star?"

She bit her lip.

"You can chase me again," she whispered, but I still heard her.

Is that what they got up to when he took her down to Kent?

Rory looked like he was vibrating with need at her words. He turned to her fully, taking her chin between the fingers of his uninjured hand.

"You want me to hunt you down and ravage you?" he asked quietly.

"Yes, please."

"Little star," he growled.

Then he was on her, their kiss messy and uncoordinated, but neither of them seemed to care as they practically tried to climb into each other. The display made it worse for me. I glanced down at my cock which strained hard against my zipper, internally cursing the fact I found anything and everything about Ash hot as fuck.

"Um… okay… wow, what the fuck?" Xav hissed at Eric, indicating them with his head.

Eric glanced at them and his eyebrows shot up.

"I thought you found them cute as fuck."

"This is not cute… it's like two rabbits going at it with each other."

Eric snorted and turned back to the stove, but not before glancing down at his crotch.

"Yeah, okay, try telling that to your dick."

"Hey!"

"I'm not the one with a hardon over Ash and Rory sucking face."

Xav turned away, for once in his life looking a little embarrassed. And I was glad I was sitting down so no one could see how aroused I was by it.

"Are you done yet or what?" he muttered. "I'm fucking starving."

"Calm down, I'm just going to plate up."

Xav stalked away and sat next to me, glancing at Ash and Rory who'd stopped kissing and were instead staring into each other's eyes.

"Did I miss the memo about it being a free for all with Ash this morning or something?"

"Isn't it a free for all with Ash every day?"

Xav stared at me.

"Did you just make a joke?"

I shrugged and sipped my coffee, not bothering to give him a response. Thankfully, Eric dumped a plate in front of Xav then and he dug in, mumbling his thanks. Eric rolled his eyes before dishing up everyone else their portions and coming to sit down next to Ash with his own. She leant over to him, her smile wide and he required no further encouragement. His hands dug in her hair as their lips met. Xav was too busy eating to make any smart remarks. A small mercy.

The rest of breakfast was a subdued affair with the mood turning a little sour. I think it all dawned on us this was it. No going back. As Xav liked to say: ride or die.

The four of us tidied up the kitchen whilst Eric went to get the supplies we needed. When he came back, we all stood in the dining room together, getting kitted up with earpieces and weapons. We'd packed everything else we needed in the car.

"Ready?" I asked, eying the rest of them.

"As I'll ever be," Eric replied shrugging.

Rory gave a sharp nod and Xav saluted.

"Ready," Ash said.

I took a deep breath.

"Let's get this show on the fucking road then."

CHAPTER THIRTY

RORY

The drive towards the city centre was quiet, as if we were all lost in our own thoughts. I sat up in front with Quinn whilst Ash was sandwiched between Xav and Eric. I tried not to think too hard about how it mirrored the way they'd been last night. Tried and failed. Ash had looked like a fucking queen. The way she'd taken all of us, begged for it, needed it. Fuck, it'd been everything. It'd taken a lot for me to come around to the idea of all of us having sex with her at the same time. I didn't want my issues to surface even though they were my best friends and I'd never had major problems with physical contact with them. When it came to it, we'd all got lost in the moment and it'd been fucking incredible.

I shook myself internally. Now was not the time to be remembering the way she'd trembled as she came around my cock or the others.

Quinn parked up one street over from where Russo's building was. A huge place which housed his offices for his investment business, but Ash told us it's where he conducted his shady shit as well. The place had a basement, which is where she suspected he was keeping Isabella. That was our aim. The boys and me. To get Isabella out.

Quinn hadn't been thrilled when Ash suggested she go after Russo alone. She'd insisted due to knowing her way around the building better than we did. We'd never been in here before. When we'd taken Ash, it'd been from Isabella and Frank's place next door in the block of flats he owned.

I think Ash also had something to prove. She'd kept telling us she wanted to be the one who destroyed Frank. Ultimately, we had to concede to her. She would not back down on it. And I knew our girl could do it. She had a ruthless streak with a thirst for vengeance when it came to Frank fucking Russo.

"Let's go," Quinn said, getting out of the car.

The rest of us piled out, gathering up our shit from the boot and locking up. We got out onto the main street and blended into the crowd before branching off down a side street and skirting our way around the building to the back entrance.

Xav checked his phone for the time as we all ducked behind the huge bins outside so we were out of sight. There were two people smoking out back. Ash had told us they were out there like clockwork at eleven in the morning every day to take a cigarette break.

She peered around before dashing out, keeping her steps silent. She shadowed the two men until they reached the backdoor. One of them used a handprint to open the door and they both disappeared inside. She ran forward, sticking her foot in the door before it closed. Then she waved us over.

We all moved quickly, reaching the door as she pulled it open, looking left and right inside.

Ash stepped into the building with the four of us crowding in behind her. We followed her down the hallway until we reached a room with a security code. Ash bashed in the numbers and it unlocked. We all piled in one by one, with Ash checking the hallway again before closing the door. The room we'd entered was full of computer equipment. It was eerily dark with only flashing lights to illuminate the room.

"Would you look at that?" Xav said, striding forward with a grin.

"Don't fucking dawdle," Quinn grunted.

Xav glared at him before setting to work with the servers. We needed to cut all the security feeds and essentially throw everything into chaos within the building by shutting it down. Whilst we infiltrated Russo's building, triggering a catalyst of events, the favours we pulled in meant we had Colm's Irish gangsters causing issues for Russo's supply lines and a few others creating noise. Attack him from several sides and drive his men to make mistakes so we could get lost in the chaos. That was the plan. Ash predicted he'd already be raging over his nephew's death and us finding Nate. We'd got word earlier he was still in the ICU in a medically induced coma, but they'd be bringing him out of it in a few days.

"Bombs a-fucking-way."

Xav had already plugged something into one of the computers. I assumed it was the virus he'd created to rip apart their firewall and hack their systems.

"How long?"

"We give it five minutes then we move."

Quinn got his phone out and fired off a few messages. Eric stood with Ash, his hand on her back as she stared at the wall in front of them. Her face was void of all expression. If I could take away what she had to do next, I would in a heartbeat. Had Ash said no, she couldn't go through with killing Russo, Quinn and I would've stepped in and taken it on. But my little star was nothing if not determined.

Quinn turned to her, his eyes dark and his expression grim. "Little girl…"

"I can do this," she whispered. "I can."

Eric frowned at the way her voice trembled on the words. I stepped forward, taking her by the hand and pulling her closer. Cupping her cheek with my uninjured hand, I stared down into her crystal blue eyes.

"Don't focus on the act itself. If you do that, you won't go through with it. Focus on what it means to rid the world of him. Think about what you have to live for. Why you're doing this. Hold on to those reasons tight, little star. Remember we love you and we'll be waiting for you at the end of it all."

She stared up at me for the longest moment.

"Thank you, Ror."

I saw in her eyes what she couldn't say. This might be the very last time we saw each other and she didn't want to say goodbye. The others might not recognise it but I did. I knew Ash was scared she wouldn't come out of this alive.

I pulled her into my arms and held her tight for a long minute. There weren't many words left to say. We'd said them all last night.

"I love you, little star," I whispered. "Forever."

She pulled away, giving me a sad smile before she hugged the other three one by one. Quinn looked down at his watch as Ash was holding Xav.

"We need to move."

Eric pulled open the door and checked the hallway. He signalled it was clear and the five of us piled out of the room. We went left and Ash went right, glancing back at us for a moment before pulling up her hood and making her way towards the central bank of lifts. We went towards where she'd told us the door to the basement was. You could access it via the lifts, but it was heavily guarded. We needed to capitalise on the element of surprise as much as we could.

"She'll be okay, won't she?" Eric murmured to Xav as we all walked.

"She has to be."

She really did have to be. If she wasn't, I don't know what the fuck any of us would do. Living without Ash didn't bear thinking about.

We'd just reached the door when all of our earpieces crackled into life.

"*People are running around like headless chickens. No one's noticed me,*" Ash said.

"Good," Quinn replied. "We need it to remain like that. We're heading down now."

He punched in the code she'd given us, but it didn't work.

"Ash… are you sure this code is right?"

"*It's Isabella's birthday. One, three, zero, eight.*"

Quinn tried again.

"It's not working."

"*Fuck, he must've changed it.*"

"Get out the way," Xav said to Quinn, nudging him with a shoulder.

Quinn put his hands up. Xav had a tiny screwdriver in his hand and was pulling apart the entire panel within minutes.

"Knew it wouldn't be this easy," he muttered.

Lucky for us we had him here, or we'd be screwed. Getting through the door would be impossible considering it looked like reinforced steel. Quinn kept checking his watch, getting more and more agitated by the minute.

"Would you stop looking at me like that?" Xav ground out.

"Like what?"

"Like I'm taking too fucking long. I know, all right? I got this."

Quinn looked away, but I could see he wanted to hurry Xav along. Eric was keeping watch a few feet away from us to make sure no one came down this way.

"Xav," he hissed. "I hate to agree with Quinn, but we've got two employees on their way."

"Fuck."

Quinn pulled a gun out, followed by Eric. Xav looked like he wanted to smash something whilst he worked with the wiring.

"Hold on… and… there."

The door made a hissing sound as it clicked off the latch. Quinn ripped it open whilst Xav hurriedly stuffed the wires back in place and screwed the panel back on. Eric backed away from the corner and we all dashed into the stairwell together, pulling the door shut behind us.

"That was a fucking close one," Eric said as we started down the steps.

"*Are you guys okay*?" came Ash's voice.

"Yes, little girl. Xav got us through at the last minute. We're going on radio silence in two minutes when we reach the bottom, okay?"

"*Yes, I'm in the lift now. I don't know if anyone saw me, but we're all in now. No going back, right*?"

"We're in this together. We'll let you know when we've got Isabella. Going dark now."

We reached the bottom of the stairwell. Quinn looked between us, his eyes filled with determination.

"This will be bloody and fucked up."

"No fucking doubt," Xav said with a shrug.

"Time to gun some fuckers down."

He turned and opened the stairwell door.

Ash was right.

There was no fucking going back now.

CHAPTER THIRTY ONE

Xavier

Quinn walked out the door first, his eyes darting around as the rest of us followed. The dank corridor was dark and had a musty smell as if no one had been down here in a long time. Ash had told us this part of the basement was where all the electrics and the boiler room was.

Quinn pointed at Rory, indicating he needed to stay in the middle. With his injury, we didn't want him getting in the firing line. We'd given him knives and he could somewhat fire a gun if he held it in his left hand and squeezed the trigger with the right.

I didn't much like having illegal guns in general, but when you lived the way we did, they were necessary. When this was done, we'd get rid of this shit and be done with the criminal underworld. Today was the culmination of years of fighting towards one goal. To kill Frank Russo. I didn't care if it was Ash who'd do the deed and not one of us. He needed to be eradicated from the world so he couldn't spread his corruption and greed any further.

We walked slowly down the corridor as Quinn turned on a torch, illuminating the way in the darkness. Eric and Rory went after Quinn and I brought up the rear. Not that we thought we had anything to fear from someone coming up behind us but you could never be too sure.

When we reached the end, Quinn peered out around the corner. He indicated it was clear and we moved on, each of us checking our surroundings. I hoisted my kitbag up on my shoulder and held my gun tight as we edged along further. There was a light at the end of this corridor with doors on our sides. Ash told us those were storage rooms so there'd be no need to check them.

We all flattened ourselves against the wall when we reached the end. Quinn had turned off the torch and looked around the corner. He held up two fingers and nodded his head towards the right. Two men up ahead. Eric indicated his gun with his head. Quinn gave us a nod. They were armed. We might have silencers on our guns, but they would still make a hell of a noise, regardless. The moment gunfire started, it would alert everyone else.

Quinn seemed to take a minute to weigh up our options, then he slid his gun back into its holster on his side and pulled out a knife instead. He waved at Rory, who grinned. Eric and I looked at each other. There was no question what those two were about to do.

Quinn and Rory silently crept out into the hallway. I took Quinn's place, keeping a lookout as the other two approached the two armed men from behind.

Idiots should be paying more attention.

Except they were completely oblivious to the threat behind them. Quinn warned us it would be a bloodbath and the Russos were about to have their first casualties.

Quinn and Rory worked in tandem, jumping the two men, holding their mouths and slitting their throats. The gurgling sounds echoing down the corridor made me flinch. They lowered the men to the floor, wiping their knives off on their clothing. Quinn waved at me. Eric and I approached them cautiously. Blood was beginning to pool on the floor so we all slipped past quickly so we wouldn't get caught out in it.

"Well, this is totally not fucked up," Eric hissed in my ear.

I gave him a grim smile. Working our way through this silently was our only choice. Right now, the building was in serious shit over us hacking their systems, but we didn't want more men down here than there already likely were. Getting trapped down in this basement before we rescued Isabella would not bode well. We'd have to fight our way out and we only had so much ammunition.

At the end of this corridor, it opened out into a larger space where there were shelving units. Ash told us beyond that would be the cages where Russo kept prisoners and a space where he conducted his interrogations. I say interrogations, it was more like a space for him to torture his unwilling victims. Something Ash had been witness to. I shuddered at the thought. Knowing she'd had to see all of that made me sick. No one should be forced to watch the man they thought was their father beat the shit out of another, let alone see him commit murder.

From what we could see there were various men stationed around the room. Fuck knows how many people they were keeping down here, but Ash mentioned they had guards around the clock. They took shifts. With their security systems down, we'd hampered their visuals. We had to strike now.

Quinn leant over to us, his expression harsh and unforgiving.

"Xav and Eric take the left, Rory and I will go right. Find Isabella, kill anyone else," he whispered. "No one is left alive, we cannot have anyone alerting upstairs, understood?"

We all nodded. I dreaded to think what the death count would be. It didn't fucking matter. We had one objective. Rescue Ash's mother and get the fuck out of here. Me and Rory would take her back to the car as agreed and Eric and Quinn would backup Ash. Thinking about her right now wouldn't help me. I was fucking worried about her safety. If she didn't come out of this, I wouldn't know what the fuck to do with myself. None of us would. Ash was our guiding fucking light. Our angel. We needed her as much as she needed us. That girl had to fucking stay alive.

Quinn pulled out his gun again and Rory did the same after they'd stashed their knives.

"I don't care if you make a fucking racket. We shoot to kill."

"You got it, man," I whispered back.

The four of us crept out into the room, Eric and I split off to the left whilst Quinn and Rory went right. We moved along the shelving unit, coming to the end and spying two men almost lounging against an empty cage.

"It's fuckin' chaos upstairs," one of them said. "Ronnie keeps radioing down. Idiot thinks that's going to fuckin' help."

"Nah, dis shit's long, fam."

I tried not to roll my eyes and glanced at Eric. Where the fuck did Russo find these fools? I was about to step forward when I heard the pop of a gun going off behind us. The two men perked up.

"What the fuck was that?" said man number one.

"A gun, you fool," said wannabe gangster number two.

Eric and I stepped out, not giving a shit about being quiet any longer.

"Hello, boys," I grinned before opening fire on both of them.

Their eyes widened and they had no fucking chance. A single shot to the head each took them both out. Man number one slid down the cage whilst wannabe gangster collapsed on the floor in a heap.

"This fucking kid clearly thought he was gangster," I muttered to Eric, stepping over them.

"You showed him who's the number one OG here."

I looked over to find him grinning.

"Oh, haha, so funny. Let's go."

To be fair, it was funny, but Eric needed to quit being such a cheeky little shit. I stifled a smile as we continued along the shelving unit until we came to the end. The men guarding this cage were on high alert with guns at the ready. They must've heard us shooting. There was someone inside, but it wasn't a female. They were huddled in a corner, their short hair matted with blood.

I leant out and popped off one round but didn't hit my target. The returning gunfire had me ducking behind the shelving again.

"You good?" I called to Eric over the sound.

"You take the one on the left, I'll go right," he replied, his expression turning dark. His green eyes held a fire in them I rarely saw. He was pissed as fuck and wanted to take it out on these fuckers.

I gave him a nod. He slipped down the shelving and popped out the other end, firing off a shot whilst I stepped out and nailed the other guy. The one Eric had fired at stared down at his chest, watching the blood pooling on his white shirt before he dropped his weapon and tried to stem it. I stepped forward and kicked him down.

"If you're going to die, do it quietly, eh?" I told him whilst Eric walked along and looked at the man in the cage.

"Xav, you got your bolt cutters?"

Quinn might have told us to kill everyone on sight, but he never said anything about the people Russo was keeping as prisoners down here. I opened my kitbag whilst holding the dying man down with a foot to his chest. Locating the cutters, I tossed them at Eric who proceeded to cut open the padlock. The man huddled in the corner looked up and I almost froze in recognition.

"Vincenzo?"

What the fuck did Russo have him down here for? Didn't he know it would piss the Italian mafia off? The man knew no bounds. No wonder we couldn't get hold of him when we were trying to plan this rescue mission.

"What are you doing here?" Eric asked.

"Fucking Russo," Vincenzo croaked out. "Leverage against my father."

"Well, shit," I said. "Get him out of there."

I might not like the guy, but he didn't deserve this shit. It reminded me he had a thing for Ash, which also pissed me off. He wasn't getting his hands on our fucking girl.

Eric stepped in and helped Vincenzo up, getting him out of the cage and setting him down on the chair outside. I decided to let the others know.

"Quinn… you there?"

There was nothing.

"Quinn? We found Villetti in one of the cages."

Eric glanced at me, concern appearing on his features.

"Rory? You there?"

"*Quinn ran off before I could stop him… I don't know where he is*," he replied thirty seconds later.

"Fuck. Okay… where are you?"

"*Still working my way through the cages on the right. Haven't found captives yet.*"

Eric picked up one of the guns from the men and handed it to Vincenzo with a raised eyebrow.

"Can you handle that?"

Vincenzo nodded. If he opened fire on us, he was a dead fucking man, but somehow I knew he wouldn't. He had as much of an axe to grind with Russo as we did.

"Shit, okay. Keep going, Rory, we'll search for Quinn too," I said before rubbing the back of the neck and lifting my foot off the dead man below me.

"Why d'you think Quinn ran off?" Eric asked.

"Fuck knows. The fool is going to get himself killed if he's not careful. He should be sticking to the fucking plan, but he's not."

All I knew is we had to find him before it was too late. I had a seriously bad feeling about this and judging by Eric's expression, he did too.

"Can you walk?" Eric asked Vincenzo.

"Yeah… What do you need me to do?"

He stood, clutching the gun like he knew how to use it and giving us both a nod.

"Help us find that fool of ours, then we'll get you out of here."

If Quinn was going to be a reckless fuck, then we'd just have to save his arse. I hoped he hadn't got himself into too much shit.

CHAPTER THIRTY TWO

Quinn

Rory and I had worked our way down the right-hand side, dispatching a fair few men in the process. I was beginning to think we might not find Isabella down here. Ash had been sure this is where Russo would be keeping her. She'd not been seen in public since we received the video of her, so chances were Ash was right. It still made me nervous. We were working on assumptions and I didn't like it. And I was seriously fucking worried about my little girl and how things were going upstairs. It made my anxiety spike to almost uncontrollable levels.

"You okay?" Rory hissed as we approached another shelving unit.

I shook my head. No point lying about it.

"She'll be fine, you know that."

I didn't feel like Ash would be. She was taking on the worst part of this operation. Going after Russo alone was the biggest risk. It wouldn't just be Frank she had to take down, but all the men between her and him. Russo would never leave himself unprotected.

"We went on radio silence so it's not like I expected to hear from her, but I'm still fucking worried," I whispered.

"Then check in with her."

I stiffened. It could jeopardise what she was doing.

"Can't, she needs to stay focused."

I knew she'd be worried about us getting to Isabella, but we'd made a promise. Fucking sworn on our lives we'd get her mother out safely. She trusted us and we couldn't let her down.

I flattened myself against the shelving unit and peered out. It spilt off in three directions. At the end of one stood a man half cast in shadows. As I met his eyes, I felt an icy chill run down my spine. It couldn't be, could it? He looked very much like Frank fucking Russo. That wasn't right. He should be up in his fucking office.

He ducked away behind the shelving unit so I couldn't be sure of it. I had to know. If that was the case, then we'd seriously fucked up and Ash was in even more danger than ever.

"Fuck," I grunted.

Then I did something stupid, but I didn't give a shit. I had to follow that man. I dashed out through the opening and heard the pop of gunfire behind me. A bullet narrowly missed me as I reached the other side and hurried off down past the shelves. I didn't look behind me to see if Rory had followed. Further popping sounds of gunfire sounded behind me, but I focused on getting after the man I'd seen. Rory could handle those men.

I got to the end and found another shelving unit to my left in the direction of where the man had disappeared to. I followed down there and when I got out into the opening, I found exactly where Russo conducted his interrogations. It was an open space with a metal chair bolted to the floor in the middle of it. I recognised it from the video he'd sent us. The chair had a sole occupant. Her blonde hair covered her face, which was hanging down on her chest. Her hands were tied together in front of her with rope and her legs cable tied to the chair.

"Isabella?" I hissed, checking the area to see if anyone else was there.

The woman raised her head slowly, her blue eyes wide. There was duct tape over her mouth, but it was her. Ash's mother. She looked gaunt and had a purple bruise across her cheek, but she was fucking well alive. She let out a muffled noise when she spied me. Thank fuck I'd found her. Now it was time to get her out of here.

I approached her slowly, checking my surroundings in case that man was lurking. Maybe this was a fucking trap. Probably, but I had no choice. Isabella was my primary aim. Keeping her alive and getting her to safety. I knelt at her feet, dropped my gun in her lap before I reached out and ripped the duct tape from her mouth.

"Quinn," she whispered.

"I'm going to get you out of here."

Her eyes went wide the next moment. Then I felt the cold press of steel at the back of my head.

"Hello, Mr Knox."

The voice wasn't quite like Frank's, more high-pitched. I raised my hands, not wanting to make any sudden movements or give him any cause to shoot me.

"Gianni Russo."

He let out a hollow laugh. So Frank had sent his brother down here to take care of Isabella. I should've fucking known.

"So you aren't stupid. Pity you fell right into my hands now, didn't you?"

Gianni didn't know the boys were down here too, or maybe he did. Either way, we'd get out of this somehow. I hoped.

"Did I? Well, that's unfortunate for me."

"You think you could come in here and take her back for that little bitch I call my niece, did you? Wrong move, fucker."

I stared at Isabella. She didn't speak, just looked at Gianni with no small amount of hatred.

"Yeah, I did. In fact, I just waltzed in here without a care in the world and decided I'd gun down all your men for the fun of it in the process."

"Shut up," he hissed, digging the gun into my skull. "You're going to tell me which one of you and your fucking friends killed my son."

Isabella gasped and glanced down at me.

"You killed Carlo?"

"Quiet, bitch," Gianni ground out. "No one is fucking talking to you."

"I think you'll find Carlo tried to kill Ash first at your behest. An eye for an eye, Gianni," I said, shrugging a little.

It wasn't exactly why we'd done it, but he didn't need to know that. I didn't give a shit Rory had murdered him either.

The man was a fucking waste of space and quite frankly, after he'd hurt Ash, I didn't have any sympathy for the fool. But if Gianni thought I would tell him who'd done it, he was barking up the wrong tree.

"You did what? Is Ash okay? Please tell me she is," Isabella cried.

"She's fine, no thanks to Carlo trying to run her off the road."

"Shut the fuck up," Gianni growled. "Answer the fucking question. Who killed him?"

"You going to let me go if I tell you?"

"Are you fucking stupid or what? You aren't leaving here alive."

I looked at my gun in Isabella's lap then back up at her, trying to send a message.

Pick up the damn gun and aim it at his head.

She could manage that even with her hands tied together if she tried. I couldn't rely on the boys finding me in time. I had to get out of this situation somehow without getting shot in the head by Russo's fucking brother.

"Then why should I tell you? Seems a little pointless when you're not giving me an incentive."

The gun pressed harder against me. I winced, keeping my hands raised. If I made one wrong move, that would be it.

"You haven't got a choice either way."

"Oh, I think I do. If you shoot me, then you'll never know. You'll go to grave wondering which one of us ended Carlo's life. Wouldn't that be tragic?"

"Fuck you, cunt. Give me the damn name."

I scoffed. He was a fine one to talk calling me a cunt when he had a gun pointed at my head.

"No."

I tried again with Isabella and the gun, but she wasn't getting the damn message. Her fear wouldn't let her see what I was trying to say.

Fuck.

How else would I get out of this fucking mess?

"I think you'll find it was me," came a voice from behind us. One I recognised well.

"What?" Gianni said as he lessened the pressure on my head.

I glanced back in time to find him turning his head before he grunted, his back arching as something hit it. I acted quickly, ducking and slapping the gun out of his hand. Spinning around, I shoved him backwards. He fell down and the knife embedded in his back dug in deeper, causing him to let out a gurgling sound. I was pretty sure it'd punctured his lung.

Rory walked over to us slowly, his hazel eyes dark with violence. He stood over Gianni and smiled.

"I killed your son. Do you want to know how?"

"You fucker!" Gianni choked out.

"I suffocated him whilst he slept. He died so quickly it was almost too easy."

Rory's voice was so casual as if it mattered not he was openly admitting he'd murdered Carlo. In all honesty, it was a little chilling, but we'd all killed today. What was one more man now? I stood up and grabbed my gun from Isabella's lap. She stared at us, her face as white as a sheet.

"Fuck you! I'm going to kill you. You fucking killed my boy! My boy! Fuck you, fucking scum—"

Bang.

The bullet left my gun and lodged itself in his skull, cutting off his diatribe against Rory and killing him instantly.

"Jesus Christ, he needed to shut up already."

Isabella started screaming. Rory stared at her in disgust whilst I walked back to her and stuck my hand over her mouth.

"Shut the fuck up."

She stared up at me, fear painting her features. Did she think we were about to gun her down too? Was she stupid? Ash would murder us.

"I'm not going to kill you. We're here to rescue you. Haven't you seen someone die before?"

She shook her head. Well, that was a fucking new one on me. Frank didn't care about murdering people in front of Ash so why would he have never done it in front of Isabella? Who the fuck knew what went on in that cunt's head.

"Are you going to keep your mouth shut if I remove my hand?"

Isabella nodded so I dropped my hand.

"Where's Ash? Where's my daughter? Did you bring her here?"

I almost sighed and looked over at Rory who'd come to stand beside me. Crouching down, I took my knife out and sawed through her bonds.

"She's here."

"Then where is she? I want to see her."

"You can't."

I cut the cable ties holding her legs and stood up, stepping back. Isabella stared at me.

"Why not?"

"She's gone after Frank."

The blood drained from her face again.

"Are the others with her?"

"No."

"You… you let her go after him alone? Are you crazy? Oh my god! He's going to kill her."

Rory and I looked at each other as Xav and Eric appeared from our left.

"Look what the cat dragged in," Xav said with a grin before he spied the body on the floor. "Oh shit, is that Gianni?"

"One and the same," I replied, shrugging.

"Well, good. Time to get this one out of here." He pointed at Isabella. "Did you let Ash know yet?"

I shook my head. Isabella was glaring at me as Xav stepped forward and helped her up from the chair.

"Nice to see you again, Mrs Russo. Pity about the circumstances. If you'd like to come with me and Rory here, we'll make sure you're safe."

She shook his hand off and crossed her arms over her chest.

"No. You are taking me to Ashleigh right now. She's in danger. You lot sent her after Frank alone. I cannot believe you. Does Viktor know about your reckless decision?"

"Yes, he knows everything. You're going with Xav and Rory, Isabella. Eric and I will handle everything else."

She threw up her hands.

"No! You do not understand. Frank will destroy her. We need to get to her right now."

I rolled my eyes, deciding to get in touch with Ash despite the risk.

"Little girl, can you hear me? We have Isabella, she's safe."

Nothing came down our earpieces. I waited another minute before trying again.

"Ash, please let us know you're okay."

Our earpieces crackled with the noise of gunfire before a muffled conversation happened which none of us could hear properly.

"Little girl, please answer me."

Then it went completely silent.

What the fuck happened to her earpiece?

The boys and I all looked at each other.

"Do you see now?" Isabella said, glaring at us.

We all turned and marched towards where Ash had told us the lifts would be. Xav grabbed Isabella's arm and tugged her along with us.

"Please tell me we're going to keep her safe, please."

"Oh, trust me, we're going to get our girl right fucking now," I ground out.

Adrenaline shot through me, flooding my veins with fire and fucking brimstone. I was going to kill that sick son of a bitch Ash had once called her father. If he harmed a fucking hair on her head, he would wish he was never fucking born.

Frank Russo was a dead fucking man walking.

CHAPTER THIRTY THREE

Ash

My hands shook as I pressed the button for the top floor in the lift. Now the boys had cut the security, I could get up there without needing to use my handprint. Who knew if Frank had revoked my access or not. Didn't matter. He probably knew I was coming for him. I had a feeling about it. He'd be waiting for me.

Hearing from the boys briefly made my heart sing but it also hurt. At least they were okay and had managed to get down to the basement without getting caught. I hoped they'd find my mother and keep her safe like they'd promised. None of them wanted me to go after Frank alone, but it had to be me. So even though I felt as though I might be dying on the inside, I stuffed my emotions in a box and steeled myself. It was time I gave the man who raised me a taste of his own fucking medicine.

I watched the numbers. Almost at the top floor now, which meant I had to prepare myself. I pulled out the gun from the holster beneath my hooded jumper. Then I pressed myself against the wall by the doors to hide from view. No doubt Frank's men would be waiting for me. Too bad they had no idea what they'd be letting themselves in for.

Frank had forced me to learn how to shoot to kill. Down in the basement, I'd spent many hours shooting targets until I could kill a man with a shot to the head with ease. Not that I'd ever needed to until now. My aim was precise, which was why I'd known what I was doing when I'd fired the gun at the tree next to Carlo's head even though I'd been injured.

The lift dinged and the doors slid open. There was a long minute of silence. I popped my head out and was immediately assaulted with gunshots going off. But what they didn't know was that I'd seen where they were now. As soon as the gunfire ceased, I struck. I stepped out and fired off three shots in quick succession, taking down each man with a single shot between the eyes.

A moment later, I heard a scream and found Frank's secretary, Adrienne, staring at the men as they collapsed on the floor and blood pooled beneath them. I walked towards her with the gun dangling at my side with slow precise steps.

"I'm not here to kill you," I said with a calm voice.

Right now, I was the daughter Frank had raised me to be. A ruthless and efficient woman who could keep her cool under pressure.

Adrienne stopped screaming abruptly and stared at me with new eyes.

"Ash? What… what are you doing here?"

I came to a standstill a few feet away, just before the hallway opened out into the lobby where her desk sat. I knew for a fact there were more men around the corner by the way

Adrienne's eyes darted to the right. That was the direction of Frank's office.

"I'm here to take what's mine."

This empire. It belonged to me. I was born to be queen and when I'd taken Frank's life, I would destroy his legacy. I would tear this whole fucking place down piece by piece, exposing his corruption and greed. He was going to fucking rue the day I came into his life. Rue the fucking day he tried to raise me up in his image. I was the secret weapon my mother had inadvertently placed within his inner circle. And it was time he realised it.

"What?"

"You heard me. Now, I suggest you duck because I'm about to rain down hell on anyone who tries to get in my way."

She froze for all of thirty seconds before she dropped to the floor and crawled under her desk. I smiled, probably looking a little manic. Then I slipped the second gun from its holster and walked out into the lobby, twisting around towards Frank's office and raising my weapons. The hail of gunfire which ensued was almost deafening, but I stood tall, not allowing anything to fucking take me down. I felt the impact of something hitting my chest, forcing me to take a step back, but I didn't stop shooting.

When everything went silent and the dust settled, there were six men on the ground and bullet holes everywhere. I looked down at myself. There was a single hole in my jumper. I winced as I felt the pain of the bullet which had embedded itself in the bulletproof vest the boys had all but insisted on me wearing. To be honest, I hadn't put up any sort of complaint. And now I was grateful.

"Fuck."

It hurt like the devil and would bruise to high hell, but I didn't have time to focus on it. I checked the number of bullets I had left, finding one clip empty. As I walked towards Frank's office, I swapped it out for the other clip after holstering one of the guns. I knew what would be waiting for me at the end of this corridor and a feeling of dread sucker-punched me in the gut.

One of the double doors was open. Beyond there was another lobby where Frank's last line of defence sat. I didn't enter the lobby, I stood off to the side and held my gun up.

"I know you're there, Berto. It's Ash… I know you think you have to protect Papa from every threat, but I don't want to kill you. I don't want to deprive Fabi of his father. He's my only friend in this fucked up world I grew up in. No one else cared about me the way he did. Everyone tried to use me except Fabi. I don't want to shoot you, so I'm going to ask you to stand down."

I took a breath. The very last thing I ever wanted was to gun down Berto Esposito. Perhaps it made me soft, but I didn't care. Fabio's family meant something to me. So I'd use every bit of leverage I had.

"You know about Isabella and Viktor Bykov… You know the truth, don't you? You know who I really am. You watched me grow up knowing I couldn't be Frank's daughter and yet you didn't say a word to him. So tell me, are you so loyal to him you'd sacrifice your life for a man who cares about no one but himself? Are you really going to make me do this?"

I gave it another minute before I stepped away from the wall and came to a standstill in the doorway. Berto stood a few feet away with his hands up. His eyes were soft as he spied me even though I had a gun pointed at him.

"Are you going to let me past?"

He took a step towards me and my hand shook.

"I won't harm you, Ash. Go ahead."

I lowered the gun and stepped into the lobby, trying to keep my nerves in check.

"You understand why I have to do this."

"I do, sweet girl. You have nothing to fear from me."

I gave him a nod before walking further in and coming to a halt at the double doors. I turned my head towards him.

"Will you stand guard for me? Make sure no one else enters this room. My boys will be coming for me… so don't shoot them, please."

He smiled.

"Frank is not happy with your choice in partners."

"Frank doesn't get a say any longer."

Berto nodded.

"Do what you have to, you can be sure I won't allow anyone in except your men."

I knew Quinn would get mad at me for doing this, but what happened next had to remain between me and Frank. So I pulled my earpiece out and left it on the chair next to the doors. Then I pushed one open, keeping my gun up and stepped into Frank's office. The office where he would take his last breath.

The man himself sat his desk with his fingers steepled. I held the gun out, aiming for his chest. I couldn't help the way my hand shook seeing him in person for the first time in months.

"Ashleigh."

"Hello, Papa."

He put a hand out, indicating the gun in mine, "Is that really necessary?"

I cocked my head to the side. Did he think I was stupid?

"Very. Did you forget you threatened to end me and the boys?"

His lip curled up into a sneer at the mention of my men.

"And where are they? Did they send you here alone and unprotected?"

I almost scoffed.

"I don't need protection. How do you think I got in here? Your men are dead."

He merely smiled at me.

"Here you complained about having to learn how to use a gun."

I wanted to smash this fucking gun across his head. His tone was condescending and it irked me. But I had to remain calm and not allow him to get under my skin. I didn't come here for small talk.

"Yes, well, your *lessons* sunk in finally. Pity for you it happened after I abandoned your sick, twisted family."

"Are you forgetting this is your family too?"

I smirked. He had no idea. How could he not have suspected? Too bad. Frank Russo was in for a fucking wake up call.

"Is it? You know, I began to question that when you all decided to start trying to kill me."

I took two steps into the room before tucking my hand into the pocket of my hooded jumper and pulling out a piece of paper. Frank's eyes fell on it and he frowned.

"What do you have there?"

I glanced at the paper, taking another step towards him.

"This? Oh well, wouldn't you like to know?"

"Do not play games with me, Ashleigh."

I laughed, unable to help myself.

"This isn't a fucking game here… *Frank*."

His eyes narrowed and his nostrils flared. I knew calling him that would piss him off.

"Your disrespectful attitude has never done you any favours."

Frank looked at the gun pointed at him again as I closed the distance and came to a standstill in front of his desk.

"You don't deserve my respect." I slammed the piece of paper down on his desk. "And this will show you why I will never have any for you ever again."

He looked down at it, trying to appear as though he didn't care but I could see in his eyes he did. I cocked my eyebrow, daring him to turn it over and look at what it said. The words printed on it would shatter everything into tiny little pieces. My life had been built on an illusion and it was high time it be unmasked.

"Go on… you know you want to."

His eyes flicked back up at me, the rage radiating off them battering me. I held strong. I was doing this for me and the boys. Taking down the king. Destroying everything he'd built. And I was doing it so we could be free.

I kept my eyes and my gun on him as I walked around his desk until I stood beside him. Shoving the gun into his skull, I took the safety off. This wasn't how I planned to kill him, but he didn't know that.

"Turn the page over, *Frank*."

He barely flinched at the cold metal against his temple.

"What do you want me to see, Ashleigh?"

I hated him calling me that so much. Irritation flooded my veins, but I kept a leash on my temper. I knew his tricks. If he thought I would lose control, he was mistaken. I'd learnt my lesson. Never again would I allow this man to make me feel small or terrorise me.

"Turn the page and read it. I won't tell you again."

He let out an audible sigh before reaching out and flipping the page over. With him distracted, I pulled the knife out of my pocket, keeping the gun trained on his head. I leant closer, watching him read the words.

"Do you see those names? Read them to me."

"Ashleigh Vittoria Russo and Viktor Mikhailovich Bykov."

"The conclusion, Frank, read it out loud."

"The alleged father is not excluded as the biological father of the tested child."

He faltered on the last words and my heart sung with joy. Now he knew the fucking truth about what Isabella had done. And the shaking of his voice told me how much it affected him.

"I am not your daughter."

He didn't say a word. I wished I could see his face, but right now, I was done. Done with this man. Done with everything he stood for. Just plain fucking done.

"I wanted you to know the truth before I kill you. I will bathe in your blood and burn your empire to the ground. Goodbye, Frank."

He let out a shuddering breath. My sympathy was well and truly gone. I raised my hand clutching the knife and slid it across his throat, digging in deep to cut through the tissue. The fool thought I would shoot him. Too fucking bad I wanted him to feel it.

His hands came up and he clutched his neck. I stepped back and spun his chair around. Blood ran from his neck, coating his white shirt as he gasped for breath and gurgled. I shouldn't have watched the life draining out of his eyes nor the gruesome sight of his blood spilling out of his body, but I couldn't stop myself. I had to see it.

His eyes pleaded with me until he lost consciousness and after that came his death. His body slumped in the chair as the blood still pumped from the open wound at his neck.

I took a step back, the gun and the knife dropping from my hands. It was done. I'd killed him. I'd murdered the man who raised me.

"He's dead," I whispered, almost unable to believe the sight of it in front of me. "I did that… I killed him."

Feeling relieved over the whole thing sickened me. I shouldn't be relieved I'd murdered a man in cold blood. Nor that I'd killed those other men without a second thought, but I was. All I could feel was a sense of relief. I was alive and Frank was dead. After fearing for my own life in the lead up to this, I was still here. Still breathing.

"Holy shit," I breathed out.

The door to the office swung open and in came all four of my men with Isabella on their heels. They all came to a standstill when they saw me.

"Little girl?"

Then I realised Frank was facing away from them now so they couldn't see what I'd done. My hands trembled at my sides. I took a deep breath, trying to steady myself.

"He's dead… I killed him."

CHAPTER THIRTY FOUR

Eric

When we'd got up to the top floor, there'd been dead bodies all over the place and one scared secretary. Isabella had a quick word with her before we'd all walked towards Frank's office, looking at the bullet hole riddled walls and wondering what the fuck Ash had done. We reached the double doors and walked through finding a man holding a gun just inside. Isabella's eyes widened when she took him in.

"Berto?"

The man's eyes softened immediately.

"Bella... are these Ash's men?" he asked, keeping his gun trained on us.

"Yes, but what are you doing here? Where's Ash?"

He nodded his head towards the doors as he lowered his gun.

"She didn't want to kill me out of respect for Fabi."

Isabella nodded slowly as the boys and I looked at each other.

"Okay, someone explain to me what the fuck is happening?" Quinn ground out.

"This is Berto Esposito, Fabio's father and Frank's right-hand man."

Berto gave us all a nod but indicated the doors with his hands.

"She is through there… with him."

Quinn made no fucking bones about striding towards the doors with us trailing him. When we got in the room, we found Ash standing at the back with Frank's chair turned towards her. Her blue eyes were wide and her face drained of all colour.

"Little girl?"

Her mouth opened and closed.

"He's dead… I killed him."

Nobody moved or said a word for a long minute. Then I was moving forward because the sight of her near fucking killed me. Our girl was alive and she looked like she was about to collapse. Ignoring the dead man in the chair next to her, I gripped her arms and pulled her away towards the windows. Then I tipped her face up to mine by her chin spying a drop of blood on her lip. I wiped it away with my thumb.

"Tell me you're not hurt."

"I got shot."

I looked her over, my eyes landing on the hole in her jumper on her chest. My hand dropped from her face and I tugged her jumper off, throwing it to the floor. The bullet had lodged itself in the vest we'd got for her.

"Does it hurt?"

She nodded, her bottom lip trembling.

"Let me get this off you then… and we'll have a look at the damage, okay?"

She let me strip it from her, then I pulled up her t-shirt finding her skin beginning to bruise where the bullet had hit. I brushed my fingers over it, checking it hadn't cracked her ribs or anything. She winced and let out a little whimper.

"I don't think you broke a rib, but this will bruise like a bitch."

"Thank god for small mercies," she replied with a sad smile.

"Beautiful…"

Her eyes filled with tears.

"I need you to kiss me, E… I need you to remind me I'm alive."

I leant down towards her, my hand cupping her face before our lips met. She let out a slight whimper and her hand pressed against my chest. My tongue swept into her mouth, kissing her for all I was fucking worth because she'd told me to remind her she was still here. When we pulled apart, the light had returned to her eyes as she blinked.

"I love you," I whispered. "And I'm seriously fucking relieved you're alive."

Her smile this time was radiant.

"I love you too."

I pulled back finding the boys had joined us. Quinn was staring down at Frank's dead body, his expression dark. Rory and Xav seemed to be waiting for me to step away. I rolled my eyes, letting Xav take my place.

"Angel."

"*Tesoro.*"

He wrapped his arms around her, cradling her to him gently.

"I was so fucking worried about you."

She pulled away and went up on her tiptoes so she could kiss him too. They whispered I love yous to each other before Xav let her go. Rory wrapped his hand around her waist and raised his hand, stroking her cheek.

"You did it, little star… I knew you would."

"I'm so happy to see you."

It was the first time since we'd left the house that Rory really smiled. He leant down and whispered something in her ear which had Ash blushing up a storm.

"You're such a bad man," she scolded, slapping his shoulder.

"You love that about me."

She shook her head, but her smile remained.

"Huh… I guess I do."

I had no idea what he said to her and I was pretty sure I didn't want to know either. Those two could keep their dirty antics to themselves. We already knew enough about each other's sex lives as it was.

Quinn stepped away from Frank's body and turned to Ash. She squeezed Rory's arm before he let her go and she took a few steps towards Quinn.

"Little girl."

Then she was in his arms and he pressed a kiss to her forehead.

"I'm so proud of you," he told her. "You've set us free, sweetheart."

They stayed like that for a long moment before he set her back on her feet. Then Ash turned and spied her mother. A grin split across her face and she practically ran towards Isabella. The two women embraced, albeit gently due to Ash's injury.

"You're alive," Ash cried.

"I'm right here, darling. I'm right here."

"I was so worried he would hurt you… but Mum… he's dead now."

"Good riddance."

Xav snorted next to me, rolling his eyes.

"Well, glad she's not mad about the whole killing business."

"We should get her out of here before she screams over a dead body again," Rory said, grimacing.

"Was it that bad?" I asked.

"Oh yes… Now, we've got to clean this mess up."

I rolled my eyes. It wasn't going to be fun scrubbing this scene given how messy it was but we had to make sure no one found out Ash had murdered Frank. Vincenzo had thankfully agreed to sort out the two men whose throats had been slit in the basement. We'd pick him up when we got out of here and make sure he got the medical attention he needed.

"Let's get on with it then. I don't want to be in this place any longer than I have to."

Xav dumped his bag on the desk and we all got to work. Ash took Isabella out into the lobby to talk to Berto, giving us all a grateful smile before she left.

It took us half an hour to deal with the mess and clean up any DNA evidence, then we packed up and left. We found

Berto had already disappeared but had given us his word on his silence. Ash knew enough about him to bury him if he ever said anything about what we'd done here today. He was free to disappear if he wanted. This way of life was over for him, and from what Ash was saying on the way down, I think he was glad of it. He could live in peace being a grandfather to his grandson, Ricardo.

"Do you want to come back with us, Mum?" Ash asked as we all walked out of the lifts together and along towards the back where we'd come into the building.

No one seemed to be about, but it didn't matter. We'd done what we came here to do.

"No, darling, I'll go to Viktor's. He and I need to have a talk."

"Okay."

Isabella stroked Ash's hair.

"Don't worry, we'll see each other tomorrow. I'm sure you're exhausted."

Ash nodded, not looking particularly put out by the prospect. I think we were all pretty drained, emotionally if not physically after all the shit we'd done today.

We met up with Vincenzo at the back door and hustled out. In the distance, we could hear sirens. It was definitely time to get the fuck out of here before the police turned up. The seven of us made our way out of the back alley and onto the main street. When we reached the car, we also found André waiting for us. Quinn must've messaged him as he stepped up to the man and had a quick word with him.

Isabella said her goodbyes to us and Ash and André took her and Vincenzo with him. The five of us piled into our own car. Quinn drove whilst Ash sat in the back with me and Xav again. She leant her head on my shoulder and within minutes had fallen asleep.

"Do you think she's really okay after that?" Xav whispered to me.

Who knew if she was or not. Ash didn't seem to be traumatised after what she'd done. We'd all known she wanted to kill Frank. Perhaps it gave her a sense of peace or freedom. We were free from him now. Free to live our lives the way we wanted. Free from all of the shit we'd dealt since the day we'd been born.

"If she's not, we'll be here for her, but I suspect she's fine, Xavi."

He looked at her before stroking his fingers across her collarbone.

"I fucking hope so."

The rest of the journey was silent. Ash didn't stir when we got out so Xav carried her out of the car into the house. He placed her down gently on the sofa. The four of us stood staring at her because we couldn't look away. Our girl had gone through hell and back today.

She opened her eyes a minute later, blinking at us.

"Boys?"

"We just want to know you're okay, little girl," Quinn said.

Ash got up, wincing a little, but she stood tall.

"I am… I promise." She took a breath. "I killed him for you. For everything he's done to you and the misery he's caused in your lives. I wanted to set you all free. And I killed him for me. Because he deserved to die for everything he put me through." She ran her fingers through her hair. "I love you, boys… so fucking much… and I can't believe it's over. We're… we're free."

I don't think any of us could help smiling. Then we all crowded her, careful to be gentle in our group hug. And I knew we'd all be okay because today we'd fucking done it. We'd ended it all for good. There was no better feeling than being with these three and Ash. No better feeling in the world.

"We love you too, Ash," the four of us said at once as if we'd suddenly become in sync with each other.

Today was the end of one chapter in our lives.

And it was time to open another.

Our future together.

CHAPTER THIRTY FIVE

Ash

In the weeks and months following Frank's death and what the press were calling '*The Massacre at Instinct Investments*,' I'd gone through a period being unable to get out of bed. Whilst I'd been prepared to take his life, the emotional strain took its toll on me. The fact I got shot hadn't helped. The bruising from the impact of the bullet made me stiff and sore. The boys had been right there, taking care of me every step of the way. Everything we'd gone through had brought us so much closer together as a quintet. We were each other's support systems and worlds. Nothing would stand in our way again.

Quinn had overseen our withdrawal from the crime families and the retirement of his *Il Diavolo* persona. They'd agreed to leave us in peace, citing we'd done them a favour by destroying Frank's empire. His company and investments fell into the hands of the board which was being overseen by my mother. She'd sold her shares and rid herself of everything to do with Frank Russo and his sick legacy.

Isabella and Viktor were remaining friends for my sake. They knew I wanted them to be amicable since they were my parents and I wasn't going to pick one over the other. Having my dad in my life had been an absolute joy and quite frankly, a lifesaver after I'd taken the life of the man who raised me. Viktor had dinner with me and the boys at least once a week and I often spent time at his house too. I didn't get on with his older brother, Gregor, but I don't think my dad blamed me for it, considering everything.

Fabio and Mandy were expecting again, something I knew his father, Berto was excited for. He'd fully retired from a life of crime and was now working in a food kitchen for the homeless. I couldn't wait to meet Fabio's new little one. We kept in touch and saw each other regularly. He was the only person I wanted to see from that life.

Nate had made a full recovery after his surgery. He returned to the US not long after his rehabilitation ended and had met someone. I don't think I could ever say I'd fully forgive him for everything, but I wished him no ill will. He had, after all, helped Quinn in infiltrating Frank's ranks. No easy feat. In his own way, he'd fought the war against the man who raised me. So for that, I was grateful.

I unlocked the front door of the house I now called home and stepped in, sighing as I smelt the scent of roast chicken, a sign Eric had dinner ready. I'd been on my feet all day and was about ready to collapse in a heap. Quinn had agreed to let me take over some of the operations at the Syndicate. Currently, I was overseeing a complete redecoration of the main floor. Whilst it meant the casino had to remain closed for a couple of weeks, it'd be worth it in the end. We wanted to move into a new era of our lives and that started with giving the place a fresh look.

I kicked off my heels and trudged into the dining room, finding the boys already seated at the table. My heart rate kicked up a notch. My beautiful men who were all looking at me with smiles and tenderness in their expressions.

"You have no idea how much I need this right now."

I slumped down in my seat and rubbed my temples. Rory reached over and stroked my shoulder.

"Hard day, little star?"

"No… just long. One of the damn builders knocked through a wall he wasn't supposed to, so Cameron was pissed off since it's creating delays. You know what he gets like."

Cameron was our project manager for the casino uplift. Most of the time, he barked orders at people and was a bit of a grumpy bastard, but he did his job well.

"You did want me to give you a job," Quinn interjected, rolling his eyes.

"I'm not complaining." I stuck my tongue out at him which only earnt me a hard stare.

"Our angel isn't afraid of hard work," Xav said, grinning as he started tucking into his food.

Eric poured me a glass of wine. I gave him a grateful nod, taking a sip and feeling the tension in my muscles begin to ease. Xav was right. I loved being able to help them run the casino. Getting out of the house at least three days a week after being locked away in here for months felt freeing. I no longer needed protection so I took every advantage to come and go as I pleased, which included another trip down to Kent with Rory. I almost blushed at the memory of our dirty weekend away full of sex and general debauchery. He'd not held back in the slightest.

It hadn't been the only time I'd gone away. Quinn and I had gone up to Edinburgh for a few days and we'd walked up Arthur's Seat together. The views made it worth the trip and the copious amounts of whisky and gin we'd ended up buying and bringing home. The boys had certainly been happy with our haul.

Eric and Xav had taken me to Budapest where we'd shared a romantic week away together. It'd involved a ton of sex, taking advantage of the mineral baths and sightseeing. Xav got drunk on too much pálinka on our last night there and passed out in bed, so Eric and I had sat out on our balcony and watched the world go by. That's when he'd dropped a little revelation on me.

"I've been thinking a lot," he'd said. "I know I should have said something earlier, but… I want us to have a family together. I want to have a baby with you, Ash… Not now obviously, but in the future."

"Really?"

He nodded reaching out a hand to me.

"Really. You're going to be an amazing mum to our kids."

He meant our kids with the boys. I was so happy, I jumped into his arms and he'd carried me back into the apartment we'd rented for the week. Since Xav was taking up the bed, he'd laid me out on the sofa and made love to me, showing me exactly how much he wanted this with me. It'd been the perfect way to end our holiday.

Those trips meant everything to me. Spending time with my boys after everything we'd gone through, away from the city we lived in, helped me heal. It reminded me our lives hadn't ended because we no longer lived in fear of Frank Russo. I had more than I could have ever imagined with my four men.

After dinner, the five of us sat outside in the garden on the patio furniture, watching the sunset with the golden hues of orange and pink spreading across the sky. Quinn had put the heat lamp on as it'd started to get chilly. I sat curled up in his lap whilst the others spread out across the seats. He stroked his fingers through my hair, each of us enjoying the peace we felt between us. Xav had hauled out a bucket of ice filled with beer and a bottle of white wine for me. Eric had set out my favourite dessert, cheesecake, on the table between us, which was severely depleted now we'd all devoured a slice each. Several empty beer bottles were strewn across the table now we'd been out here awhile.

"Did you ever think we'd be here like this?" I asked, my voice low and full of emotion.

"Honestly, no," Quinn replied. "I wasn't sure we'd ever succeed in bringing the empire down."

It'd been over eight months since this all started. Since the day they'd taken me. It felt like the longest time of my life. In the aftermath of Frank's death, we'd dealt with a lot of heat from the press because of who I'd been to him and someone tipping them off about my unorthodox relationship with the boys. I'd refused any interviews about my life with them. The speculation had died down after while thankfully. There were always more scandals for them to report on.

The police had no leads about what happened at Frank's building. It's not as though they had no idea who Frank was in the criminal underworld. I'm not sure the higher-ups really cared much he'd been taken out, but they still had to do their jobs and investigate the circumstances of his death and the other lives we'd taken that day. It meant we'd done a thorough job in covering our tracks but I expected no less from my boys. They were nothing if not efficient.

"I'm glad it's over… Do you miss being *Il Diavolo*?"

He snorted and rolled his eyes.

"Fuck no."

Quinn's stress levels had massively improved over the last few months. He'd been far more relaxed and less liable to lose his temper. I think he was glad of the reduced workload and it pleased me no end to see him so content.

"You'd be happy if you never heard that name again," Eric said, sipping his beer.

"You're telling me," Quinn muttered.

I grinned, stroking his chest.

"As long as you never stop being my sir, I'll never mention it again," I whispered.

His devious grin set my body on fire.

"I'll hold you to that, little girl."

I shivered, which I'm sure he noticed as his hand drifted down from my hair and his fingers dusted over my bare shoulder. Punishment between us tended to be a part of foreplay now. I still acted up occasionally so he'd use his palm on me. I'm not sure Quinn minded having to instil discipline in me repeatedly. It certainly benefited him afterwards when he fucked me without mercy.

"Oh shit, I forgot… you got some mail, angel," Xav said, sitting up and dragging something out of his back pocket, which he handed to Eric who gave it to Rory.

I sat up and took it from him, staring down at the two letters. They both looked official and my heart raced. I had a feeling I knew exactly what they contained and I almost couldn't hold back my excitement. My fingers tore open the first one and trembled as I read the contents. I didn't stop to take it in as I ripped open the envelope of the second one and read it too.

"Are you going to hold us in suspense forever?" Quinn asked. "You're practically vibrating."

I put my hand to my mouth as tears welled in my eyes. It'd finally happened. All the paperwork had duly been filed and now I had the irrefutable documentation showing who I really was. I jumped up out of Quinn's lap and did a little victory dance, not caring about four sets of amused and confused eyes on me.

"This, my amazing, wonderful and incredibly sexy boyfriends, is the best possible news in the world," I practically sang as I carefully placed the letters on the table.

I levelled my gaze with each one of them, smiling from ear to ear.

"Allow me to introduce to you to your new and improved girlfriend… Ashleigh Bykov."

"What? The paperwork came through?" Xav asked, eyebrows shooting up.

I nodded, pressing my hands to my heart as I couldn't contain my excitement.

"And I got my updated birth certificate too. I can't wait to tell Dad, he's going to be so happy."

It might not seem much to anyone else but letting go of my Russo heritage meant everything to me. It closed the door on that chapter of my life completely.

Xav jumped up and enveloped me in a hug.

"I'm so fucking proud of you, angel."

"Thank you for everything you did to help me with this, *tesoro*. It means the world to me."

He'd been the one to research how to do it all, go through the proper legal channels and helped me fill out the paperwork.

"You know I'd do anything for you. You own my fucking heart."

We heard a cough from beside us.

"And that fool does too, but don't tell him, he'll get all smug and shit about it."

I snorted and pulled away in time to see Eric rolling his eyes. Xav glanced over at him with a grin.

"Aww, man, you know I fucking well love you, you big idiot."

"You're the only idiot here," Eric muttered, but he was smiling too.

He got up and hugged me too, nuzzling my hair with his nose.

"I can't wait to *tame* you, Miss Bykov," he whispered and I squirmed in his arms.

There'd be plenty of taming from him. I was well and truly under his spell, intoxicated by the wildly sensual man underneath his gentlemanly exterior.

"I'd like to see you try."

He grabbed a handful of my behind, pressing me harder against him.

"Brave words, hellcat, brave fucking words."

I kissed his cheek before pulling away, giving him a wink.

My eyes fell on Rory who smiled at me before letting out a grunt as I jumped into his lap, straddling his thighs. Wrapping my arms around his neck, I stared down into his hazel eyes as he tipped his head up me. His hands gripped my hips in a possessive hold which only made me wriggle in his lap, something I'm not so sure he appreciated judging by the way his eyes darkened.

"Are you happy?"

I nodded, biting down on my lip.

"I can see it in your eyes, you're shining so brightly, little star, I'm in awe."

My heart tightened so hard, I thought I might die a thousand times over. The intense feeling of joy coursed through my veins, spreading like wildfire.

"Ror…"

He smiled and I swear to god I'd never seen such happiness and peace radiating from him before.

"I'm yours, forever," he whispered. "You own my heart."

I held back from outright crying over his words and settled for kissing him instead. A gentle, tender kiss which demonstrated the depth of our affection for each other.

He let me go when I pulled away and I found Quinn standing and staring down at me with those stunning dark eyes of his.

"This calls for a celebration, little girl."

I cocked an eyebrow.

"What kind of celebration?"

His eyes filled with heat and my skin prickled.

"The kind involving stripping you down and pleasuring you until you're screaming our names."

Then I found myself hoisted up and flipped over his shoulder. He turned and started towards the patio doors. He paused at them, looking back over his other shoulder.

"Coming boys?"

I raised my head to find the three of them looking particularly eager as Quinn carried me through into the conservatory. Then I realised what Quinn intended.

"Wait! All four of you again?"

Quinn slapped my arse and I yelped.

"You're damn fucking right all four of us, little girl. You belong to us and we're going to make sure you know it."

I smiled all the way up to my bedroom. I might belong to them, but they belonged to me too. We were permanent. Our quintet was imperfectly perfect. We were it for each other. I loved them and they loved me. And that was all I could ever want in this world.

The five of us as one.

Forever.

EPILOGUE

Ash

Eight years later

The front door slammed and I stepped out of the kitchen in time to see Aurora rushing towards me, dragging Eric along behind her.

"Mummy, Mummy, Mummy!"

She let go of Eric's hand and slammed into my legs, wrapping her small arms around me. I grinned and stroked her dark hair.

"Hello, sweetie, how was your first day at school?"

My beautiful girl had turned five over the summer and started full time at school today. Aurora was Quinn's daughter and a cheeky little madam, which he constantly said she'd got from me. She'd inherited her temper from him. It caused no end of drama in our household. Especially since she was the only other female and liked to boss her brothers around. We'd named her Aurora as a tribute to Rory and his love of the night's sky as he and Quinn were like brothers to each other.

"I had so much fun, Mummy. I met this girl called Colleen and she's the same age as me and has blonde hair like you. She's really pretty, Mummy. I want to be her friend."

I smiled at Eric who'd picked her up from school.

"She sounds lovely. I'm sure she'd be happy to be your friend. Now, Mummy has to finish up in the kitchen so why don't you go find the boys, okay? I think they're in the playroom with Xav."

Aurora pulled away and pouted, crossing her arms over her chest and stomping her foot.

"I want to see Daddy!"

She was talking about Quinn.

"You know Daddy is busy, sweetie. You can tell him all about your first day later, I promise. Now, please go see the boys as Grandpa and Grandma will be here soon."

Her arms fell and her eyes lit up.

"YAY! Grandpa and Gran-Gran."

Then she rushed off towards the playroom.

"How was she really?" I asked, stepping up to Eric who leant down and kissed me.

"Just fine, beautiful. Her teacher said she's sure Rora will fit right in. You know how she outgoing she is."

"More like boisterous."

He chuckled.

"And here I thought you wanted a girl."

I trudged back into the kitchen with him on my heels.

"You know, I'd rather it'd been with you, then she might have had an even temper."

He snorted and rubbed my back, glancing over at Rory who held our baby boy in his arm and was reading a comic at the counter.

"You not helping our girl prepare Viktor's birthday dinner?"

Rory stuck his finger up at Eric and stroked our son's head. Cole had been born six months ago. He had a tuff of dirty blonde hair and hazel eyes like his daddy. Rory doted on him, surprisingly the most hands-on dad out of the four of them. To be honest, I needed all the help I could get with a baby boy, two toddlers and a boisterous daughter running around the house all day. I was glad Aurora had started school now.

"You can help me instead."

"Your wish is my command, hellcat."

I shoved him and rolled my eyes, getting back to the stove where I'd left the curry simmering. We were having quite the feast tonight. Four different types of curry, homemade naans and rice along with salads and a huge chocolate birthday cake for dessert. Since it was Viktor's fiftieth birthday, I'd wanted to go all out for him.

"Raphi, get back here, you cheeky little monkey," Xav's voice echoed down the hallway.

My little boy with chestnut hair and green eyes ran into the kitchen and charged around the counter, giggling away to himself. Xav followed in afterwards, looking particularly aggrieved. Eric was quick to grab his son by his collar and pick him up. Raphael had come along two years ago and looked like a mini version of his father.

"Jesus Christ, your son is ridiculously fast," Xav complained, as he leant against the kitchen island. "He's wearing me out."

"As if anyone could wear you out," Eric retorted give Xav a soft smile.

Those two were still as in love as ever. We'd never been anything but open with the kids about our rather unorthodox relationship. We knew it might be an issue when they started going to school and met other kids. We had explained it to Aurora's headteacher so they could deal with any problems that could potentially arise. Knowing my little girl, she'd likely tell any kids who gave her shit for it where to go.

"Daddy, is I in twuble?" Raphael asked, putting his hands on Eric's cheeks.

"No, Raphi, you're not, but you have to stop running away from Xav, okay? He's just trying to look after you."

"NO! Give it back!" came Duke's voice from behind us.

He was backing into the room with Aurora, a toy between them as they wrestled for control of it. This was a usual occurrence between brother and sister so hardly surprised me.

"Daddy, Rora won't give it back!" he screeched.

Xav rolled his eyes and walked over to the two struggling children, taking the toy off both of them.

"If you two can't play nice, neither of you gets it."

"But Xav! I wanted it first!" Aurora said, stamping her foot.

"Aurora, you know you need to play nicely with your brothers," I called to her as I stirred one of the pots of curry bubbling away on the stove.

"But Mummy—"

"No buts. Do you want me to tell Daddy you haven't been behaving?"

Her dark eyes widened.

"NO! Please don't, Mummy!"

I held back from smirking. The only person Aurora rarely misbehaved for was Quinn. She was such a daddy's girl.

"Well, apologise to your brother then."

Aurora pouted but turned to Duke.

"Sorry."

He stuck his tongue out at her.

"Duke, do not do that to your sister. Accept her apology like a good boy."

He put his arms out to her and Aurora let him hug her.

"Sorry, Rora. Love you."

"Love you too, smelly bum."

Xav rolled his eyes as things were about to kick off. Duke was three and a half with blonde hair and sky blue eyes. He was beautiful and would be a heartbreaker when he grew up, but he was also naughty and forever winding his sister up. Their relationship mirrored Quinn and Xav's which amused me no end.

"I AM NOT A SMELLY BUM!"

"Oh Jesus, here we go again," Xav muttered, taking Duke by the hand and pulling him away from his sister.

"Daddy, Rora is being mean to me."

"I know, Dukey, your sister needs to learn some manners."

Aurora stuck her tongue out at Xav but I decided to ignore it as Quinn walked into the room.

"What on earth is all this racket?"

"DADDY!" Aurora screeched, jumping up and down and rushing towards Quinn.

He picked her up and kissed her cheek.

"Hello, sweetheart, how was school?"

"I loved it, Daddy. Didn't have to be with smelly boys all day."

"Your brothers are not smelly, Rora. What have I told you about saying that?"

Quinn was forever telling her to be good to her brothers just as I was. She loved them, but since she was the oldest, she often bossed them around, which drove Duke crazy. He hated how demanding his sister was. Raphael didn't seem to mind so much. He was the quieter out of the two boys, but it didn't mean he was any less of a troublemaker.

"Sorry, Daddy."

The doorbell rang. Quinn set Aurora down and smiled at me from across the room, mouthing *'I love you.'* My heart thumped against my chest and my hands went instinctively to the infinity pendant necklace around my neck. The one he'd given me all those years ago when he'd first declared his love for me. To this day, I'd never taken it off. Our love had only grown over the past eight years.

Quinn was still as beautiful as he had been when we'd met, but now he had a more distinguished look with his hair greying at his temples. I'd never get over the way his dark eyes roamed across me, caressing my skin nor the sharp pain of his palm when I misbehaved. We kept it behind closed doors now we had the kids.

No matter how much time passed, I still loved all my men wholeheartedly. And with our little family, I felt complete.

"I'll get that. Come on, Rora, let's go say hello to Grandpa and Grandma, okay?"

Quinn took her hand, leading her out of the kitchen. Eric set Raphael down and he ran over to Xav and Duke.

"I'll set the table," Eric told me, pressing a kiss to my temple and grabbing the plates I'd left on the counter.

"Thank you."

I spooned the curries into serving dishes whilst Xav took the boys out into the living room to say hello to their grandparents.

"Is Cole okay?" I asked Rory over my shoulder.

"He's fine, little star. I'm sure Bella will want to hold him."

My mother had fallen over herself with joy at being a grandmother. She loved the kids to bits and was over here a lot to spend time with them. To be honest, I didn't mind since the kids were a handful even for the five of us and having her babysit them gave us time to ourselves. Something we didn't always get much of these days.

I walked over and leant down, pressing a kiss to my baby boy's head. He gurgled and reached out with his hand. I let him take my finger, my heart soaring. Rory stared at me over the top of our son's head, smiling softly.

"You think he's going to be quiet like you?"

Cole rarely cried and was such a smiley boy who had an infectious laugh. I loved him to bits.

"No, I think he's going to be a chatty little man who will drive us both up the wall."

"Lucky for us he can't talk yet then, we already have three kids who talk non-stop."

I leant over and kissed Rory.

"Too right," he grinned as I pulled away.

"Where is my grandson?" came Isabella's voice as she stepped into the kitchen.

"Aren't you going to say hello to your daughter first?"

I walked over to her and we embraced.

"Hello, darling. Everything in here smells wonderful. Now, where is my little Cole?"

I rolled my eyes, pulling back and waving at Rory who'd stood up with our baby in his arms. Isabella's eyes shone as she went over to him.

"Hello, Rory, I hope you're well."

"Yes, all good, Bella."

The boys had taken to calling her that now she was part of the family. Rory handed Cole over to her and she stroked his little face.

"You are the cutest little munchkin," she cooed as she took him out of the kitchen. "Grandma is going to spoil you. Yes, I am. Yes, I am."

Eric came back in the room to help me carry all the dishes into the dining room. Rory gave us a hand and once the table was set, I called for everyone to come through from the living room. It was still the afternoon, but with the kids' bedtimes being early evening, I always did dinner for them long before then.

As soon as I spied my dad, I rushed straight into his arms and hugged him tightly.

"Happy birthday, Dad."

"Thank you, *kotik*. This all looks wonderful."

I smiled as I pulled back and kissed his cheek.

"A wonderful feast for a wonderful father."

He grinned, stroking my face before we turned to the table. The boys had started dishing up for the kids. Duke was hanging off Xav's arm and driving him crazy.

"Dukey, Raphi… come over here, boys."

The two of them rushed towards me in an instant. Raphi put his arms up as Duke wrapped his arm around my leg.

"Up, Mummy, up!"

I laughed and hoisted my little chestnut-haired boy up into my arms.

"Are you being a good boy for Xav and Daddy?"

He nodded and leant his head against my shoulder, wrapping his small arm around my neck.

"Lub you, Mummy."

"I love you too, my baby boy."

"Raphi's not a baby, Mummy, Cole is," Duke chimed in, putting his arms up to me.

"I can't carry both of you at the same time, Dukey."

Thankfully, Viktor picked Duke up and ruffled his blonde hair. I leant over and kissed my son on the forehead which made him smile.

"I love you more than Raphi does, Mummy."

I snorted. Duke was always trying to one-up his siblings.

"If you say so."

"I DO! Grandpa, I don't fink Mummy believes me."

Raphael ignored him and kept hugging me whilst sticking his thumb in his mouth, a habit he'd picked up from when he'd been a baby. Eric and I had attempted to discourage him, but our son had held strong against us.

"Your mummy knows you love her, Duke, and she loves you very much too."

Duke grinned and looked like he was about to explode with happiness.

"Dukey, come here and get your dinner," Xav called.

Viktor set my son down and he ran over to his father. I carried Raphi over to the table and sat down with him as Eric placed a plate in front of us.

"You want some din-dins, Raphi?"

He nodded and sat up, his thumb popping out of his mouth.

"Mummy, help."

I chuckled.

"Mummy will help you. Now, make sure to blow on it because it's hot, okay?"

I'd made the kids a mild curry because none of them could take spice yet, but they all enjoyed the variety of meals we prepared for them. I spooned up a little portion and Raphael blew on it before I fed him. Eric watched us with love and affection in his eyes. Shit, I really loved my men so much and my babies. They meant the world to me.

I watched my family tuck into the dinner I'd made for them. Xav sat with Duke in his lap, the two of them wolfing down their meals. Eric was beside me and Raphael, making sure to serve me up a plate alongside his. My mum still had Cole, but Rory was hovering next to her with his own plate. Viktor had sat down and Aurora had joined him, the two of them having a conversation about school. And Quinn sat next to her, staring down at his daughter with so much love, it threatened to make my heart burst.

Here we all were, my family, celebrating my dad's birthday together. And I really couldn't ask for more. My soul felt content and complete. My heart was on fire. I had the love of my men and my babies along with my parents. Nothing in the world could be better than this feeling.

Looking back at the years we'd spent together, our love had only grown. With each baby who'd come along, our bond had only become stronger. The nine of us were a solid family unit who'd stay together no matter what. Having kids had been our biggest challenge yet, and we were surviving it the only way we knew how. By sticking together as one.

As unorthodox as our quintet was, we worked so well because of the love and determination we shared. And as the boys looked up at me, their affection shining in their eyes, I knew I'd found my place and my home in the world.

It was here with Quinn, Xavier, Eric and Rory.

My heart. My soul. My entire being belonged to them.

And theirs belonged to me too.

The End

ACKNOWELDGEMENTS

Thank you so much for taking the time to read this book. I really appreciate all of my readers and hope this book gave you as much joy reading it as I did writing it.

Thank you to my partner in writing crime, Sab. I could gush over our friendship all day and how much you support me. This last book would not exist without your badgering me into getting it written. You made sure I gave our quintet a satisfying ending and for that, I'm forever grateful. Thank you for always standing by me and my crazy ideas!

To Elle – honestly, I'm so grateful we met online. The constant support we give each other has been such an integral part of my author journey. From bouncing ideas off each other to discussing cover art, there's never a dull day. Thank you for everything!

To my wonderful readers, thank you for following me down this path into a dark reverse harem unlike anything I've ever written before. It's been quite the journey and I appreciate all your support and love for my books so, so much!

To my friends and family who have always supported me no matter what. Thank you for being here for me.

And finally, to my husband who is my everything. Thank you for supporting me through this crazy author journey and allowing me the freedom to write. I love you to the stars and back.

ABOUT THE AUTHOR

Sarah writes dark, contemporary, erotic and paranormal romances. They adore all forms of steamy romance and can always be found with a book or ten on their Kindle. They love anti-heroes, alpha males and flawed characters with a little bit of darkness lurking within. Their writing buddies nicknamed Sarah: 'The Queen of Steam' for their pulse racing sex scenes which will leave you a little hot under the collar.

Born and raised in Sussex, UK near the Ashdown Forest, they grew up climbing trees and building Lego towns with their younger brother. Sarah fell in love with novels as teenager reading their aunt's historical regency romances. They have always loved the supernatural and exploring the darker side of romance and fantasy novels.

Sarah currently resides in the Scottish Highlands with their husband. Music is one of their biggest inspirations and they always have something on in the background whilst writing. They are an avid gamer and are often found hogging their husband's Xbox.

Made in the USA
Middletown, DE
19 May 2024

54546651R00203